THE GHOST

AND THE
HALLOWEEN HAUNT

HAUNTING DANIELLE

HAUNTING DANIELLE - BOOK 22

THE GHOST
AND THE
HALLOWEEN HAUNT

USA TODAY BESTSELLING AUTHOR
BOBBI HOLMES

The Ghost and the Halloween Haunt
(Haunting Danielle, Book 22)
A Novel
By Bobbi Holmes
Cover Design: Elizabeth Mackey

Copyright © 2019 Bobbi Holmes
Robeth Publishing, LLC
All Rights Reserved.
robeth.net

ROBETH
PUBLISHING, LLC

ISBN: 978-1-949977-52-3

Dedicated to my husband, Don.
For always encouraging me to follow my dreams.
I love you.

ONE

Perched high in the Douglas fir, their bare feet dangling from a branch, the two ghosts looked down at the mourners. Although, technically speaking, those gathered for the funeral could hardly be called mourners. Annabelle and Kat doubted any of the people below had ever met the deceased, considering they had passed decades earlier. Both were murdered for the sake of greed and jealousy, and only recently had their remains been discovered and finally put to rest.

Annabelle and Kat looked as if they could be granddaughter and grandmother—although Annabelle, who appeared to be in her early twenties, had died before her elderly looking companion had even been born.

"Mama would've boxed my ears had I showed up at a funeral wearing slacks," Annabelle declared, taking note of all the women below wearing pants instead of dresses.

"It's more casual now than it was in your day," Kat reminded her. It was not the first time they'd had this conversation. After spending countless hours confined to a cemetery, there were rarely new topics to discuss.

"That's obvious. I don't know when the last time was that I saw any woman or girl wearing—or carrying—a respectable pair of wrist gloves. Of course, I suppose white gloves would look silly with slacks."

"Even in my time we wore white gloves. I had the loveliest pair with a little row of pearls along their pinky seams." Kat smiled at the memory. "I imagine the mothers of many of the younger women here today would tell you they also wore white gloves at one time." With a sigh she added, "Styles change."

"I don't like it," Annabelle grumbled. "And hats. I rarely see pretty hats these days. Just straw hats to keep the sun out of their eyes. Nothing fashionable."

Kat peeked up at the straw hat perched on her own head and gave a chuckle yet reserved comment.

"Did I tell you I met Maisy Faye Morton right before she moved on?" Annabelle asked. The funeral they were attending was for Maisy Faye Morton and her fiancé, Kenneth Bakken.

"Yes, dear. You have mentioned that—numerous times."

"I'm just glad they finally found her body." Annabelle studied the crowd below.

"Dreadful affair," Kat said, adding several tsk, tsk, tsks to her comment.

Poorly concealed in the evergreen branches of the tree, the ghosts might be noticed by an attending medium had one bothered to look up. Which none had done thus far.

"Have you seen Virginia?" Annabelle asked, looking around. "She usually likes watching these."

Before Kat could respond, Annabelle squealed, "Oh, it's a baby!" She pointed down to a stroller being pushed by a redheaded woman. "I do adore babies. Abe and I were going to have four. Two boys and two girls. I'm tempted to pop down and say hello. At least with a baby I'll get a response."

"I imagine if you pop down now, more than the little one will notice." Kat then pointed to the three women now standing under a nearby shade tree with the baby. One was the redheaded woman who had been pushing the stroller moments earlier. "The brunette in the middle, that is Danielle Boatman."

Annabelle squinted her eyes and leaned forward, staring intently at the woman. "You mean Danielle Marlow now." Annabelle shook her head in disbelief. She still could not get used to the idea Walt Marlow had not just managed to leap back into the living world, but he was married again. And then, as if a thought suddenly occurred to her, she turned to Kat and said, "That must mean Walt Marlow is here somewhere!"

Kat shrugged. "I suppose he is."

Annabelle quickly scanned the crowd. With a gasp she pointed to a man below. "It's him!" She then shook her head and said, "I should have known it might be him. Look, he's the only man down there wearing a proper hat. Not a silly baseball cap that seems to be all the rage."

Kat stared down at the tall man wearing the fedora hat. It sat cockily on his dark head, a perfect companion to his tailored three-piece suit. He was undoubtably the most formally dressed man in the crowd. He turned in her direction, yet did not look up. She caught a glimpse of his handsome profile.

With curious eyes, Annabelle studied Walt from afar. "You suppose it's true what they say? He can see ghosts?"

"According to Eva he can," Kat reminded her.

"Oh, Eva…" Annabelle rolled her eyes and groaned.

"I don't understand why you have such a problem with Eva," Kat said. "It's hardly her fault."

"It just doesn't seem fair. You and I are stuck here in this cemetery while Eva is free to gallivant all over the countryside!"

"Death, as life, is not always fair," Kat reminded her.

"Oh hooey," Annabelle scoffed.

"And no one is making you stay here. You are free to move on."

"You know why I can't. Eva is free to move on too—and free to traipse all around town. Heavens, she's even free to leave town!" Annabelle grumbled.

"We each have our own path. I suppose whatever Eva is meant to do on this plane goes beyond the confines of this cemetery."

"And ours doesn't?" Annabelle asked.

"Apparently not. And I do appreciate how Eva comes around regularly now that Angela has moved on. It's nice to have someone reliable keeping us informed. Hard to depend on those souls passing through to give us updates on the living. Always in a rush."

"I suppose." Annabelle shrugged and looked back down at Walt. "It is so strange to think he is actually alive now. All those years—decades—I waited for his spirit to come. I wanted to make him tell me. I can't move on until I know."

"You knew he was confined to Marlow House. It's not like he could drop by the cemetery for a chat."

"I assumed he would eventually decide to move on. And as we

both know, spirits more often than not visit their grave before doing so," Annabelle explained.

"He did come to talk to Angela before she moved on," Kat reminded her.

"Yes, I know. By then he was already alive. And I didn't even realize he was at the cemetery until he was ready to leave. Not to mention Angela was here at the time. I didn't want to talk to him in front of her. He left before I had a chance to approach him alone."

"Well, he's here now." Kat nodded toward the subject of their conversation.

"Oh yes, I can just imagine how that conversation would turn out," Annabelle scoffed. "Especially if it's true what they say— Marlow is surrounded by a number of mediums. I seriously doubt he would actually tell me the truth if I ask him in front of an audience—in front of his wife. Of course he would lie. Does he really want the friends he has made in his new life to know what he is capable of?"

"Annabelle," Kat said gently, "if you are so certain, then I really don't understand why you don't just move on. What are you waiting for? It is time."

"Because I can't," Annabelle said softly. "Something is keeping me here. I just know it's tied to Walt Marlow and what I must ask him. I need to do it for Abe."

"If you don't want to ask him here, there is another option," Kat said.

Annabelle frowned questioningly.

"What's just a week away?" Kat asked.

Annabelle groaned and rolled her eyes. "Halloween."

Kat laughed. "Every year I've suggested Halloween. And every year I get the same response. You've been hanging around here for almost a hundred years waiting for Walt's spirit to show up. What are you going to do, wait another hundred years for his live self to show up alone?"

"I don't suspect Walt Marlow will actually live for a hundred years. Of course, who knows. Maybe he isn't just a medium now, maybe he's immortal," Annabelle suggested.

"I seriously doubt that. But I am beginning to think you don't actually want to talk to him."

"It's just that—well, it seemed so forward, me popping into

Marlow House uninvited on Halloween. My mother always told me a proper young woman does not just show up at a man's doorstep."

"In case you haven't noticed, you are no longer a proper young woman. You are a ghost," Kat reminded her.

Annabelle shrugged.

"What are you talking about?" Virginia asked when she suddenly appeared, sitting next to Kat on the end of the branch.

"Halloween," Annabelle told her.

"Are you going somewhere this year?" Virginia asked.

"I just reminded Annabelle it was her chance to see Walt Marlow. Talk to him," Kat explained.

"He's here now," Virginia said in a quiet voice. "I saw him. And he saw me."

"Did he recognize you?" Annabelle asked.

"He smiled at me when he walked by. But I don't believe he recognized me. Not sure why he would. That was an awful long time ago. And I don't believe for a moment he thought I was a ghost."

The three sat in silence for a few minutes, watching the crowd below as it began to disperse. Many of the mourners headed to the parking lot. Finally, Virginia broke the silence.

"Halloween…I forgot it was almost here. It comes and goes before I have time to think about it. I told myself last year to watch for the changes in the trees. They would tell me when it was almost here again," Virginia whispered. The two other spirits turned to her and stared.

"What are you saying?" Annabelle asked.

"Perhaps I should look at it again. I wonder sometimes if there is something I have forgotten. It has been so long." Virginia turned to Annabelle and added, "Unlike you, when I venture out, I have no one to look for but myself. I think you should go to Marlow House this Halloween. Find Abe."

TWO

It was a peculiar sight. The infant, bundled securely in a blue baby blanket, seemingly floated from one end of the Marlow House living room to the next and back again, while Lily Miller Bartley half-heartedly attempted to keep up with the adult conversation. They were discussing the final preparations for the upcoming Marlow Haunted House, which was to open on Friday and run until Halloween, the following Tuesday.

It was difficult for Lily to focus. She kept looking back to her son and cringing, fearful something might happen and he would suddenly fall to the floor. But then she would glance at Walt, who sat with Danielle on the sofa, and he would flash her a smile and give her a reassuring nod, letting her know he was backup, and he would let nothing bad happen to Connor Daniel Bartley, who had just fallen fast asleep.

"Evan is going to come over tomorrow and help us finish up with the decorations," Danielle said as she looked over the list of to-do items on the yellow legal pad of paper in her hands. Glancing up from her notes, she smiled at Marie Nichols, who lovingly paced the floor with the sleeping bundle. Had Marie been alive, Danielle would never have approved of the ninety-one-year-old woman walking around her living room holding a sleeping infant, fearful she might fall or stumble. But now that she was dead, it seemed as if there were a variety of things Marie could once again do.

Everyone in the room—Walt and Danielle Marlow, Chris Johnson (aka Chris Glandon), Heather Donovan, and Eva Thorndike could see Marie. Everyone except Lily. While Lily knew Marie was there—carrying her son—she couldn't see the ghost, which was why the scene made her far more uncomfortable than it made anyone else in the room. Lily also could not see Eva. That was because Eva, like Marie, was a spirit.

"You don't suppose Marie might suddenly lose her ability to harness energy?" Lily asked nervously.

Marie stopped pacing, still holding the sleeping babe tight to her chest, and looked to Lily. "Oh, don't worry, dear, I won't let anything happen to this precious boy." Just the night before Marie had discovered to her delight that Connor was able to see and hear her, as she had been able to see Eva when she was a baby.

In the next moment Danielle let Lily know what Marie had just said.

"Are you sure?" Lily squeaked.

"Danielle, please tell Lily she has nothing to fear," Eva said. "Spirits—unlike those in the living realm—have limited free will. The universe would never—and I mean never—allow a spirit to drop an innocent babe on the floor. Which means they won't suddenly pull the plug—so to speak—on Marie's powers. And it also means innocent babies are relatively protected from any mischief a spirit might attempt to impose. Such as if Marie herself decided to drop dear Connor."

"Oh, Eva! I would never do such a thing!" Marie gasped, quickly dropping a kiss on the baby's forehead.

"I never said you would, dear," Eva countered.

Once again, Danielle repeated for Lily's benefit what the spirits had just said.

PEARL HUCKABEE DISLIKED BEING CALLED middle-aged. After all, it wasn't that long ago that she was on a women's softball team. Okay, maybe it had been about ten years, but she could still throw a mean pitch. Standing just under five seven, willowy thin with gray hair and eyes, someone had once called her wiry. She didn't like being called wiry any more than she liked being called middle-aged.

Absently thumbing through the morning newspaper, she thought about her new life in Frederickport, paying scant attention to the printed words on the pages before her. She loved living in what had been her grandmother's home, bringing back cherished childhood memories. She tried not to think about the human remains that had been recently discovered in her backyard—remains that had been there since before her grandparents had purchased the property. It was rather creepy to realize they had been there when she and her cousins had played in the yard those many years ago. She tried not to dwell on all that unpleasantness.

"Put it out of your mind, Pearl," she told herself. "That has nothing to do with you or your family."

Reaching over to the side table, she picked up her cup of hot tea. Taking a sip, she flipped to the back page of the newspaper. In the next moment an ad caught her attention, and she found herself spitting out the hot liquid, dampening the newspaper as she began to sputter, her eyes never leaving the advertisement.

The ad was for a Halloween haunted house, which was to begin in just two days—at Marlow House. Slamming the cup back on the saucer and splashing tea all over the side table, Pearl ignored the mess she had just made and continued to stare at the ad, her hands angrily clutching the newspaper.

"Why are you doing this?" Pearl screeched. "I know why you are doing this! You have more money than you know what to do with. It isn't for the money!" Pearl shouted to the empty room, her gaze still fixed on the haunted house ad. "You're doing this to torment me! Getting your revenge because I got your illegal boardinghouse closed down!"

Standing up, Pearl rolled up the newspaper and shoved it under one arm, holding it there as she marched out of her house, heading next door to give the Marlows a piece of her mind. Perhaps there would be nothing she could do about the haunted house—it seemed the city of Frederickport let the Marlows do just about whatever they wanted—but she wasn't going to make this easy for them.

"Perhaps I should run for city council," Pearl muttered as she made her way down the front walk. "After all, if it wasn't for me, they would still be illegally operating a business in a residential neighborhood."

Her stride determined, the newspaper still tucked under one arm, Pearl plodded up the sidewalk toward Marlow House. She passed its south gate. It led up the driveway into their side yard. While the gate was closed, its padlock was not latched. Yet she had no intention of entering from that way. Pearl intended to use their front door.

When she reached the front gate a moment later, she found it open. Entering, she started up the walkway when motion from one of the front windows caught her eye. With a frown she stood there a moment, staring at what she believed was the living room window. If she didn't know better, it looked as if something was floating around in the room. *What are they up to?* she asked herself. Curious, Pearl decided to take a closer look.

Ducking down so the shrubbery along the front of the house would block her from view should someone from inside look out, Pearl stealthily made her way to the living room window. She paused a moment and glanced over her shoulder, making sure no one was walking up the sidewalk. It would be just her luck to have that annoying redhead from across the street come barging over about now.

Stepping off the walkway and onto the mossy ground, she crept closer to the window, careful to conceal herself from whoever might be inside. Crouching behind a leafy shrub—it covered the lower right corner of the window—she used her hands to part the branches, peeking through them and into the living room.

Pearl ducked down lower because, as it turned out, there were a number of people sitting in the room. It appeared to be some sort of gathering of the neighborhood. One she hadn't been invited to. Not that she wanted to be invited, she reminded herself.

There had been no reason to worry about the redhead from across the street sneaking up on her. Pearl spied her sitting in one of the chairs facing the couch. Sitting next to her in the other chair was that man from down the street, and on the sofa sat the Marlows. There was someone sitting on the floor with that troublesome pit bull, and she was fairly certain it was her other neighbor. *Such a nasty girl, that one—she gets perverse delight in scaring me with that vicious dog,* Pearl thought.

Gritting her teeth over the thought of a pit bull residing in her neighborhood—something she would work to outlaw should she someday become a city council member, she spied what she had seen a moment before—something floating by. *Was it some remote-control toy?* she wondered. Whatever it was, it was wrapped in what appeared to be a blue blanket. Pearl frowned, trying to identify the object. No one in the room seemed to be manning controls for the slowly floating bundle, which confounded Pearl.

A moment later the unidentified object shifted directions and, when doing so, revealed what was wrapped inside. A baby!

Stunned, Pearl stood up, staring in disbelief as the baby floated by the window. It turned its face in her direction and opened its eyes. Looking into her face, it let out a cry.

LILY, who had finally managed to give her full attention to the conversation at hand—a discussion of the upcoming haunted house fundraiser and what still needed to be done—heard Connor let out a sob. She, along with everyone in the room, looked in his direction.

Standing at the window behind Marie and the once sleeping baby was Pearl Huckabee from next door. Her gray eyes wide, she stared blankly in the window. The next moment, she disappeared.

Marie, who had stopped pacing and started bouncing Connor gently, soothing him, looked in annoyance at the window.

"That horrid woman scared him!" Marie said.

In the next moment Lily jumped up and took Connor, who was no longer crying.

Marie stuck her head out the window—literally through the glass pane—and looked down. A moment later she pulled her head back inside and turned to the others.

"It looks as if that dreadful woman has fainted," Marie said matter-of-factly.

Lily took Connor to the parlor while the others rushed outside to Pearl. Just as they reached her, she was coming to. Now muddy from falling on the damp ground, Pearl looked up to her neighbors, who all stood over her, looking down curiously. The dazed woman blinked up at the four people—not seeing the two ghosts who accompanied them. A moment later Walt and Chris each offered a hand to help her up. Scowling at the men, Pearl refused to take their assistance. She stumbled to her feet. Both men withdrew their hands without comment.

"There is a baby flying around in your living room!" Pearl blurted.

Danielle smiled at Pearl. "Oh, so you saw that? Pretty impressive, huh?"

Pearl narrowed her eyes and looked back in the window. No one was in the room now, and nothing was floating about. "What's going on here?"

"Odd question coming from a Peeping Tom," Heather snarked.

Pearl glared at Heather. "I am not a Peeping Tom!"

In unison, they all arched their brows. "You were looking into our window," Walt reminded her.

"I...I simply came over here to talk to you about..." Pearl stammered and then looked around for the newspaper, realizing she must have dropped it when she had fainted. She found it sticking out from the shrub she had been hiding behind. Snatching up the paper, she folded it to show the ad and then held it up for all to see. "I came over to talk about this!"

"Ahh. Well, then I guess you know why there was a baby floating around in our living room," Danielle said sweetly.

"I do?" Pearl muttered in confusion.

"Sure." Danielle smiled again. "It's one of the tricks we're trying out for our haunted house. Pretty impressive, wasn't it? I bet you really thought the baby was floating. He wasn't, of course. Babies don't float."

Drawing her forehead into a scowl, Pearl looked from Danielle to the rest of the neighbors. They all smiled at her, which she found unsettling. Without saying another word, Pearl turned and hurried back to her house, newspaper in hand.

THREE

Ian Bartley, who wrote under the pen name Jon Altar, sat at his computer in his home office, researching telekinesis and psychokinesis. The research wasn't for a future article or book—it was more personal than that. His golden retriever, Sadie, napped on the floor nearby, and his battered old Cubs baseball cap sat on his desk next to his now empty coffee cup.

He had just finished reading an online article when Sadie jumped up and gave a little woof, her tail wagging. The dog dashed from the room, and Ian assumed Lily must have returned home from Marlow House with their son. He couldn't believe the baby would be a month old tomorrow. It seemed like just yesterday Connor had been born. Just yesterday that Walt had moved a downed tree limb out of their way so they could reach the hospital in time. How Walt actually managed to move that heavy tree limb had been preoccupying Ian's thoughts, which was the reason for his recent internet search on telekinesis and psychokinesis. A moment later Lily walked into the room with their son.

"Still working?" Lily asked after dropping a kiss on Ian's lips. He remained sitting in his desk chair, but accepted the kiss and then reached out and gently stroked Connor's cheek. The baby squirmed restlessly in his mother's arms, but he did not cry.

"Just doing some research," he said.

"You mind if I sit in here while I feed him?" Lily asked, taking a seat on the rocking chair they had recently added to the room.

Ian swiveled his chair to face his wife and son. Lily hadn't waited for an answer, which only made him smile. Leaning back, he watched as she opened her blouse and released one of her breasts. A moment later Connor latched on to the nipple and began to greedily nurse, making little cooing sounds as he did.

"You do that so naturally," Ian said in awe.

Looking up from their son, she flashed Ian a smile and then glanced back at Connor, gently stroking the side of his cheek. "It is natural."

"Have I told you lately how much I love you?" he asked in a soft voice.

Lily grinned. "Before I left this morning. But I always love hearing it. I love you too, Ian." She stared down at Connor and sighed. "I still can't wrap my head around the fact we created something this perfect."

"How was he over at Walt and Danielle's?" Ian asked.

"He got a little fussy, but then Marie insisted on taking him."

"Marie?"

Lily looked up at Ian and giggled. "Marie confessed she stopped in last night to check on Connor, and he could see her—like she could see Eva when she was a baby. And by how Connor reacted to Marie—which was weird for me, since I couldn't see Marie—he is obviously drawn to her. She walked him a little bit after he got fussy, and he immediately fell asleep."

"I'm trying to imagine that—watching Marie walk him, but not being able to see her." Ian cringed.

"Yeah, I know. It was a little nerve-racking, but according to Dani, Eva claims the universe would never allow Marie to drop him —whatever that really means. Oh, and Pearl Huckabee saw."

"Saw what?"

"She came over this morning. I suspect to bitch about the upcoming haunted house, considering she had the newspaper ad with her—"

"I saw the ad this morning. Turned out good," Ian interjected.

"Well, she never really got to talking about the haunted house. When she was coming up the front walk, she must have noticed our son floating around the living room, so she went to get a closer look.

Poor Connor, he woke up to her angry mug staring at him through the window, and she made him cry."

"She saw Marie carrying him?" Ian recalled the time he had witnessed the wine bottle and glasses floating in the Marlow House kitchen before he was aware of the existence of ghosts.

"Yep. And she fainted. Right there in Dani's front shrubbery. Thankfully she didn't knock her head or anything, or I imagine she would be suing Dani about now."

"So what did you tell her?"

"I didn't tell her anything. I took Connor in the parlor while they all went outside to check on her. I guess she was just coming to when they got outside. Dani told her it was one of the tricks they were practicing for the haunted house."

"And she believed that?" Ian asked.

"You would have believed it," Lily reminded him, referring to the wine bottle and glasses. "And I actually told you the truth." She had told him the truth, but at the time he had chosen to believe some sleight-of-hand trick was responsible for the floating objects, not energy from a ghost.

Ian shrugged. "So then what did she say?"

"I guess not much. She bolted and went home. But we all assume her original reason for coming over was to protest the haunted house, but after she fainted, she was just too flustered."

"So how are the plans coming?"

Before answering, Lily glanced down and moved Connor from one breast to the other. "Good. I think it will be fun. Tomorrow Evan is coming over after school to help finish decorating."

"Is Eddy coming too?" Ian asked, referring to Evan's older brother.

Lily shook her head. "No. He has a scout meeting. So, what are you working on?"

"Not really work. But I've been doing more research on telekinesis and psychokinesis."

"I'm not sure why Walt moving that tree limb has you so obsessed. After all, he's been doing stuff like that since you met him."

"I suppose it's because Walt is no longer a ghost. And picking up something the size of that tree limb is a far cry from bending a spoon. Which is typically the extent of what those who claim to have telekinetic or psychokinetic powers normally do. I just don't understand it."

"I don't imagine we're meant to. As for me, I don't understand the difference between telekinesis and psychokinesis," Lily said.

"Kinesis means movement," Ian explained. "While psycho means mind and tele means far off. Some of the articles I've come across claim the terms are basically interchangeable, while others say there is a subtle difference between the two. But considering most reputable sources say the power of the mind to move objects is unproven, then I don't suppose it matters."

"But you know it isn't fiction."

"Yes. But is it really telekinesis or psychokinesis?" Ian asked. "Or just a convenient label Danielle suggested to explain the power?"

"I don't imagine you will find the answer online," Lily said.

"I did read something interesting." Ian swiveled his chair to face his computer. "Let me find the article." A moment later he pulled up the webpage he had read earlier.

"What is it?" Lily asked, facing her husband's back as he used his computer.

"It's an article that was posted earlier this month, by a Benjamin Radford, on Live Science dot com. The headline is 'Psychokinesis: Facts About Mind Over Matter.' It's rather interesting."

"What does it say?"

"Basically that it's a phenomenon that remains unproven. According to the article, some researchers believe if psychokinesis exists, it only works on small objects."

Lily chuckled. "I guess they didn't see what Walt did with the tree."

"The article mentioned one person who had garnered public attention for his self-proclaimed power of psychokinesis, but when put to the test, he couldn't perform and later confessed to perpetrating a hoax. And another notable who claims he has the power—everything he's done can be duplicated by magicians. Most rational people understand magicians aren't performing actual magic."

"Which illustrates why Dani doesn't just come out and announce to the world that she can see ghosts," Lily said.

"What do you mean?" Ian turned in his chair and looked at Lily. He noticed Connor had fallen asleep at her breast, his small mouth still making soft sucking sounds.

"I remember back when Heather had the idea to write a book about the haunting of Presley House. She hoped Dani would back her up so people would believe her. But the fact is, the world of science is skeptical —which is understandable. And as long as magicians can perform amazing sleight of hand, trying to convince a nonbeliever there really are ghosts is going to be impossible. Look at you. It almost broke us up. You certainly didn't believe what your eyes—what I was telling you."

"Very true," Ian said with a nod. He then turned to the computer and said, "Oh, there was something else I found interesting." He then began to read from the article, " '...*Some people even link psychokinesis to the spiritual world, suggesting for example that some reports of ghosts—such as poltergeists—are not manifestations of the undead at all, but instead the unconscious releases of a person's psychic anger or angst.' "*

Lily chuckled. "It's sort of funny, if you think about it. Both ghosts and psychokinesis are difficult concepts to wrap your head around. But they decide to go with the psychokinesis instead of ghost." She then stood up.

"Where are you going?" Ian turned around in the chair again, facing Lily and his sleeping son.

"I'm going to put Connor down in his crib. And then how about we get some lunch?" Lily suggested.

Ian stood up. "I'll meet you in the kitchen. We have some roast beef left. Want me to make us sandwiches?"

"Sounds great!" Lily paused at the doorway and turned to face Ian. "Just an FYI, don't say anything in the nursery you don't want someone else to hear."

Ian frowned. "Why? I don't think Connor is going to be repeating what he hears at home. At least, not for a couple of years."

"Marie asked me—through Dani—if I had any objections to her visiting Connor. She doesn't want to invade our privacy—you know, just popping in here uninvited. So she said she would enter through the outside wall, directly into his room. I told her it was okay."

ALMOST FIFTEEN MINUTES later Lily joined Ian in the kitchen. Two plates sat on the breakfast bar, each holding a roast beef sandwich, dill pickle spear, and potato chips.

"What took you so long?" Ian asked.

"Connor woke up, and I had to change his diaper. But once I put him in his crib, he went right back to sleep." Lily sat down at the breakfast bar and watched as Ian set a tall glass of iced tea in front of her.

"Looks delicious," Lily said, picking up half of her sandwich. "Thanks."

"No, thank you," Ian said, dropping a kiss on her cheek as he took the seat next to her.

Before taking a bite, Lily said, "Guess what Chris told us?"

"What?" Ian asked, picking up his glass of tea and taking a sip.

"Pete Rogers's house sold. Chris is going to have new neighbors."

"Really? I didn't know it was for sale. There wasn't a sign."

Lily shrugged. "If you think about it, there wasn't a sign when we bought this house—"

"I was living here," Ian reminded her.

"Yeah, but Adam had a buyer lined up—before us—and he never put up a sign. Same for Pearl's house."

"True. So how did he find out? Did he meet them yet?" Ian asked.

"No. Adam called him this morning. He doesn't know who bought the house, but he heard they're going to be full-time residents and are moving in any day. It was a quick escrow."

"I wonder if Rogers still owned the property?" Ian asked.

"I don't know. But considering his age and the sentence he got, he's probably going to die in prison. He was never going to be moving back to that house."

FOUR

The pit bull no longer slept in her crate at night. Although, when left alone at home—which was rare—Chris crated her. According to Walt, she didn't mind. In fact, Hunny felt safer in her crate when left alone, and she preferred its door latched. Fact was, the world often scared Hunny. If alone, she wanted to be securely tucked in her wire den, and at night, she preferred sleeping close to Chris, snuggled against his back as the two shared his king-size bed.

Chris stirred first on Thursday morning. He stumbled out of bed wearing just boxers and made his way to the bathroom, absently combing his fingers through his sandy-colored hair. Hunny lifted her head and watched him for a moment before jumping off the bed and following him to the bathroom. She sat patiently outside the closed door, waiting. A few minutes later he came out of the bathroom and found her sitting by the door, staring at him, her tail wagging.

"Come on, girl," Chris said before taking her outside.

TWENTY MINUTES LATER, Chris, coffee cup in hand, stepped out onto his front porch. Just as he was about to bend down to pick up his morning newspaper, he noticed a car sitting in the driveway next door. Both the passenger and driver doors were wide open and the car appeared to be empty. But next to the vehicle stood a man and woman, and with them a young girl who looked to be about Evan MacDonald's age.

The child stood quietly by the woman as the two adults engaged in a heated discussion. The man seemed angry and pointed to the street. Chris glanced in the direction the man pointed and spied a moving van driving in their direction.

For a brief moment Chris had considered walking next door and introducing himself to who he assumed were his new neighbors, but he didn't think barging in while they were clearly arguing would be a terrific first meeting. Instead he bent down to pick up the newspaper just as the moving van pulled up in front of what had been Pete Rogers's house and parked in the street. Before going back inside his house, Chris glanced over to his new neighbors and watched as the woman marched into her house, the little girl following her. In turn, the man slammed the passenger door shut on his car and then stomped around to the driver's side of the vehicle. The next moment he backed the car out of the driveway and parked along the street, while the moving van pulled into the now empty driveway.

"I'll meet them later," Chris muttered to himself as he went inside his house.

Thirty minutes later a knock came at his front door. Chris wondered briefly if it might be his new neighbors coming to introduce themselves. But once he opened the door, he found Adam Nichols standing on his doorstep.

"Morning, Chris," Adam said cheerfully, holding up an Old Salts Bakery sack. Hunny, who stood between the men, wagged her tail at Adam and tried to nose the bag, but Adam held it out of her reach.

Chris looked at Adam's offering. "Cinnamon rolls?" He gave Hunny a silent hand command to get back. She obeyed.

Adam nodded and said, "You mentioned you weren't going to the office today."

Chris opened the door wider. "No, I'm helping set up the haunted house."

Adam stepped inside.

"So what did I do to deserve cinnamon rolls?" Chris asked, closing the door behind them.

"Trying to put you in a good mood," Adam said, walking into

the kitchen and tossing the sack on the counter. He helped himself to a cup of coffee.

"I use these sometimes to coax Heather out of one of her surly moods." Chris picked up the sack, pulled out a cinnamon roll, and took a bite.

"Does it work?" Adam asked. He helped himself to a roll and then took it and his now full coffee cup to the breakfast bar and sat down. Chris joined him.

Chris shrugged. "Old Salts cinnamon rolls are pretty good, but they aren't magic. So what do you need?"

"It's not what I need, it is what you need," Adam said, pulling his cinnamon roll in half.

"When have I heard that before?" Chris chuckled and took another bite of his roll.

"You told me last week you might be interested in buying some more oceanfront property?"

"I might have been interested in Pete Rogers's house had I known it was on the market."

Adam shrugged. "I didn't know it was for sale either. The courts are handling Rogers's estate. The house never showed up on MLS."

Chris shrugged. "No problem. So where are these properties?"

The two discussed real estate for almost thirty minutes when the conversation turned to local gossip.

"So have you met your new neighbor?" Adam asked. He now sat on the sofa across from Chris, their empty coffee cups abandoned on the breakfast bar.

"No. But I saw them this morning. At least I assume it was them."

"I noticed the moving van when I drove up," Adam said. "But there was nobody outside. So what are they like? Young? Old?"

"Family." Chris shrugged. "Looked to be in their early forties, I guess. There was a little girl with them. Don't know if they have any other kids. I considered going over and introducing myself, but when I saw them, they appeared to be having a fight. Didn't think it would be a good time to barge in."

Adam chuckled. "Yeah, moving can be stressful for some people. More than once I've had to calm down a buyer when something didn't go as they expected."

"I wonder what Rogers is going to do with the proceeds from

the house. See if he can find a lawyer that can get his sentence reduced?" Chris suggested.

"You know, Rogers already had money—most inherited from his wife. But between you and me, a good portion of his estate has already gone to Mel, settling a wrongful death claim against him for her mother, along with damages for his attempt to kidnap her. When the court is done distributing the funds from the Beach Drive sale, Rogers won't be seeing any of it," Adam explained.

"I heard the house next door belonged to his wife."

"The original house did," Adam said. "Actually it belonged to his wife's parents. But that house—well, most of it—burned down not long after she died. He rebuilt it, only keeping that corner section."

"You mean the brick section?" Chris asked. The southwest corner of what had been Pete Rogers's house—about four feet on the south wall and four feet on the west wall—was made of brick.

Adam nodded. "From what my grandmother once told me, the fire didn't take the house down to the ground, but it destroyed much of it. Rogers had the debris hauled away and kept the foundation and rebuilt on it, adding a garage. But he left that section. It was the only part of the original house he didn't have torn down. I used to think it had once been a fireplace and they had removed the chimney after the fire."

"It wasn't?" Chris asked.

"No. The original house was wood frame, but it had that brick corner. I always assumed it had been a fireplace, but Pete said it hadn't been."

"I always figured it was an abandoned fireplace."

"Have you ever been inside Pete's house?" Adam asked.

"A couple of times."

"So you saw the brick section from the inside and the copper panel?"

Chris frowned. "I guess I've never been to that part of the house. What is it?"

"That brick section is built like a four-foot square, from floor to ceiling, and on one of the brick walls inside the house it's covered with a copper panel. The panel is engraved with the name of the builder."

"That's different."

"I think the original house was built the same year as Marlow House."

Chris arched his brow. "Really?"

"Yeah. I suspect that's why Pete left the section up. Not that he was ever that interested in local history, but I think he figured if he went to sell the house someday, it might add value to the property."

"Interesting," Chris muttered.

"You know what I recently discovered?" Adam asked.

"What?"

"After I heard the house had sold, I did a little digging into old titles. That property was originally owned by the Marlows. Which isn't all that surprising, considering Frederick Marlow once owned a ton of land in this area. But he was the one who originally had the house built, the one that burned down. And it was Walt Marlow who sold the property to Pete's in-laws. Not to his in-laws exactly. To his father-in-law's parents."

"Really? Did Marie know that?" Chris asked.

Adam shrugged. "If she did, she never mentioned it to me."

WHEN CHRIS WALKED Adam to his car later that morning, the moving van was still in the neighbor's driveway and the movers were in the process of taking a mattress up the walkway. Chris stood in his driveway for a moment, watching as Adam drove off, giving him a final goodbye wave. Just as he turned to his house, he heard someone calling, "Hello!"

Looking in the direction of the new neighbors, Chris spied the man walking toward him. He was smiling, no longer looking angry, as he had the first time Chris had seen him.

"Hello!" the man called again when he reached Chris, extending his hand in greeting.

Chris accepted the handshake. "Welcome to the neighborhood. I assume you are my new neighbor?"

"Yes, my name is Austin Crawford."

"Chris Johnson here, nice to meet you."

When the handshake ended, Austin placed his balled fists on his hips and glanced briefly at his house and then back to Chris. The woman Chris had seen Austin arguing with earlier was walking toward them. She flashed them a smile.

"This is my wife, Mia. Honey, this is Chris Johnson, our neighbor." Austin introduced them after his wife reached them.

"So nice to meet you," she beamed.

Austin wrapped his right arm around his wife and pulled her closer to his side. He smiled at Chris. "So tell me, is it true what our real estate agent told us? No kids in this neighborhood?"

"I'm afraid not," Chris said, thinking of the little girl he had seen earlier. There wouldn't be any neighborhood kids for her to play with. "Just Connor, but he's only a month old."

"Yes!" Austin said gleefully, giving his free hand a fist pump.

"Oh hush." His wife laughed, nudging him with one hip. She smiled up at Chris. "You have to excuse my husband. He isn't fond of children."

"It's not like I hate them." Austin shrugged. "But I don't want to live on a street with a bunch of noisy kids hanging around." He looked at Chris and asked, "Am I right?"

Chris smiled dully and looked past the man at Pete Rogers's old house. The young girl stood inside, looking out the window at them. Chris's cellphone began to ring.

Pulling the cellphone from his pocket, he looked at it briefly and then said, "Excuse me, I have to take this call. It was nice meeting you both."

The couple said a brief goodbye and watched as Chris walked away, his back to them and his cellphone at his ear. They turned toward their house. When Chris was out of earshot, the woman said, "Oh my god, he is gorgeous!"

"Shut up," her husband muttered, dropping his arm from her shoulder.

"Oh, come on, he is. Is he an actor or something? A model? Dang, and I thought the only thing I would have to look at here was a great ocean view."

FIVE

On Thursday afternoon Walt stood in his living room, holding a plastic bag filled with what looked like cotton. He read its label: *Spiderwebs*.

"I guess you can buy about anything these days," Walt said as he tossed the bag to Chris. Also with them in the living room were Heather and Danielle, each woman busy sorting through large paper sacks filled with Halloween decorations.

Holding the plastic bag filled with faux spiderwebs, Chris paused a moment and said, "You know what I need to finish decorating? I know it would really help."

Heather glanced up from the bag she was sorting through. "What?"

"A big slice of Danielle's double fudge chocolate cake," Chris said.

"Sounds like a good idea to me," Walt chimed in.

Danielle chuckled. "Decorate first; cake later."

"Slave driver," Chris said as he ripped the plastic bag open. "I hope you have more than this."

"More than enough," Danielle said, taking another bag of spiderwebs out of her sack and throwing it at Chris.

"Hey, wait a minute." Chris used his wrist to dodge the incoming missile. It fell to the floor. "One at a time."

"I got some great spiders," Heather said as she pulled a handful of plastic spiders out of her bag.

"Perpetuating another myth," Walt said.

"What myth is that?" Danielle asked as she checked her to-do list.

"That haunted houses are covered in spiderwebs. Marlow House was haunted for almost a hundred years, and I am proud to say we were virtually spiderweb-free," Walt boasted.

"That's only because its previous living owner had the presence of mind to hire people like Joanne to keep it clean," Danielle reminded him.

"Here it is!" Heather shouted as she pulled a small tube out of her bag.

"What's that for?" Walt asked, eyeing the tube.

"It's for Max," Heather explained.

"But first Walt needs to explain it to him," Danielle said.

"Explain what exactly?" Walt asked, taking the tube from Heather and reading its label.

"It's fairly obvious," Heather said impatiently. "A haunted house needs a black cat. Max is almost a black cat—almost."

"Aww," Walt said, handing the tube back to Heather. "You intend to blacken his white-tipped ears?"

"They said this is nontoxic, will cover the white fur, and will easily wash off," Danielle said. "But I don't want Max going around trying to rub it off and getting black dye all over the place. I thought you could explain it to him."

Walt took back the tube of black dye and said, "Let's see how this works." He glanced around, looking for Max.

———

PEARL HUCKABEE STARED out her bedroom window at the morbid sight below. Headstones lined her neighbor's backyard, transforming it into what looked like a cemetery. When stopping at the hardware store earlier that day, she had overheard two women discussing the unsightly decorations. Although, it seemed as if no one shared Pearl's opinion that the decorations were in fact unsightly.

"I heard they've fixed the backyard to look like a cemetery. They've added headstones," one young woman told her much older companion, discussing the haunted house decorations going up at Marlow House.

"I don't know why they needed to go to all that trouble, considering the house next door is practically a real cemetery!" the older woman joked, referring to the bodies recently discovered in Pearl's backyard.

"You mean Beach Drive Cemetery?" the younger woman said with a laugh.

The two women had no idea Pearl, who stood behind them in the checkout line, listening to their conversation, owned the property where the bodies had been found.

After taking a final look at the sight below, Pearl closed her curtains so she wouldn't have to look at it anymore. Hopefully they would remove the headstones as soon as this haunted house nonsense was over.

She then headed downstairs. A few minutes later she walked outside to get her mail. Making her way toward her front gate, she noticed the traffic had already increased on Beach Drive. A moment later she took several envelopes from her mailbox and glowered at the passing vehicles. They slowed down when reaching Marlow House to read the makeshift sign that had been posted on the front fence. It listed the hours of operation for the upcoming haunted house. Actually, it listed when the haunted house tour would begin each day, but it didn't state when it would close. Pearl had read the sign earlier and had even called the city office complaining. According to them, Danielle had taken out a permit for the sign, and it would be removed by November second. Once again, there was nothing she could do. She just hoped they would be closing early each evening.

Just as she closed the door on her mailbox, she noticed a large truck coming up the street. As it passed her house, she read the sign on the side of the vehicle: *Bellemore Construction, Frederickport, OR.* Pearl frowned and craned her neck toward the street, watching as the truck parked at Marlow House. Unlike the other vehicles, it wasn't just passing by.

Pearl thought about how she had looked for a contractor to do some repairs after moving into her house. She couldn't recall a Bellemore Construction company in the area. She wondered if they were new in town—and she wondered what they were doing next door. What kind of work were the Marlows planning now?

"They'd just better get a permit," Pearl grumbled, turning back toward her house and starting up the walk. Just before she reached her front porch, she heard a meow. Looking north, to the fence separating her property from the Marlows', she spied a large black cat sitting in the tree, looking at her.

At first glance she thought it was the Marlows' cat. But then she noticed something different. It was all black. The cat did not have white-tipped ears.

Pearl glared at the feline, mentally daring it to jump into her yard. "Mr. Stray, how about a quick trip down to the pound? I don't need any feral cats hanging around here."

The next moment the black cat jumped down off the tree, disappearing into the Marlows' backyard.

THE BELLEMORE BROTHERS stood on the sidewalk at the front gate leading up to Marlow House and stared up at the Second Empire Victorian with its mansard roofline.

"We're really here," the elder brother, Cecil, said in awe, taking in the sight.

"It's gorgeous," the younger brother, Chester, muttered. "But it looks pretty good. Not sure they're going to need us."

"The house is old," Cecil reminded him. "It may look good on the outside, but I can't believe it doesn't need some work. And it would be easier for us if we had access to the house."

Chester nodded to the haunted house sign hanging on the fence. "Looks like they plan to turn the place into a haunted house for Halloween. I suppose that would be one way for us to get inside."

Cecil shook his head at the suggestion. "With all those other people hanging around? I don't think so."

Chester let out a sigh and said, "Let's go introduce ourselves."

DANIELLE ABSENTLY RUBBED her fingertips with a tissue, attempting to wipe off the black dye that had gotten on her when applying the makeup to Max's ears. Although the cat had sat perfectly still while she covered his white fur, he immediately dashed from the room and headed outside when she had finished. She wondered if he was going across the street to show Sadie his new look—or perhaps to Heather's to show her calico, Bella, or perhaps down to see Hunny. She hoped it wasn't to see Hunny. The poor pitty didn't need another thing to be scared of—like a new black cat in the neighborhood.

Just as she tossed the tissue into the trash, she heard the doorbell ring. Looking up, she called, "I'll get it." Walt, Chris and Heather were busy hanging spiderwebs, with Walt attaching the webbing to the higher points of the ceiling. Unlike Heather and Chris, Walt could reach those areas without a ladder—and without actually using his hands.

"Hello," Danielle greeted a few minutes later after she opened her front door. Standing on her porch were two extremely large thirtysomething men. It wasn't as if either was overweight, just tall, even taller than Walt, with physical frames matching their height. They were dressed similarly with new blue jeans and crisp white long-sleeve linen shirts over broad shoulders. Each had prematurely gray hair, and if she was to guess, she would say they were brothers considering their remarkable resemblance to each other.

"Hello," one greeted her. "Is Mr. Marlow available?"

"Mr. Marlow is currently busy. We're decorating for the haunted house, and I'm afraid my husband is in the middle of hanging spiderwebs. I'm Mrs. Marlow. Can I help you?" Danielle asked politely.

The other man pulled a business card from his pocket and handed it to her. "Hello, Mrs. Marlow. My name is Cecil Bellemore, and this is my brother, Chester."

Danielle looked down at the business card and read it aloud. "Bellemore Construction?"

Chester nodded. "Yes. We specialize in Victorian house renovation."

"We are new in Frederickport," Cecil explained. "And we wanted to introduce ourselves. Your house is beautiful, and we understand it is one of the oldest houses in town."

"It's nice to meet you both…" Danielle said, looking down a bit confused at the business card. She looked back up and said, "But as you can see, Marlow House doesn't really need renovating."

Cecil smiled. "You are right; your house is lovely. But old houses like this often need repairs—I noticed some shingles on your mansard roofline look as if they could use some attention."

"You are a roofer?" Danielle asked.

"When it comes to this style of house, we do it all," Cecil explained. "And when the time comes that Marlow House needs some attention, we hope you think of us."

Danielle looked at the card again. "That is nice to know." She looked back up to the men. "Umm, I see on the card your business is in Frederickport. Do we really have that many Victorian houses around here to keep you busy?"

"We are general contractors," Chester explained. "We don't just work on Victorians. But they are our specialty, and we're going around today, introducing ourselves to homeowners—like yourself."

"Well, I'll certainly keep your card and show it to my husband. And if we ever need some work, we will definitely keep you in mind. But right now, I really need to get back to decorating."

"KEEPING us in mind is not what I wanted to hear," Cecil grumbled after he got back into the driver's seat of their truck.

"What did you expect? *'Come right in, gentlemen, and get to work?'*" Chester snarked.

"I figured she might at least offer to take us on a tour of the house. But she seemed awful anxious to get rid of us."

"She did say they were in the middle of decorating for the haunted house and had to get back to it. Our timing was off." Chester, now in the passenger seat, hooked his seatbelt.

"I suppose." Cecil shoved the key into the ignition.

"I still think we should have told her who our grandfather was," Chester said.

Cecil furrowed his brows at his brother. "Absolutely not. You don't know how much she knows."

"There is no way she knows about all that. You read her website. She's posted all that historical stuff on it, and nothing about it or our grandfather. We should tell her about him," Chester insisted. "It could prove to be our pass into Marlow House."

"Or get the door slammed on us forever."

SIX

It had been about five years since Frederickport Police Chief Edward MacDonald's wife had died from cancer—five years raising their two small sons alone. He glanced in the rearview mirror at his youngest boy, Evan, who sat alone in the back seat, absently playing with a pair of wax vampire teeth.

The eight-year-old boy so resembled his late wife it sometimes made Edward ache to look at him—especially when the sunlight hit Evan's face at just the right angle, brushing over the tip of his delicate nose, the large brown eyes and those long, long lashes.

People often told him his oldest son, Eddy Junior, was his mini-me, with his blue-gray eyes and smile. But Eddy's laugh, that was his mother's. It made Edward smile, a gentle reminder that his wife had left behind something tangible of herself in both sons before moving on. And she had moved on—it was something he understood more now than he had five years ago.

Five years ago he had questioned it all. What was the meaning of life? When we died, was it just over? Was there a heaven or simply a long sleep? Why did his wife have to die so young?

But then he met Danielle Boatman, and everything changed. Danielle proved to him that death was simply a doorway into the next step of our voyage. Why his wife had to leave so soon, he still didn't understand, but it was comforting to know—really know—that her death did not mean the end for her.

Meeting Danielle also meant he was not alone in regard to raising his sons. While his sister, Sissy, and her husband, Bruce, had always been there to help, as had his wife's parents, who made a concerted effort to be a part of their grandsons' lives—Danielle and her friends helped him understand and deal with Evan's unique gift —a gift that his sister, grandparents and Eddy Jr. were not aware of. Evan, like Danielle, could see ghosts. Had it not been for them, Edward shuddered to think what might have been the fate of his youngest. Children who seemingly spoke to imaginary people often ended up labeled as mentally ill.

Now driving up Beach Drive, the chief pulled over to the side-walk in front of Marlow House and parked his car. Evan looked up at his father and smiled.

"I understand Chris is buying pizza when you're finished deco-rating," MacDonald said as he turned off his ignition and unhooked his seatbelt.

"You going to stay?" Evan asked.

The chief shook his head. "Sorry. I have to get back to work and later pick up your brother from his scout meeting. Danielle said she would get you home."

"I could spend the night," Evan suggested with a hopeful grin.

The chief laughed and opened his car door. "What, you wouldn't be scared spending the night in a haunted house?"

Evan shook his head. Still holding his wax vampire teeth, he fumbled with his seatbelt, unlatching it. "Nahh. I'm not scared of no ghost."

With a grin Edward stepped out of the car and muttered, "No, you aren't."

AFTER EDWARD WALKED Evan up to the front door of Marlow House and chatted for a few minutes with Danielle, he left his son to help finish decorating for the haunted house.

They put Evan in charge of spider detail, which meant he was to place plastic spiders in the spiderweb tunnel they had created in the living room. Walt stayed to help him reach the high spots.

In the kitchen Heather busily transformed the room into a witch's workshop while Eva offered suggestions. The onetime silent screen star viewed the area as a movie set and enthusiastically threw herself into the project, which Heather found somewhat amusing.

On the counter Heather artfully arranged glass bottles with decorative labels she had printed off on her computer. Small plastic mice filled one jar; its label read *mice*. Another jar label read *bats*, another *eyeballs*, *warts*, *eye of newt*, *frogs*, and so on. She filled each jar with the items—or a plastic replica—according to the label. The jar labeled *poison* contained cola instead of actual poison. One jar went without a label. It needed none. It appeared to contain a severed head.

In the downstairs bedroom Chris arranged the wooden casket he had brought over, Marie helping him move the heavy object. Before starting on the spiderweb tunnel, Evan had found the ghoulish box fascinating and had even climbed in for a moment, wanting to see what it felt like.

But now he was busy in the living room, and Danielle stood for a moment at the open bedroom doorway looking in. Hands on her hips, she shook her head.

"Seriously, Chris, don't you feel a little guilty having a ninety-one-year-old woman move that thing?" Danielle teased.

Chris paused a moment and looked over to Danielle, flashing her his crooked grin. "No, not particularly."

Marie laughed. "Death does have its perks."

Danielle walked into the room and looked down at the casket. "Where did you get that thing, anyway?"

"I had Norman order it for me," Chris said.

"Umm…what do you plan to do with it after Halloween?" Danielle asked.

"I figure if this goes well, you might want to make it an annual tradition," Chris explained. "So next year you'll already have the casket."

Danielle groaned. "Certainly you aren't going to leave it here?"

"Don't worry, dear," Marie said, now stretched out in the casket, trying it out. "I'll move it to the basement for you." To prove her point, the casket lifted into the air, Marie still inside. She giggled.

Danielle shook her head in amusement and walked into the entry hall. She made her way back to the living room to check on the progress of the spider tunnel. When she got there, she found Evan floating in the air and laughing as he placed plastic spiders up near the ceiling.

"Walt, what is he doing up there?" Danielle asked. "I thought you were going to put the spiders in the high places?"

"This is more fun," Walt told her.

"Oh yeah!" Evan stretched out his arms, clutching a few plastic spiders in one hand. "I can fly!"

Danielle glanced to the window and noticed the shades were closed. *At least he had the presence of mind to shut the front blinds*, Danielle thought.

Later that afternoon, after the completion of the spiderweb tunnel, Walt reopened the blinds in the living room. The others returned to the room to discuss what kind of pizzas to order. Evan stood at the front window, looking outside and listening to the conversation, when he noticed a girl standing out on the sidewalk, looking up to the house.

"I bet she's waiting for the haunted house to open," Evan said, still looking out at the girl.

Chris glanced outside. "That's my new neighbor."

"She looks about your age," Danielle said after looking out the window.

"You should go introduce yourself," Walt suggested.

Evan shrugged and turned from the window and then plopped down on a chair. "She's a girl."

Chris chuckled and then rustled Evan's hair good-naturedly. "Trust me, kid, that is not a bad thing."

"You should go say hello," Heather said. "Nothing worse than moving to a new neighborhood where you don't know anyone."

"Heather has a point," Walt said.

"It would be the nice thing to do," Marie chimed in.

Eva nodded. "Yes, it would."

"Aw, come on, Evan. You have no problem hanging out with a couple of ghosts, climbing in a casket, and flying around the room, but you are afraid of a girl?" Chris teased.

Evan frowned. "I'm not afraid."

Chris cocked a brow at the boy, silently challenging him.

Evan glanced over to the window for a moment and then let out a sigh. He stood up. "Okay, I'll go say hello."

"HI," Evan greeted her, walking down the front walkway toward the street.

Untidy blond curls fell to the girl's shoulders, while large blue eyes looked questioning at Evan. She seemed startled at his greeting, and for a brief moment, it looked as if she was about to bolt. Instead, she blinked her eyes several times and asked, "Do you live here?" She looked back up at Marlow House briefly and then to Evan.

Evan shook his head. "No. My friends do. I'm helping them decorate for the haunted house."

She nodded to the sign on the fence. "I just read that. A haunted house for Halloween?"

"Yes. It's going to be really cool. Are you going to come?" he asked.

She shrugged. "I don't know."

Evan stepped out onto the sidewalk. "My name's Evan MacDonald. My friend Chris said you moved into the house next door to him." He pointed up the street toward Chris's house.

"My name's Ginny," she told him.

Evan glanced over Ginny, noting the ragged dress she wore and oversized sweater. "Do you know what class you're going to be in?"

She frowned. "Class?"

"At school."

"I don't know." She dug her hands deep in her pockets. "My father always said it was a waste to send a girl to school."

Evan looked confused. "Uhh…why is that?"

She shrugged. "But my father died. So I went to live with my aunt and uncle. I don't think they were very happy about it."

"Where's your mother?" Evan asked.

She shrugged again. "She's dead too."

"Oh, I'm really sorry. My mom died too," he explained.

Instead of commenting on Evan's mother, she asked, "Do you like to climb trees?"

"Well, sure. Do you?" He frowned.

She nodded. "I like getting up really high in a tree—where no one can see me."

"I didn't know girls like to climb trees."

Ginny flashed him a scowl. "Why wouldn't a girl like to climb trees? That is just silly."

"What else do you like to do?" he asked.

"I don't really like playing with dolls," she confessed. "I know some girls do, but I just don't understand why. I'd rather play hide-and-seek or build a sand castle on the beach or climb a tree. Or go fishing."

"You like to fish?"

"Yeah. Do you?"

Evan nodded.

She looked back up to the house. "I think I would like to go to the haunted house. It sounds like fun."

"It doesn't start until tomorrow," Evan said.

"Oh." She stuck her hands deep in her sweater pockets and looked around, as if trying to figure out what to say next.

Finally Evan asked, "What do you want to be for Halloween?"

Ginny studied Evan a minute and then said, "A ghost."

Evan grinned. "That's what I'm going to be. Danielle said she would help me make a ghost costume tomorrow. I'm going to work in the haunted house and be a ghost."

"How do you make a ghost costume?" she asked.

"From an old sheet, of course," he explained. "How are you going to make your costume?"

She shrugged. "I don't know. I really haven't thought about it. I've never dressed up for Halloween before."

Evan's eyes widened in surprise. "Never?"

Ginny shook her head.

"If you want, I bet Danielle would help you make a ghost costume when she helps me. And if your aunt and uncle will let you, you could help me at the haunted house. I'm going to be jumping out at people, wearing my costume. We could have two ghosts jumping out if you wanted to help."

"You think she would let me?" Ginny asked excitedly.

He nodded. "Danielle is really nice. She and Walt own Marlow House."

"I heard Marlow House is really haunted," Ginny whispered.

Evan nibbled his lower lip and glanced behind him at Marlow House. "Some people say that."

"Have you ever seen a ghost there?" she asked in a whisper, her eyes wide in anticipation of his answer.

"Umm…" Evan shifted his weight from one foot to the other.

"Do you believe in ghosts?" Ginny asked.

SEVEN

Danielle decided to run errands alone on Friday morning, leaving Walt at home to oversee the final touches for the haunted house. According to the online calendar Danielle had referenced, sunset would fall about six fifteen that evening, which was why they planned to open the haunted house at 7:00 p.m. The fundraiser would run through Halloween evening.

Her first stop was the police station to see Police Chief MacDonald. Her next stop would be the museum. They had been selling advance tickets, and she wanted to pick them up and deposit the money in the bank account she had set up for the event.

When Danielle arrived at the police station that morning, she found Officers Joe Morelli and Brian Henderson having coffee in the front waiting area.

"Morning, gentlemen," Danielle greeted them cheerfully when she joined them.

"Morning, Danielle, you all ready for your haunted house?" Joe asked.

"Just about." Danielle grinned.

"The chief tells us Evan has been helping you decorate," Brian said.

Danielle nodded. "Yes, and both boys are going to be helping this weekend. It should be fun."

"There is one nice thing about Halloween these days," Brian said after taking a sip of coffee.

"What's that?" Danielle asked.

"We don't have to deal with Presley House anymore."

Joe let out a gruff laugh. "You are right there. What a pain that used to be."

"I almost got killed in that fire," Danielle reminded them.

Brian shrugged. "But you didn't. I've always said you're like a cat. Land on your feet."

Danielle scrunched her nose at Brian. "Whatever."

Joe cringed. "Yeah, that was pretty terrifying seeing you three coming out of those flames. That place was always a magnet for trouble on Halloween."

"It was a shame to lose that house," Danielle said. "But I'm just grateful Lily and I didn't lose our lives."

Ten minutes later Danielle was alone with the chief in his office, enjoying a cup of coffee Brian had brought her.

"It is a refreshing change seeing you and Brian get along," the chief said after Brian left his office, closing the door behind him.

Danielle lifted her cup to the chief in mock salute and said, "And I always enjoy a cup of coffee."

The chief smiled and leaned back in his chair, his own coffee mug in hand. "Evan tells me he met a new friend."

"Yes, Ginny. She moved in with her aunt and uncle to Pete Rogers's old house," Danielle explained. "She seems like a sweet girl."

"Evan tells me she lost both her parents."

Danielle nodded. "That's what she told Evan."

The chief shook his head in sympathy. "I suspect that might have been a bonding moment for Evan. I don't think he's ever had a friend who, like him, doesn't have a mother."

"When I was little, I had a friend who had lost her mother. When we were in high school, she once told me how it always made her feel different. Everyone else had a mother but her."

The chief nodded. "Yes. I've talked about this with both boys. It's not uncommon for a child who has lost a parent to feel different from his friends. It really bothered Evan that she lost both parents."

"I have to admit we had to give Evan a little nudge to go introduce himself to her. After all, she is a girl." Danielle chuckled.

"The way he was talking about her last night, he didn't seem to have a problem with her being a girl."

"No, they hit it off. In fact, he brought her inside and introduced us to her and then gave her a tour of the house. We invited her to stay for pizza, but she said she had to get home. She's returning this afternoon so I can make her and Evan ghost costumes. Evan asked if she could help during the haunted house, and I said yes, as long as it was okay with her aunt and uncle."

"I know both boys are looking forward to it," the chief said. "Eddy tells me you're going to wrap him up like a mummy, and he gets to wander the house."

"Yes. Chris is wrapping up like a mummy, too. Actually it's more like a mummy costume, no actual wrapping involved. I don't know if Evan told you, but Chris got us a real casket, which they set up in the downstairs bedroom. Chris plans to lie in it and pop up to scare people when they come through."

"Yes, Evan told me all about it. He thought it was very cool," MacDonald told her. "Umm…are you planning to have Eddy get in the casket?"

Danielle grinned and shook her head. "I don't want to scar your eldest child. So no. But I will have to tell you, Evan climbed right in to check it out. It didn't seem to bother him at all."

AFTER LEAVING THE POLICE STATION, Danielle headed over to the museum. Overhead gray clouds filled the sky, and in the distance she spied a flash of lightning. While a stormy night might provide the right ambiance for the event, Danielle wasn't thrilled with the thought of wet and muddy shoes tromping through her house.

She pulled into the museum parking lot and parked her car. After turning off the engine, she glanced to her left and noticed a truck parked several spaces over. On its door it read *Bellemore Construction*. She frowned, trying to remember why that name sounded familiar. Just as she pulled the key from the ignition, she had her answer when two men got into the truck before driving off.

A few minutes later Danielle walked into the museum and was greeted by Millie Samson.

"Are you here to collect the ticket money?" Millie asked when Danielle walked into the museum gift store.

"Yes. How did the presale go?" Danielle asked.

"It looks like this is going to be a success!" Millie said before handing Danielle an envelope.

"I noticed the Bellemore brothers leaving the museum. Are they going to be doing some work here?" Danielle asked.

"Who?" Millie frowned.

"The two men who left just a minute ago," Danielle explained.

"They never told me their name."

"I met them yesterday. They're new in town. Stopped by Marlow House and introduced themselves. They're general contractors. They own the Bellemore Construction company. Apparently they specialize in Victorian house renovation," Danielle told her.

"That might explain all the questions they asked. They seemed very curious about some of the older homes—especially those built when the town was first founded. What did you say their name was again?" Millie asked.

"Bellemore."

Millie frowned as she considered the name.

"What is it?" Danielle asked.

"There is just something familiar about that name. Hmm…what is it?"

Danielle shrugged. "Doesn't sound familiar to me."

"I know!" Millie said at last. "That was the name of the man who built Marlow House!"

"Frederick Marlow built Marlow House," Danielle reminded her.

Millie smiled at Danielle and shook her head. "No. He had the house built, but he wasn't the one who built it. It was built by a man named Bellemore. I remember coming across that information when we put together the Marlow exhibit. Bellemore built a number of the older homes in town. I believe he died not long after Frederick Marlow did."

"I doubt it's the same Bellemore family," Danielle said.

"It is a small world, but I suspect you're right."

"Did they happen to say where they were from?" Danielle asked.

"No. Just that they recently moved to town and would like to learn more about the community. They seemed most interested in the older homes. But if you say they specialize in Victorian restorations, I suppose that makes sense they would be asking where the older houses are."

"I DON'T THINK I can eat in this room with that head looking at me," Danielle said as she stood in the kitchen, holding the bag of burgers she had picked up for lunch. She glared down at the jar with the head. It looked insanely real.

Walt eyed the ghoulish Halloween decoration and said, "I swear the eyes follow you."

"I have to say, the kitchen looks pretty creepy. How about we eat in the library?" Danielle suggested.

Fifteen minutes later Walt and Danielle sat in the library eating lunch.

"I don't imagine we'll be doing much cooking in our kitchen until after Halloween," Danielle said before taking a bite of her burger.

"No. While Heather did an amazing job, it's not very appetizing."

Danielle chuckled and took another bite. A few minutes later she asked, "Do you remember a man named Bellemore? According to Millie, he built Marlow House."

Walt nodded. "Certainly. Chester Bellemore. He did good work, but I never cared for the man."

"Chester?" Danielle frowned.

"Yes. How did his name happen to come up?"

"Are you sure his first name was Chester?" she asked.

"Yes, why?"

Danielle shook her head in disbelief. "Weird coincidence. Remember those men who stopped by yesterday?"

"The ones handing out their business cards?" Walt asked. "They did construction?"

"Yes. I don't think I mentioned it before. But their last name was Bellemore, and their company is Bellemore Construction." She then went on to tell Walt about her visit to the museum.

When she was done, Walt said, "I seriously doubt it's the same Bellemore family."

"But one of the brothers was named Chester."

"So?"

"Don't you think it's an odd coincidence?"

Walt shrugged. "I suppose it's possible he's a great-grandson or something."

"Millie said Bellemore died right after your grandfather."

After wiping the corners of his mouth with a napkin, Walt said, "Yes. He was probably in his seventies by then. His son also worked for my grandfather—Thomas Bellemore. Thomas was not happy when I sold the company. Although, I suppose in retrospect, I can't say I blame him. But I think he was most upset when I sold a house he wanted to buy to someone else."

"Why did you do that?" she asked.

"It wasn't intentional," Walt said with a shrug. "After Grandfather died, I sold off a number of properties. I certainly didn't feel I needed to check with Thomas Bellemore to see if he wanted to purchase something. It was only after the house sold that he came to me, furious. Said I shouldn't have sold it and asked me to cancel the deal and sell it to him."

"What did you tell him?" Danielle asked.

"That it was too late. In fact, it was the house next door to Chris."

"You don't mean Pete Rogers's old house?"

"I suppose it was," Walt said. "Chris mentioned it to me last night after Evan made friends with his new neighbor. Adam told Chris I used to own that property. Apparently the original house— the one I sold—burned down some time ago, and they rebuilt on the spot."

"And you used to own it?" Danielle said in surprise.

"My grandfather did. I owned it just a short time. I haven't thought about that house in years. And the times we've been over at Chris's, it never occurred to me I once owned the property next door. But like I said, that was a long time ago, and my family used to own a lot of property in Frederickport."

"Marie once mentioned to me her family home was one of the first houses built on that side of the street."

"True, but the house that used to be next door to Chris's was almost as old."

EIGHT

Crumpling the paper that had held her now eaten burger, Danielle balled it up and stuffed it in the to-go paper sack. Grabbing a napkin off a nearby table, she wiped her mouth and then said, "From what I understand, that house was owned for years by Pete Rogers's in-laws. His wife inherited the house, and then he got it."

"I sold it to the Michaelses," Walt told her.

"I'm pretty sure that was Pete's wife's maiden name," Danielle said. "I bet the ones you sold it to were his wife's grandparents, not parents."

"When I knew the Michaelses, they didn't have any children. Although, they were raising his sister's child. That's why I agreed to sell them the house."

"Why is that?" Danielle asked.

"Michaels's sister married a no-good rummy," Walt told her.

"Umm, is that some sort of ethnic slur?" Danielle asked.

Walt chuckled. "I have no idea what his ethnicity was, other than he was white and habitually unemployed. But he drank a lot and was a bum. They lived in a broken-down house outside town, and his wife used to clean houses. Not sure what he ever did but drink and run moonshine. Not good moonshine, either."

"And you would know." Danielle snickered.

Walt shrugged. "The bad stuff could kill you, or at least make you go blind. I was surprised he hadn't lost his sight before he burned down his house, killing him and his wife. Their daughter managed to escape."

"Did he burn it down on purpose?" Danielle asked.

"I doubt it. I don't think he was the type to kill himself, but he didn't have a problem knocking around his wife and kid."

"Nice guy," Danielle said dryly.

"Anyway, Michaels and his wife took in the child, but they were renting a room in town. The three of them couldn't very well live in one small room at the boardinghouse, they needed someplace to live, so I gave them a good deal on the house," Walt explained.

"A house with an ocean view. For someone struggling, it sounds pretty extravagant."

"From what I remember, they used some money from a life insurance policy his sister had to help buy the property."

"Who was living in the house before you sold it to Michaels? You mentioned Bellemore wanted to buy it," Danielle asked. She stuffed the used napkin she had been holding into the to-go sack and looked at Walt, waiting for him to continue.

Walt considered the question a moment, trying to remember the tenants' names. Finally he said, "Fortune. Abe and Annabelle Fortune. I suppose had he not run off, I wouldn't have thought about selling the house."

"Was it just a rental?" Danielle asked.

"Not really. It was owned by my grandfather's company. Fortune worked for my grandfather—never cared for the guy. Always seemed like he was hiding something. Anyway, not long after my grandfather died and it was announced I would be selling the company, Fortune took off. Left his pretty wife high and dry. I couldn't help feeling sorry for her. She came to my house demanding I tell her what I'd done with him."

"She thought you had something to do with him leaving?" Danielle asked.

"To be honest, I was never sure what she really thought. She was so distraught. He'd been gone for a couple of weeks, and she was frantic to find him. She came pounding on my door in tears. I wasn't sure what to do. One of her friends showed up a few minutes later. I suspect they knew she was planning to come over here, and they were checking on her. The friend calmed her down and took her home."

"How sad." Danielle considered what Walt had just told her and then frowned at him. "Are you saying you evicted that poor distraught woman?"

Walt shook his head. "No. I would have let her stay and worked out something. But she died days later."

"What happened?"

"Some fisherman found her on the beach early one morning. She was soaking wet, freezing cold and delirious. She died later that morning but not before telling them she had been looking for her husband—insisting he had been calling for her, begging for her help."

"Did she go mad in her grief?" Danielle asked.

"Not sure what happened. I went to her funeral," Walt explained. "There I ran into the friend who had calmed her down at my house and took her home. She felt guilty, believing she should have done more to help. According to her, Annabelle had been having dreams about her husband—dreams where he begged for her to help him. Annabelle, in her grief, had come to believe they weren't just dreams, that he was really calling for her."

"How soon after that did you sell the house to Michaels? You said Bellemore wanted the house, but you had already sold it."

"Thomas had gone to London for his father's funeral. That's where Chester Bellemore was originally from, where he wanted to be buried. While he was gone, I announced my intentions to sell the company."

"What did he do for the Marlow Shipping Line?" Danielle asked.

"The elder Bellemore had worked for my grandfather for years, supervising the construction of Marlow's various real estate interests and later managing the properties. His son had been groomed to take over. But now I was selling the business and disinvesting in properties. I wouldn't be needing him."

"I don't imagine he was thrilled with you."

"No. But the father had made a fortune from our family, which Thomas had just inherited after his father's death. It wasn't as if he was going to starve. He returned to Frederickport after Annabelle's funeral. Until then, he had no idea Abe Fortune had taken off, or that Abe's wife had died of exposure."

"Or of a broken heart," Danielle muttered.

"Yes, probably more the broken heart," Walt agreed. "Bellemore's son was furious when he returned and learned I was selling the house. He said I should have given him the first right of refusal, claimed my grandfather had always promised him the house. It was the first I'd heard about it, but I had already agreed to sell it to Michaels, and I was not about to go back on my word. Plus, I didn't particularly want Bellemore as a neighbor."

"So he left town after that?" Danielle asked.

"Yes, but not before breaking into Michaels's house before they moved in," Walt said.

"Seriously? Why would he break in?"

"Technically speaking, the first time he didn't really break in, considering he had his own key and his job until that point had included managing that property. I found him in the house just hours after he had returned from Europe. He told me he had heard about Abe and Annabelle and wanted to know if it was true. That's when he offered to buy the house."

"And the other time?"

"When I refused to sell him the house, I asked for the key back. The Fortunes' personal property had already been removed, the house cleaned. There was just some furniture, which I was leaving for the new owners. Nothing of any real value. But then I caught him in the house later that night. I didn't call the police, and he didn't stick around and explain why he was there, or how he had gotten in. I imagine he had another key."

"You think he was looking for something?" she suggested.

"Perhaps, but like I said, we'd already removed all the Fortunes' personal property. When I arrived, he just left without a word. I never saw him again. I heard he left town three days later."

Danielle stood up and gathered all the trash from their lunch. She stuffed it all in the paper to-go sack.

"Did the Michaelses turn out to be better neighbors than Bellemore?" Danielle asked.

"Since Bellemore was never my neighbor, I have no way to compare. But I really didn't have much to do with them. We ran in different crowds. From what I recall, they were pretty involved with their church. Unlike his late brother-in-law, I don't think Michaels ever took a drink of alcohol. I believe he was quite content with prohibition."

"What happened to the niece?" she asked.

"No idea. When I returned from Europe, she was no longer living with them."

"Interesting how things work out," Danielle murmured, holding the trash from their lunch.

"How so?" Walt asked.

"You sold that house to a couple raising their niece—and Pete Rogers did the same. The Crawfords are raising their niece. Weird how things work out," Danielle said as she turned and headed for the doorway.

In the kitchen a few minutes later, Danielle tossed the trash in the bin and glanced around, taking in the kitchen's new look for the haunted house. Tonight Heather would come dressed as a witch, brewing up something in a cauldron on the stove. She chuckled at the thought and then turned to one of the overhead counters to grab a glass.

A moment later she filled the glass with ice and water. Turning from the sink, she leaned back against the counter and took a sip. Her gaze moved around the room and landed on the mock severed head in the jar. She cringed. It was the creepiest and most realistic prop they had added. However, it was nothing more than a rubber Halloween mask, but how it had been placed in the jar, at first glance it looked eerily real.

Danielle stared a moment at the gruesome sight. It seemed to look at her. And then, to her astonishment the corners of its mouth lifted up as the head shifted slightly in the jar, giving Danielle a ghoulish grin.

Letting out a scream from the unexpected sight, the glass slipped from her hand, shattering on the floor, sending glass and water around her feet.

Walt rushed into the kitchen. "What is it?" He looked down at the broken glass on the floor.

"Did you do that?" Danielle squeaked. She pointed nervously to the head in the jar. It was no longer smiling, but looked exactly as it had when she had first come into the kitchen.

Walt looked at the jar and frowned. "Did I do what?"

Danielle stared at the mock severed head and shook her head. "I...I must be imagining things."

NINE

It began as a light sprinkle and then accelerated until the afternoon rain pelted the rooftop in a noisy serenade. Ginny wondered if the persistent downpour would keep others away from the haunted house. She hoped not. It wouldn't keep her away.

Sitting quietly at the kitchen table, she listened to the rain and watched as Austin made ham sandwiches while Mia unpacked a box of dishes. Neither one had spoken a word in the last hour—not since their last argument. They fought a lot. But Ginny was used to fighting. It was her normal.

Today she wore blue jeans and a blouse. The jeans were just like the ones Danielle had been wearing. Ginny liked Danielle. She had been nice and had offered her pizza. Jeans would probably work better with a ghost costume than a dress, Ginny told herself.

Glancing around the kitchen, Ginny thought the place didn't feel like home. She couldn't imagine it ever would. With a sigh she let her mind wander, and she thought about Evan and the haunted house. It seemed like forever since she had made a new friend, and she liked Evan.

Evan was brave, she thought, and fun. He had given her a tour of Marlow House before she had left last night. Nothing seemed to scare him. Not the casket in the downstairs bedroom or giving her a tour of the large spooky house without an adult escorting them. He laughed at the head floating in the bottle in the kitchen. For a moment she actually thought it might be real. But what impressed her most, Evan was not afraid of ghosts.

Letting her mind wander, she failed to notice Austin had turned abruptly from the kitchen counter and practically slammed the plate with the sandwich in front of her on the table. It made her jump in surprise. She looked down at the sandwich. He hadn't cut it in half.

"Go ahead and eat," he said gruffly and then added, "and then we need to get back to unpacking. There is a lot we need to do before you have to go to school on Monday."

ACCORDING TO EVAN, he wouldn't be at Marlow House until after 4 p.m., after he got out of school and went home to change his clothes. Ginny had some time to kill before meeting him. Leaving Austin and Mia in the kitchen, she wandered through the house, looking around.

"No, this doesn't feel like home," she muttered.

Now in the living room, she looked over to its peculiar brick corner. She walked over to take a closer look. Standing just a few inches from the brick wall, she cocked her head and studied the brass panel affixed to the wall. The next moment the doorbell rang.

She had no idea who it was, but she didn't want someone coming in and possibly asking her questions. Considering everything that had happened in the last twenty-four hours, that was entirely possible. If that happened, what would Austin and Mia think?

Glancing around, she spied the stack of boxes along the other wall. It would be a good place to hide, she thought.

"GO AHEAD AND LOOK AROUND," Ginny heard Austin say ten minutes later. She peeked out from behind the boxes and watched as he led two men into the living room. "My wife and I are going to be outside if you need us. But go ahead and look around. Let us know what you think." A moment later he left the room.

The two men stood in silence as if waiting for something. After a few moments one of the men walked over to the living room window and looked outside. "They're on the side patio."

"Is that it?" the other man asked, pointing to the brick corner.

Ginny watched as the two men hurried toward the brick corner and immediately began inspecting it, running their hands over the brass panel.

"This is it, Cecil," one said excitedly.

"Not so loud, Chester, they could come in at any minute," Cecil scolded.

Lowering his voice, Chester said, "When the lady at the museum told us they'd kept the brick section of the original house, I couldn't believe we'd be lucky enough for it to be this section of brick."

"I can't believe nothing was discovered when they tore down the original structure."

"I'm sure she would have said something if they had."

"Now what?" Cecil asked.

"Now you need to turn on that charm of yours. But first, we'd better check out the rest of the house before we try closing the deal."

Ginny waited for the men to leave before coming out of her hiding place. She wondered what they were up to—and who were they?

HEATHER STEPPED out onto the sidewalk in front of her house and looked up the street toward Marlow House. The rain had stopped about twenty minutes earlier. She spied Pearl Huckabee standing next door on the sidewalk in front of her house. It looked as if she was busy hanging something on her fence. *Signs?* Heather asked herself.

Heading toward Marlow House, she paused when she reached Pearl. Glancing at the signs now posted on Pearl's fence, Heather chuckled. In a black marker Pearl had written NO TRESPASSING!

"Getting into the holiday spirit?" Heather snarked.

Pearl scowled at Heather. "It's not the holiday season."

"Halloween's next week. That sort of kicks off the holiday season."

"Nothing but an excuse for teenagers to get into mischief and children to beg for candy."

"Does that mean you aren't handing out Halloween candy this year?" Heather asked.

"I don't believe in Halloween. It's a pagan holiday!"

"So you aren't coming to the haunted house?" Heather asked. "Not sure we're going to have the baby flying around, but there is going to be some cool stuff."

Pearl glared at Heather. "You know perfectly well I have no intention of going to that haunted house! I just hope vandals don't do much damage considering all the riffraff it will be attracting for the next few days!"

Heather rolled her eyes. "You really need to lighten up, Mrs. Huckabee."

Normally Heather would take a shortcut through the side yard gate at Marlow House, yet it was locked due to the fact they had already set the yard up to look like a cemetery, complete with realistic headstones. She wondered wryly how Pearl liked looking out her bedroom window at a makeshift cemetery.

When Heather reached Marlow House's front gate, she spied someone sitting on the steps leading to the front door. Pushing through the gate, she got a better look. It was Evan's little friend from up the street.

"Hello," Heather greeted her when she reached the girl. "Your name is Ginny, right?"

Ginny nodded. "Yes."

"What are you doing out here?" Heather asked, glancing around.

"I'm waiting for Evan," Ginny told her. "He said he would be here around four o'clock."

Heather glanced at her watch. "Then he should be here within the next ten minutes. I imagine the chief is dropping him off after school."

"The chief?" Ginny frowned.

"Yeah, Evan's dad. His father is Police Chief MacDonald."

Ginny's eyes widened. "Oh. And he's going to be bringing Evan?" Ginny stood up and glanced around as if she were planning an escape.

"Yeah." Heather studied Ginny curiously.

"Who else is coming over?" Ginny asked.

"You mean before we open for the haunted house? Because we open at seven, and after that, I have no idea who will be here." Heather grinned.

"I mean before…before they open." Ginny's gaze darted to the street and then back to Heather.

"Everyone who was here last night. You met everyone. Evan's older brother is coming too, but from what I understand, he won't be here until about a half an hour until we open. Why?"

"Is Evan's father staying? I mean until the haunted house?"

Heather shrugged. "I doubt it. Why? Is there something wrong?"

Ginny shook her head quickly. "No. I'm just cold."

"I saw you sitting on the front step. I imagine it was wet from the rain. Do you need to run home to change?"

Ginny reached behind herself and touched the seat of her pants. She shook her head. "No, the step wasn't wet."

Heather glanced up at the overhang covering the front porch and shrugged. She looked back to Ginny and said, "Well, if you're cold, let's go inside, and you can wait for Evan there."

"HEY, CHIEF," Danielle greeted him when she opened the front door at four thirty on Friday afternoon. An anxious Evan stood by his father's side.

"Sorry we're late," the chief said as they walked into the house. "I thought this kid was going to explode if I didn't hurry up and get him here."

"Hey, Evan." Danielle smiled down at the boy. "You ready to make your ghost costume?"

"Yeah, but I need to get Ginny so she can make hers too," Evan said.

"Don't worry about Ginny, she is already here. She's in the parlor."

"Then I can meet her," the chief said.

A few minutes later Danielle led the way into the parlor. Ginny stood in the middle of the room, hidden under a sheet. Slits had already been cut for her eyes, but the holes had not yet been cut, so it was impossible for anyone to see the eyes peeking out.

"I assume you're Ginny?" The chief laughed.

Ginny nodded her head exuberantly.

The chief laughed again.

"This is my dad, Ginny," Evan introduced them.

Ginny's sheet-covered hand waved at the chief.

Evan looked at Danielle and frowned. "I thought you were going to paint our faces white instead of us wearing a sheet over our heads?"

"Ginny said her aunt doesn't like her to wear any face makeup, so I thought the old-fashioned ghost costume would work for her. We'll do the face paint for you. And I'll be adding an outside layer of tulle netting to give you both a more ghostly look." Danielle grinned down at Evan.

The chief glanced at his watch. "I need to get going. You kids have fun. It was nice meeting you, Ginny—sort of." The chief chuckled.

Danielle walked the chief back out into the entry hall, leaving the two children alone in the parlor.

"I'll be back when I bring Eddy. Maybe I'll go through the haunted tour," the chief told her. "I can be your test run."

When Danielle returned to the parlor, Ginny was no longer wearing the sheet, and the two children sat on the sofa together.

"Danielle, I have a question for you," Evan said.

"What is that?" Danielle asked, taking a seat on the chair facing them.

"Ginny and I were talking about what ghosts...umm...what they might look like if they were real."

Danielle arched her brow at Evan. "Hmm, really? And what do they look like?"

"Like people," Evan said. "Sometimes people you can see through, but not always."

Danielle grinned. "So what was the question?"

"Why do people dress up in sheets when they pretend to be ghosts?" Ginny asked. "Why do people think ghosts look like sheets?"

"Ahh...I don't think people actually believe ghosts look like sheets. And most movies with ghosts in them, well, they normally do look like people—often transparent, see-through people."

"So why the sheets?" Evan asked.

"Because a long time ago—I think it was in England—poorer people often wrapped their dead in old sheets after they died to bury them in. They couldn't afford coffins."

"You mean like mummies?" Evan asked.

Danielle nodded. "Yeah, pretty much. And so if someone

wanted to scare someone, they might dress up in torn sheets to make the people think they had been buried and were coming back from the dead. I suppose after a while, people just started using a sheet to dress up like a ghost, instead of wrapping up like a mummy."

"So my brother and I are both dressing up as ghosts this year?" Evan asked.

Danielle laughed. "I suppose, in a way. More like you're both dressing up as the dead."

TEN

Sergeant Joe Morelli had grabbed a quick take-out burger for lunch on Friday so that he could get a haircut. His naturally curly, thick dark hair had needed taming. His girlfriend, Kelly Bartley, preferred his hair a bit longer. Not so that it reached his collar, but long enough so that she could loop a finger through one of his errant curls. But shorter and tamer was more professional, and if Joe was anything, he tried to be professional.

The cut was hardly a buzz, but the curls were gone. Standing at six feet, the shorter cut gave his husky stature a no-nonsense appearance as opposed to what Kelly privately called his teddy-bear look.

He stopped by the break room before heading home and found Brian Henderson sitting alone at a table, drinking a cup of coffee. He paused at the door and looked in.

"I thought you swore off coffee in the afternoon?" Joe asked.

Brian turned to the younger officer and smiled. "I'm working tonight. I need the caffeine."

Joe stepped into the room. "Double shift?"

"I'm covering for Gary," Brian said before taking another sip.

Joe nodded and helped himself to a cup of coffee. He then took a seat at the table with Brian.

"You going to the haunted house this weekend?" Brian asked.

"Kelly and I are going Saturday. Tonight we're babysitting." Joe grinned. He raised his cup and said, "So I'll probably need the caffeine too."

"Babysitting?"

"Kelly's nephew. It's the first time she's watching him. Lily and Ian want to help at the open house tonight, so we agreed to sit with him."

"What about the other nights? I thought it was running through Halloween?"

"Just one of them will help on the other nights. Not sure which one. I think they're making tonight more of a date night. First one since the baby was born. They're going out to an early dinner and then over to Marlow House at about six thirty," Joe explained. "But knowing Lily, I can't believe she won't be popping in every fifteen minutes, checking on Connor."

Brian chuckled and took another sip of coffee.

"So when are you going to take the haunted house tour?" Joe asked.

Brian arched his brows at Joe. "Me? I'm not."

"If you don't have anyone to go with, you're welcome to go with Kelly and me," Joe invited.

"Thanks. But no thanks." Brian set his now empty cup on the table.

"Why not?"

"I've seen enough odd things over at Marlow House to last me a lifetime. I don't need to pay to see more. No, thanks."

"It will be fun. And it is for a good cause."

Brian shook his head. "No. I'm not going. I have no desire to tour a haunted house and have the chief's sons jump out at me wearing sheets."

"If it makes you feel any better, it's not really haunted," Joe teased.

Unsmiling, Brian stared at Joe and then asked, "Are you sure about that?"

AFTER JOE LEFT a few minutes later, Brian remained alone in the break room. He looked down at his empty coffee mug and absently rubbed one finger around its rim while thinking of Marlow House.

"Are you sure the house isn't haunted?" Brian whispered to the empty room.

Leaning back in the chair, he closed his eyes and thought about the strange occurrences he had witnessed at Marlow House over the last few years. There was the time it felt as if someone had slugged him in the entry hall, sending him to the floor. It had all happened so quick. He had foolishly grabbed at Lily right before it had happened, and he had eventually convinced himself he must have slipped. Perhaps his own hand flailed against his face in the fall, giving him the sensation of being slugged.

But there was another time—even more bizarre—that he kept telling himself it had to have been the alcohol. That was the only logical explanation. It had been at Ian's bachelor party, which had been moved from Ian's house to Marlow House. It wasn't just the fact some invisible entity dumped beer on him—it was the towel floating in the library to help wipe him up. *A freaking floating towel.*

Brian shook his head at the thought. "It had to be the booze," he muttered. Perhaps, but it had still seemed so real. There had also been other incidents—numerous ones.

Heather Donovan had once told him she could see ghosts, even claiming she had seen Walt Marlow. There had been that time he had asked Evan who he was waving at and the boy had said *Walt Marlow.* And he wasn't talking about the Walt Marlow who had once gone by his middle name, Clint.

Clint Marlow—now the other Walt—that was an entirely different story. It was as if the ghost of Walt Marlow—if there really had been a ghost—had taken over his distant cousin's body. Of course, that was a ridiculous thought, and the only explanation for the Marlow then and now sharing the same handwriting and finger-prints—someone from the here and now was messing with him. Who and why? He had no idea, but it sent his normally rational world off-kilter, and to make matters worse was the chief's blasé reaction to it all.

Of course, strange sightings didn't just occur at Marlow House. There was that time he was at the grocery store and he could swear cereal boxes fell off the shelf, only to return on their own. Walt Marlow had been there, but neither man mentioned what had just happened. *Or perhaps nothing had happened. I must have imagined it all,* Brian told himself. *Maybe I am simply losing it.*

He stood up and took his coffee cup to the sink. "No, I don't need to go through a haunted house," Brian muttered as he washed the cup.

THE CHIEF STEPPED out of his office and spied Brian coming down the hallway. He stopped a moment and turned to the officer.

"I understand you're working for Gary tonight?" the chief asked.

"Yes. You heading home?" Brian asked.

The chief glanced at his watch. "I have to pick up Eddy—he went over to one of his friends' houses after school. They're working on some scout project. But I have to take him over to Marlow House after we grab a bite to eat. He's helping with the haunted house. You going?"

Brian smiled and shook his head. "No. Not interested."

"You should at least stop over and check out their side yard," the chief suggested.

"I heard. In fact, I got a call on it earlier. A complaint from a neighbor."

The chief grinned. "Pearl Huckabee?"

Brian nodded. "That will teach me to give a chronic complainer my business card."

MacDonald chuckled and then glanced at his watch again. "I'd better get going."

WHEN MACDONALD ARRIVED LATER at Marlow House with Eddy Junior, he found a hub of activity as they prepared for their first opening of the haunted house. Danielle gave Eddy his costume. They weren't actually wrapping him with strips torn from a sheet— he would be slipping on what could best be described as a mummy costume.

"That's interesting," the chief said, taking a closer look at the pair of pants that had strips of white sheet covering it, with bell-bottom-like cuffs large enough to conceal Eddy's shoes.

"We didn't think it would be a good idea to wrap him up in sheets—makes it a little difficult if he has to use the bathroom. And considering the haunted house is going on all week, we figured a costume he could slip on and off might be the best thing. We also had an adult one made for Chris," Danielle explained as Eddy took hold of his costume, preparing to go to the bathroom to put it on. "Ian will help you with it. He helped Chris with his," Danielle told Eddy.

In the next moment a loud groan interrupted them and they looked to the downstairs bedroom door. Stumbling from the room in their direction, arms outstretched in front of its body, was what appeared to be a mummy.

Eddy giggled and said, "Oh cool!"

A few minutes later, after Eddy and Ian retreated to the downstairs bathroom and Chris stumbled back to his coffin, Danielle stood in the entry hall with the chief and Walt.

The chief looked Walt up and down, noting his vintage suit. There was something familiar about it. He thought about it a moment and then remembered. It looked like the suit Walt had worn in the portrait. "That is definitely a blast to the distant past. Where'd you get it?"

"I ordered it online. Walt is dressed up as the ghost of Marlow House—Walt Marlow." Danielle chuckled.

The chief arched his brow. "You are going as yourself?"

Walt shrugged. "I'll be hanging out in the library with my portrait."

Danielle held Walt's right hand and gave it a little squeeze. She flashed him a smile and said, "I rather like you in that suit."

"Where is Evan?" the chief asked, glancing around.

"He and Ginny are upstairs," Danielle explained. "They'll be slipping in and out of rooms on the second floor, scaring people. Eva will be orchestrating them—of course Ginny doesn't know that. She thinks Evan will be telling her what to do. But he will just be passing on what Eva tells him."

"I didn't get a chance to really meet the girl," the chief said. "She was covered in a sheet."

"They both look very ghostly." Walt chuckled.

"You would know." Danielle snickered, giving him a little tap with one hip. She looked back to the chief and said, "She seems like a very nice little girl."

"There is something familiar about her. I swear I have seen her before—but I can't remember where," Walt said.

"Maybe you've seen her around town," the chief suggested.

"It's my understanding they just moved in yesterday," Walt said.

"It doesn't mean they haven't been in town," the chief reminded him. "They obviously have been here before, when they bought the house."

Walt nodded. "True."

"I've been so busy I haven't had a chance to go down and introduce myself to her aunt and uncle," Danielle said.

"They didn't come up here and introduce themselves? I assumed they would since she's helping tonight," the chief said.

Danielle shook her head. "No. I get the feeling she's a free-range kid."

Walt scowled at Danielle. "A what?"

"You know, she's left to her own devices. But it isn't that she doesn't have rules, and while her aunt and uncle might not closely monitor her, it appears she respects their rules, considering what I've seen so far."

"Free-range kids I've seen are often neglected and go hungry," the chief said with a frown of concern.

"I wouldn't worry about that. She hasn't come across as underfed or hungry," Danielle said. "Heck, she turned down pizza."

The chief nodded. "That's good to know. I was a little concerned. She told Evan her aunt and uncle weren't thrilled she came to live with them."

Danielle scrunched up her nose. "Yeah, Evan told us that too."

ELEVEN

Clad in a floor-length pink terrycloth robe, fuzzy slippers and rollers in her hair, Pearl stood by her front gate. With her arms stubbornly folded across her chest, she looked up the sidewalk toward Marlow House. Overhead, the quarter moon partially lit the sky. Pearl had hoped the morning rain would have continued into the night, believing that would put a damper on the haunted house. But the rain had long since stopped, and by the line of cars up her street, it was obvious the fundraiser had been a success. At least for the first night.

She glanced at her watch. It was almost ten p.m. Earlier that evening she'd had an unpleasant encounter with her dreadful neighbor Heather Donovan, who was walking over to Marlow House, and later, the Bartleys from across the street had joined her. She wondered how many of the neighbors approved of the Marlows turning their home into a haunted house for Halloween. She certainly would not appreciate strangers tromping through her home.

Glancing across the street to the Bartley house, she noticed their porch light on. With a grunt she turned and made her way up to her front door.

AT THE BARTLEYS', Joe and Kelly sat with baby Connor while Ian and Lily were across the street helping with the haunted house. Kelly had just changed Connor's diaper and returned him to his crib. He began to fuss.

"I think he wants his teddy bear," Joe said, carrying the stuffed Winnie the Pooh from the rocker to the crib. He placed it next to the squirming baby.

Kelly snatched up the bear. "No. He can't sleep with that."

Joe, who now stood by Kelly's side, frowned at her. "Why not? I thought Lily said it was his favorite."

Now clutching the bear in her arms, Kelly said in a whisper, "Goodness, Joe, he's only a month old. I doubt he's even aware of the bear. I've read how these things get dusty—which isn't good for a baby. And it could smother him."

Kelly carried the stuffed animal over to the rocking chair and set it down.

Joe shrugged. "My mother said I always slept with a teddy bear."

"And it's a good thing it didn't kill you," Kelly teased as she grabbed Joe's hand and dragged him out of the room.

ACROSS THE STREET at Marlow House, Lily manned the ticket booth. She had just let a large group in, and for the moment things had settled down, and she didn't see any new cars pulling up.

"How's it going?" Danielle asked when she came to check on Lily a few minutes later.

"Good," Lily said with a grin. "But how is it going in there?"

"I think everyone is having a great time. But Chris might have made poor Susan Mitchell pee her pants when he popped out of that casket," Danielle told her.

Lily chuckled.

"Everyone seems to be having a wonderful time," Marie said when she appeared the next moment.

"Although I have to say, it is killing me being away from Connor this long," Lily groaned.

"You were over there an hour ago to feed him," Danielle reminded her.

"I know. But still. I've never left him with Kelly before."

"Ask Lily if she would like me to pop over and check on Connor," Marie offered.

Danielle glanced quickly to Marie and then to Lily. "Marie is here. She offered to go over and check on Connor for you."

Lily perked up. "Really? I know this sounds awful," Lily said in a whisper, "but I would like to know how Kelly really does with him. Makes me wish I had put cameras in—but Ian is not thrilled with the idea."

"I'll go check and make sure everything is okay," Marie said before vanishing.

WHEN MARIE ARRIVED AT THE BARTLEYS', she found Kelly and Joe sitting in the living room watching television while Connor cried in the crib in the nursery.

"He's crying!" Marie said anxiously.

"He's still crying," Joe said, glancing over to the hallway leading to the nursery.

Kelly, who sat next to Joe on the sofa, gave his knee a pat. "He's okay. Sometimes a baby just needs to cry. I don't want a spoiled nephew."

"Spoiled? How do you spoil an infant?" Marie snapped. "He's only a month old!"

Marie heard what sounded like a scratch on the wall. She glanced around and frowned. "Where is Sadie?"

Kelly glanced toward the direction of Ian's home office. "If Sadie scratches up that door, my brother is going to kill me."

"I don't know why you shut her in there," Joe said.

"Why did you do that?" Marie asked deaf ears.

"Because she keeps trying to get into the baby's room," Kelly said.

"I thought Ian said Sadie always sleeps in Connor's room?" Joe asked.

Kelly turned to Joe and rolled her eyes. "Yes. But while Connor is my responsibility, I certainly am not going to risk it."

"Risk what?" Joe frowned.

"Sadie is a big dog. And I'm sure she's jealous of Connor," Kelly began.

"She is not jealous!" Marie snapped.

"You think Sadie would hurt him?" Joe asked.

"I certainly hope not. But I won't take the chance while we're watching him."

Joe and Kelly hadn't seen Marie when she popped into the living room with them, and they didn't notice when she popped out, going to the baby's nursery.

"Oh, sweet boy, what is wrong?" Marie cooed down to the baby.

Connor's angry red face looked up to Marie, his little hands drawn into fists as he took a deep breath, preparing to let out another wail. But once he caught a glimpse of her smiling face, he seemed to relax, and instead of letting out a cry, he gurgled up to the ghost.

"Where is your Pooh Bear?" Marie asked as she glanced around the room. She spied it on the rocking chair. The next moment it floated over to her. Snatching it out of the air, she placed it in the crib next to Connor. He began to giggle.

"You just needed your Pooh Bear, didn't you?"

He responded with a little laugh.

"We need to get you to sleep," Marie whispered. Although it wasn't necessary to whisper. Even if she shouted, the only ones who would hear were Connor and Sadie.

Leaning over the crib, Marie began to sing a soft lullaby. Transfixed on her face, Connor listened to her sing a moment before letting out a little sleepy yawn. He relaxed, unfisted his hands and closed his eyes. Within minutes he was fast asleep. Marie watched him for a few minutes and then went to see Sadie.

"Don't bark," Marie said the moment she entered Ian's home office. The golden retriever, who had been sitting by the door, looked over at the ghost and began wagging her tail.

"He's alright, Sadie," Marie told the dog. "He's sleeping now, poor dear."

Looking at Marie, Sadie cocked her head.

"I suppose I can't fault Kelly. She doesn't know you as well as I do."

Sadie tilted her head in the other direction, her eyes still on Marie.

"Yes, I understand Kelly has known you since you were a puppy. But you can't talk to her, can you?…What does that matter?…Well, she is just trying to keep the baby safe, and she might be a bit overzealous about it, but I suppose that is better than having it the other way," Marie said.

Sadie made a grunting sound.

Marie nodded. "I have to agree. I'm not sure the point of making that poor boy cry like that. He obviously misses his mommy and daddy." She smiled at the dog and added, "And his Sadie."

"He stopped crying," Joe said from the living room. Both Joe and Kelly looked toward the hallway.

"I don't hear Sadie scratching the door either," Kelly added.

"Maybe you should go check on him," Joe suggested.

Kelly frowned and turned to Joe. "Why? Do you think something's wrong?"

Joe shrugged. "I don't know. But he was crying pretty good and just stopped."

Kelly jumped up from the sofa and ran to the baby's room, Joe at her heels. Once at the nursery doorway she peeked inside. She could see Connor in the crib. He wasn't moving, but from where she stood, she could see the gentle rise and fall of his chest.

"He's breathing!" Kelly whispered in relief.

"Breathing is good," Joe muttered under his breath.

They practically tiptoed over to the crib. Now standing by its side, they looked down at the sleeping baby.

Kelly smiled at her nephew and was about to turn from the crib when she spied something that was not supposed to be there. She let out a loud gasp, the unexpected sound jerking the baby from his sleep. Connor began to cry.

The next moment Marie reentered the room from the home office to find Kelly picking up the crying baby, attempting to soothe him.

"You woke him up!" Joe said at the same time as Marie asked, "Why did you wake him up?"

Awkwardly holding the baby and attempting to soothe him with gentle pats to his back, Kelly looked to Joe. "How did that thing get in the crib?"

Joe looked down and spied the Winnie the Pooh. He frowned and then glanced over at the rocking chair and back to the crib.

Connor stopped crying and a moment later fell asleep on his aunt's shoulder as she continued to hold him.

"It was on the chair," Joe said numbly.

"You need to check the house. Someone has obviously been in here," Kelly said, looking around nervously.

"Oh my," Marie muttered. "I suppose I shouldn't have left the stuffed animal in the crib after he fell asleep."

Before leaving the room, Joe checked the closets and window and then left Kelly in the nursery, locking the door behind him.

Marie groaned. "Oh dear, I do feel a bit like Lucy right now…I have some 'splaining to do."

When Joe returned ten minutes later, he said, "Everything is locked up. There is nothing."

"Well, someone was in here," Kelly insisted. "That stuffed animal didn't move to the crib on its own."

"True, it had some help," Marie mumbled.

Gently, Kelly placed the sleeping baby back in the crib. She then went out to the living room and called Lily.

"Who are you calling?" Joe asked.

Kelly shushed him, keeping the phone to her ear. A moment later Lily answered.

"Is something wrong?" Lily asked anxiously.

"No," Kelly lied. "Connor is sleeping. I just wondered how you're doing over there."

"It's been pretty busy, haven't even been able to leave to go to the bathroom, and another group is just coming up, so I'd better get off the phone."

"What about Ian?" Kelly asked in a rush.

"What do you mean?" Lily asked.

"Has he had any downtime?"

"Umm, no. Not sure what you mean. He's been with people all night. But I really have to go."

When Kelly got off the phone the next moment, Joe asked, "What was that about?"

"I thought maybe one of them came over here and checked on Connor, came in the back door. But they didn't. I think you should let Sadie out of the office."

"Why? I thought you wanted to keep her away from the baby."

"I might have been wrong. According to Ian, Sadie practically stands guard over Connor. She likes sleeping by his crib. Knowing Sadie, I don't think she's going to let someone near that baby."

"I still don't see how anyone could have gotten in here," Joe said.

"I even checked outside by the windows. I would be able to tell if someone was walking around out there since it is so muddy."

"So how did the stuffed animal get in the crib?" Kelly snapped.

Instead of trying to answer the question, Joe stared dumbly at Kelly for a moment. The next minute he left the room and let Sadie out of the office. The dog immediately rushed into the nursery and planted herself next to the crib.

"Perhaps this worked out after all," Marie said cheerfully, looking down at the content dog and then over to the sleeping baby. While the dog and baby might have been worry-free, Kelly and Joe looked troubled, still trying to figure out how the stuffed animal had moved across the room from the rocking chair and into the baby's crib.

TWELVE

A small wooden table and two kitchen chairs had been set up on Marlow House's front porch under the overhang for ticket sales and admission to the haunted house. Bundled in a green parka, knit cap and leather gloves, Lily had been manning the table for most of the evening.

"Why don't you head on home," Danielle told Lily when she joined her on the porch. It was almost eleven thirty. "I can take over."

"Not sure if I want to go home." Lily snickered. With her arms crossed over her chest, she rubbed her shoulders with gloved hands.

"You mean you aren't ready to deal with the magic Pooh Bear?"

"Pretty much." Lily stood up and shivered. "But I would like to go home and take a hot shower. So you'll have to tell Ian about it before he comes home. Give him the heads-up. I haven't had a chance to tell him what happened."

"How are you going to handle it when they tell you?"

"I think I'm going to look at them like they're crazy. Give a condescending nod, and tell them I know how exhausting it can be watching a baby. Sometimes our mind plays tricks on us." Lily grinned.

"And that will work?"

Lily shrugged. "Or I could just tell them Marie's ghost put the stuffed animal in the crib."

Danielle laughed and gave her friend a hug, telling her good-night, thanking her for helping, and extending well wishes for a peaceful night's rest. After Lily left a few minutes later, Danielle watched her cross the street to go home. She was curious to find out in the morning how it all went—what conclusion would ultimately be drawn regarding the stuffed animal moving from the rocker to the crib.

Now sitting where Lily had been a few minutes earlier, Danielle pulled her cellphone from her pocket. She checked to see if there were any new text messages from any of the haunted house crew. There weren't. Just as she set her phone on the table, the front door opened, and Ginny walked outside, no longer dressed as a ghost.

"I have to go home," Ginny said. "I left the costume in the parlor. I hope you'll let me help tomorrow. It was lots of fun."

"Certainly. But let me get someone to walk you home."

Ginny shook her head. "No, you don't need to. My uncle is here."

Danielle glanced to the street. "He is? I would like to meet him."

"He's down the street," Ginny explained. "He told me to come home at eleven thirty, that he would meet me halfway. I looked out the upstairs window and saw him. He's down the street waiting for me. But I have to go. Bye!" The next moment Ginny rushed off the porch and down the walkway and into the dark night.

"Well, I guess I'll just have to meet him tomorrow," Danielle muttered to herself.

IT WAS after midnight and the front gate at Marlow House had been latched with a *"closed"* sign attached to ward off any lingering haunted house customers. Ian and Chris brought the table and chair indoors from the front porch, and all the foyer lights were turned on, transforming what had been a dark forbidding dwelling into a brightly illuminated home.

It was decided Evan and Eddy could wear their costumes home. It would save them time getting ready for Saturday night. Both boys were sleepy, and the chief hoped they would still be awake by the time they arrived home. He didn't want either of them sleeping in their costumes.

The moment Eddy climbed into the back of his father's car, he stretched out on the seat and promptly fell asleep. MacDonald looked down at his exhausted son and shook his head. "I knew I should have had you guys take those off before we left."

"Where am I going to sit? Eddy is taking up the whole seat," Evan whined.

The chief looked from his sleeping son to his youngest, who stood shivering on the sidewalk. "Go ahead and sit up front."

"Wow, you never let me sit in the front!" Evan said excitedly, rushing to the passenger side of the car.

The chief leaned into the back seat and awkwardly belted in his sleeping son. He then slammed the car door shut.

"This is just for tonight," the chief told Evan as he climbed into the car and buckled up.

A moment later MacDonald steered the vehicle away from the sidewalk, turned the car around, and began heading down the street.

Unlike his older brother, Evan was much too wound up to sleep. He looked out at the dark night, playing over in his mind all that had happened that evening. It had been so much fun, especially since he had the privilege of helping with the haunted house and wasn't just touring it like many of his friends.

He was just thinking about how Eva had helped them when to his surprise the headlights of the car fell on what appeared to be a man walking in the middle of the dark road. Evan expected his father to hit the brakes, but when he didn't, Evan shouted, "Stop! Look out!"

MacDonald slammed on his brakes, his heart now racing. He looked around, but saw nothing. "What?"

From the back seat Eddy groaned and woke up, grumbling, "What is going on?"

Evan pointed to the man they had almost run over. "There! You almost hit him." Evan watched the man run toward Marlow House.

"Hit who?" MacDonald asked with a frown.

"What's going on?" Eddy whined again from the back seat.

"Right there!" Evan insisted, now wiggling out of his seatbelt so he could sit on his knees and turn in the seat to have a better look. He pointed toward Marlow House, and in the next moment he watched as the man disappeared.

WALT, Danielle, Chris, Heather, Ian, Marie and Eva sat in the living room, winding down from the long evening and exchanging ideas on what they should do different the next night.

"It's late," Chris said with a yawn. "I think we should all sleep in. Tomorrow I'll buy lunch, and we can all go over this then." He yawned again.

Ian glanced down at the cellphone in his hand, reading a text message. He looked up and said, "No. We can go over this now. No reason for us to rush home."

Danielle chuckled. "Kelly and Joe are still at your house, aren't they?"

Tucking his phone back in his shirt pocket, Ian nodded. "They want to talk to me about how someone must have gotten into the house. They don't want to leave Lily and Connor alone."

"Oh dear. I am so sorry, Ian," Marie muttered. Danielle relayed Marie's comments to Ian.

"It's okay, Marie. Actually, it's kind of funny." Ian grinned.

"Right. That's why you're sitting there and don't want to go home," Chris teased.

"Hey, I feel your and Lily's pain. Remember the time Walt decided to pack for Cheryl?" Danielle asked.

"I was just trying to help," Walt said in his defense.

"That was before Heather and I moved here," Chris said. "But I've heard the story, and it did make me laugh."

"Wasn't so funny when they thought it was evidence I'd killed my cousin," Danielle reminded them.

Ian stood up. "Okay, if you braved the ghostly suitcase fiasco, I suppose I can deal with flying Winnie the Pooh."

"I prefer possessed Winnie the Pooh." Heather snickered.

"Take that back!" Danielle said in mock seriousness. "Winnie's sweetness is almost sacred!"

Heather stood up and stretched, giving a yawn. "Whatever. I gotta go sleep."

Chris stood. "Me too. It was fun, guys. I'll walk you home, Heather."

"Thank you. Protect me from all the ghouls and goblins," Heather said.

"Nah. If we run into any ghouls or goblins, you're on your own," Chris told her.

Danielle and Walt stood.

"Yes, it was a good night," Danielle said.

"One advantage of not having a flesh and blood body, I've nothing that needs to be rejuvenated weighing me down. The night is young! I think I'll pop over to the Astoria cemetery and catch up with a few friends." Eva looked to Marie. "Would you like to join me? There are a few souls I'd like you to meet."

"That sounds like fun!" Marie said before she and Eva vanished.

"Well, goodbye to you too!" Danielle called out.

"Which one left?" Ian asked.

"They both did. I have to wonder what Adam would think about his grandmother gallivanting at all hours of the night with a silent screen star," Danielle mused.

STANDING under the hot stream of water, Danielle closed her eyes. She hadn't realized how tired she was until she had stripped off her clothes and stepped into the shower. Twenty minutes later she stepped back into her bedroom, her hair now damp from the recent shampoo.

"You were in there a while," Walt said as Danielle approached the bed. She wore fleece pajama bottoms, a long-sleeved T-shirt, and her damp hair was combed straight.

Leaning against the pile of pillows stacked in front of the headboard, a book in his hand and light coming from the lamp on his nightstand, he watched as his wife climbed into bed with him. With his left hand he lifted the blanket, welcoming Danielle under the covers.

"It just felt so good, I didn't want to get out." She snuggled up next to Walt. He closed his book and set it on the nightstand. With his left arm he drew her close, giving her a loving pat.

"It was fun tonight, wasn't it?" Walt asked.

"I'm actually surprised I got into the whole haunted house thing, especially considering my experiences."

"What, that you lived in a haunted house for two years?" He gave her another pat.

"I never really thought of Marlow House in those terms—I mean, not a haunted house like you would associate with Halloween. Those are supposed to be scary. Marlow House has always been comforting to me, even when it was a haunted house.

No, before, when I thought of a Halloween-like haunted house, I thought of Presley House. And that, well, not a comforting memory."

Walt reached over and turned off the lamp, sending the room into darkness. He snuggled down and took his wife in his arms, holding her.

"That is all behind you," Walt said as he kissed the top of her head. "Only fun haunted houses for you."

Danielle giggled and then moved closer in his arms, her head resting on his warm hard chest. She could feel his heart beat. They lay quietly together for a few minutes when suddenly a loud thud broke the silence. They both sat up.

"What has Max tipped over now?" Danielle groaned.

Walt reached out and turned on the bedside lamp.

The next moment they heard a meow and then felt something—a cat—jump onto their bed with them.

Walt looked down at Max. He studied him a moment.

"Max just told me the sound woke him," Walt said.

Before Danielle could question Walt, they heard another crash, as if something had broken on the hardwood floor downstairs.

"Someone is in the house with us," Danielle whispered. "Should I call the police?"

"Stay here," Walt said, climbing out of bed.

Danielle reached out and grabbed at his arm. "No! It's dangerous!"

Another crash came from downstairs. Walt looked at Danielle and then glanced to the closed bedroom door.

"Okay," he whispered. "You'd better call the police."

THIRTEEN

Lucy's Diner was the only restaurant in Frederickport open twenty-four hours. It was a popular stop for late night fishermen, workers getting off the late shift, and partiers who had closed down the local bars and needed something to eat before heading home.

Knowing Brian's second shift was about to end, Joe had given him a call after leaving the Bartleys', asking him to meet them at Lucy's Diner. Brian arrived first and was already seated at a booth, looking over the menu, when Joe and Kelly walked into the restaurant.

"Did babysitting work up your appetites?" Brian asked when they walked up to his booth. "I thought there was some sort of rule about keeping the refrigerator filled with snacks for your sitter."

"I wanted to talk to you," Joe said after he scooted into the bench seat after Kelly.

"You won't believe what happened tonight," Kelly said as she picked up a menu.

Joe then went on to tell Brian what had happened at the Bartleys', with Kelly periodically interjecting a comment. He paused a moment when the server came to take their order, but continued with the story after the server left the table.

"What did Lily and Ian say?" Brian asked. "I bet Lily was freaked."

"No. That's the odd thing. She didn't seem upset at all," Kelly said.

Brian frowned. "Seriously?"

Kelly nodded. "I don't think she believed it happened."

"She thinks you just imagined it all?" Brian asked.

"Lily said something about how exhausting it can be to look after a baby. That there is just so much to do and think about that she often goes to do something, forgetting she had already done it," Kelly explained.

"Ahh." Brian nodded. "She thinks one of you put the stuffed animal in the crib and just forgot about it."

"Yes," Joe said. "But that is not what happened. I saw Kelly set the stuffed animal on the chair, and we both left the room together. We were on the couch the entire time, watching television."

"Any chance Sadie put it in the crib?" Brian asked.

"Sadie?" Kelly frowned.

"Sure. Sadie is a smart dog. Maybe they taught her to fetch the stuffed animal and drop it in the crib. I could see something like that happening," Brian suggested.

"That would be a possibility if Sadie wasn't shut in Ian's office at the time," Joe said.

"So what do you think happened?" Brian asked.

"I'm thinking the only thing that could have happened, someone came in the back door from the beach. There were a lot of people driving up and down Beach Drive tonight. Someone came in. Not sure why. Maybe just a prank, and when they left, they locked the back door."

"So it wasn't locked earlier?" Brian asked.

Kelly cringed. "We didn't check it. But we should have."

Brian let out a sigh and sat back in his seat. "Maybe Pearl Huckabee was right."

"Right how?" Joe asked.

"She didn't think the haunted house was a good idea—that it would bring too many people and riffraff to the neighborhood. Apparently it brought one prankster a little too close to the baby."

AFTER LEAVING THE DINER, Brian decided to take a drive down

Beach Drive instead of heading straight home. While he wasn't sure what he expected to find when he turned down the street, he certainly hadn't expected to see two Frederickport Police cars parked outside Marlow House and Walt and Danielle standing on the front porch.

Parking his car behind one of the other police cars, Brian then got out of the vehicle and sprinted up to the house.

"Did they call for backup?" Danielle asked, half kidding, when Brian reached them.

"What's going on?" Brian asked.

One of the officers standing with Walt and Danielle proceeded to fill Brian in on what had happened.

"All the doors were locked, so we have to assume whoever it was locked it on the way out," the officer said.

"Very considerate," Walt scoffed.

"Yeah, after breaking my vase and tipping over several chairs," Danielle said. "I'm just glad the vase is the only thing they broke."

"We're thinking it might have been someone who came for the haunted house and didn't leave," the officer suggested.

"I really don't know how that could have happened," Danielle argued. "I was careful to keep track, making sure everyone who came through the front door left."

"Someone obviously didn't leave," the officer said.

"Perhaps they came back later, through an open door," Brian suggested.

Danielle shook her head. "We checked all the doors. But I suppose it's possible someone came in through the pet door. A small child could get through it. Of course, they would have to climb the fence or tree to get in. We have that gate locked."

"We were just going," the officer told Brian as he shut his notepad.

Brian glanced at the front door and then looked at Danielle. "You think I could come in for a moment? I need to talk to you both about something."

Danielle looked down at her wrist, but then realized she wasn't wearing her watch. She imagined if she stayed up a couple more hours, she could probably watch the sun come up.

Flashing Brian a weary smile, she said, "Sure, why not."

A few minutes later Walt and Danielle sat with Brian in the parlor, both wearing robes over their nightclothes. Outside, the two police cars that had answered Danielle's 911 call were just driving away.

"I think whoever broke in here tonight may be the same one who broke into the Bartleys' earlier," Brian told them after he took a seat on the chair facing the sofa.

"Umm, are you talking about Connor's Winnie the Pooh ending up in the crib?" Danielle asked.

"You know about that?"

"Umm…yeah…Lily told me." Danielle wondered if she should have pretended she didn't know, considering she hadn't really talked to Lily since she had left earlier that evening, and as far as Kelly knew, Lily wouldn't know what had happened until Kelly told her.

"I'm thinking it's probably kids—hyped up with Halloween and the haunted house. Look at the mischief they used to do at Presley House," Brian said. "Now with Presley House gone, they're turning to Marlow House."

"We had a very nice group tonight," Danielle argued. "It wasn't just teenagers. We had a lot of families and businesspeople in town. Sure, there were some teens, but they were all respectful."

"Someone broke into your house and started throwing things around," Brian argued.

Danielle took a deep breath. "Yes…"

"And I suspect it's the same person who broke in across the street," Brian argued.

AFTER BRIAN LEFT, Walt and Danielle locked the front door and went upstairs to their bedroom.

"If we want to find out who broke into our house, it's just going to muddle things with Brian thinking this has something to do with Connor's stuffed animal," Danielle said with a groan as she slipped off her robe and tossed it over a chair.

"We can talk to the chief in the morning," Walt suggested. "If he knows Marie is the one who moved that stuffed animal, maybe he can do something to steer his people away from trying to tie the two together."

"I'll have to call him," Danielle said. "He told me he wasn't working this weekend."

Danielle left to use the bathroom and returned a few minutes later. Walt was already in bed waiting for her. When she reached the side of the bed, he lifted the top corner of the blanket so she could crawl in.

Just as Walt reached over to turn off the table lamp, Danielle said, "I have an idea."

"It always terrifies me when you say those words," Walt teased.

"Oh hush." Danielle giggled. "But I have an idea to get Joe and Kelly to stop worrying about that stuffed animal, and for the police to realize it's not connected to what happened here."

"Go on," Walt urged.

"Lily needs to confess," Danielle said.

"What do you mean?" Walt frowned down at her.

"Think about it. It was the first time Lily has left Connor with anyone. She was naturally nervous. So maybe she went over there to check on him. Not wanting Kelly and Joe to know what a nervous Nelly she was being, she slipped in the back door, using her key. When she heard Connor crying, she snuck into the nursery. Seeing the stuffed animal on the chair, she used it to calm him down, and when she left, she forgot to put it back. So when they told her about the stuffed animal being in the crib, she felt foolish, and instead of fessing up, she said nothing."

"IT MAKES ME SOUND LIKE AN IDIOT," Lily said the next morning after Danielle made the suggestion.

Walt and Danielle sat with Lily and Ian in the Bartley living room, drinking coffee. Baby Connor sat on his mother's lap, nursing while a baby blanket concealed Lily's breasts.

"Not an idiot, exactly," Ian argued.

Lily rolled her eyes and said, "Then you tell them you snuck over here and gave Connor his stuffed animal. Anyway, I'm kind of annoyed with your sister for not letting him have it in the first place, and to lock Sadie in the office! What was that all about?"

"My sister was just being overcautious," Ian said. "She's never been around babies much."

Lily let out a sigh and looked down at her son. Leaning over, she kissed the top of his bald head and then said, "I suppose I shouldn't fault her for being too cautious."

"I tell you what, let me be the fall guy," Ian said.

Lily looked at Ian. "Seriously?"

Ian shrugged. "Yeah, she is my sister, and if she has to be annoyed at one of us for sneaking over here, it's probably best it be me and not you."

"True," Lily said with a nod. "She loves you. She will forgive you."

"She loves you too," Ian argued.

"Okay, now that we have that settled, we need to figure out who broke into Marlow House last night," Danielle said.

AFTER LEAVING THE BARTLEYS', Walt and Danielle walked to their garage to get the Packard so they could drive to the MacDonald residence. When they arrived, the boys had just woken up and were eating cereal in front of the television, watching cartoons. The chief guided Walt and Danielle to his study so they could talk in private.

"Yes, I heard about what happened last night. Joe just called. So it was Ian who snuck in the house?" the chief asked.

"Actually it was Marie," Walt said. Danielle then went on to tell the chief what had happened the previous night.

"We wanted you to know the cases weren't connected," Walt explained. "Which is why Danielle came up with that story. You know how good she is about fabricating alternate stories." He gave her a wink and she in turn rolled her eyes at him.

"The way Brian was talking, I got the feeling he was starting to side with Pearl, that the haunted house was a bad idea," Danielle said. "But if we could just figure out who broke in last night…"

The chief let out a sigh and leaned back in his chair. "I've this gut feeling whatever was going on in your house last night was similar to what was going on across the street in Connor's nursery."

"What are you talking about? Marie wasn't even there when someone broke the vase and tipped over the chairs," Danielle argued.

MacDonald let out another sigh and said, "Last night when we were going home, I almost ran over a man. Evan shouted for me to stop."

Danielle's eyes widened. "Oh my gosh, that must have scared you."

"I didn't even see him," the chief said.

"Why do people always walk around on dark streets during Halloween?" Danielle asked. "A good way to get run over."

"No. I mean I didn't see him at all. It was like there was no one there," the chief clarified.

"So Evan thought there was someone in the street, but there wasn't?" Danielle asked.

The chief shook his head. "No. I suspect he was there. He walked toward Marlow House and disappeared. I didn't see him. But Evan did."

FOURTEEN

M ax strolled down the hallway like a miniature panther on patrol duty. Walt had explained how someone had broken in the previous night to cause mischief. Tipping over chairs and knocking a vase off a table—it didn't seem like such a bad thing to Max. Actually, it sounded like a good time. However, Max didn't like strangers on his turf. And he certainly didn't like anyone messing with his Danielle.

Walt and Danielle had left for the morning, and Max wasn't sure when they planned to return. Until they did, it was his job to keep an eye on things. With his tail swishing like a silky black flag, he made his way into the kitchen, intending to slip out the pet door and patrol the perimeter of the property. He was just a few feet from the back door when a male voice startled him.

"Hello, Max."

Max's back immediately arched, the black fur standing on end as the feline slowly turned toward the unwelcome intruder.

"It's been a long time," the intruder said. "You're getting fat. Becoming lazy in your old age? Although, as I recall, all you ever did was sleep."

Max responded with a hiss.

The intruder laughed. "Oh, come on. What kind of greeting is that for an old friend?"

The cat snarled and backed up.

"Oh, you're a scaredy-cat now?" The intruder laughed. "I must say, you're hurting my feelings. I thought we were friends."

No longer hissing or growling, Max sat down, staring at the intruder with his golden eyes while his back remained hunched and his tail swished nervously.

"Where is she, Max? Where is Danielle? I need to see her."

Max stared but made no sound.

"Oh, she's with him, is she? I heard he's magically come to life. How is that even possible?"

Max growled.

"Married? Death just isn't fair, is it? Rules are different for everyone. Although, now that I think about it, life was that way. Different rules for different people. Always seemed whatever deck I ended up with was short a few cards."

Max growled again.

"Don't be so rude, Max. I just want to talk to her."

Max stared at him.

The intruder frowned. "Of course not. Why would I do something silly like that? That's something a cat does. Are you sure you aren't responsible and just trying to blame me?"

Abruptly Max turned and raced out the pet door, sending it swinging back and forth.

"Nice to see you again too!" he called after Max and then muttered, "Stupid cat. You were always useless."

The intruder turned from the back door and headed for the hallway, looking for a good hiding spot to hang out in until Danielle returned.

―――――――

WHILE MAX HID in the side yard near the garage, waiting for Walt and Danielle to get home, up the street Chris had just stepped out on his front porch to grab his morning newspaper. He had overslept —something he had intended to do considering how late he got home the previous evening *(which was actually the morning, if he wanted to get technical about it).*

While picking up the newspaper, Chris noticed his new neighbors driving away. Parked in front of the house was a pickup truck. Two men in work clothes carried building supplies from the back of the truck up to the Crawfords' front porch. Chris assumed his new neighbors were having some work done to the house.

Ten minutes later Chris had just settled in his living room recliner with a cup of coffee and the newspaper when a text message came over his phone. Setting his coffee on the end table, he picked up his phone and read the message. It was from Danielle, reminding him of his promise to take them all to lunch. Chris chuckled and then sent a response.

PEARL COVE'S hostess sat them at a booth overlooking the ocean. Danielle always preferred these booths earlier in the day, when the late afternoon sun wasn't yet blaring in the window. Sitting to her right was Walt, and to her left Lily, with baby Conner on Lily's lap, and next to them Ian. On the other side of Walt sat Heather and Chris.

"My sister is annoyed with me," Ian announced. "Since I didn't trust her enough that I had to sneak over to the house and check on Connor."

"Better you than me," Lily teased, giving Connor a gentle bump in her arms to keep him quiet, yet the pacifier he eagerly sucked seemed to be doing the trick.

"I still can't believe she locked poor Sadie in the office," Heather said.

"At least they're no longer obsessing over the idea someone broke into your house," Chris pointed out.

"No, it's just Marlow House we need to worry about," Danielle grumbled. She then told them what the chief had said about Evan seeing a ghost the previous night.

"So maybe it wasn't an actual person who'd come to the haunted house and came back to cause mischief?" Ian said.

"I still say someone could have hidden somewhere and just didn't leave when we locked up," Chris added.

Danielle shook her head. "No. Lily and I were pretty careful about monitoring who came in and left."

"I've been thinking about that," Lily said hesitantly. "That last group of teenagers, one of them could have slipped back in after they left. That's when I used the bathroom."

"I think Lily has a point. Plus, even if Evan saw some spirit last night—well, it is Halloween," Heather said. "And spirits wandering around like that typically haven't harnessed enough energy to tip over chairs and break things."

"But Marie does," Ian argued.

Heather shrugged. "She is an exception. Like Walt."

"Like me how?" Walt asked Heather.

Heather looked over at Walt. "I don't know any other ghost who has come back over to this side. Traditional reincarnation doesn't count."

"What did you mean it is Halloween?" Lily asked Heather.

"Traditionally, Halloween is the time of year spirits try to communicate with the living," Heather explained.

"Technically speaking, it isn't Halloween yet," Ian reminded her.

"I don't think it's a particular day as much as a season. Maybe even the entire month. Remember Harvey," Heather reminded them.

"I would rather not," Danielle groaned.

"Yes, that's right. Harvey would go to Presley House every October," Lily recalled.

"Thankfully, Harvey has moved on. There hasn't been a reporting of a haunting over there since the fire," Danielle said.

"So what does Harvey have to do with any of this?" Ian asked.

"He doesn't," Danielle said. "It's just that some believe that during this time of year, earthbound spirits can more easily contact the living."

Lily giggled.

Danielle glanced to her friend and frowned. "What's so funny?"

"Calling them earthbound spirits—like the name of that crazy cult," Lily explained.

"The cult obviously had it wrong," Danielle said. "To them all living people were earthbound spirits. Their spirits trapped in their bodies and doomed to keep returning until they learned whatever it was they needed to learn before moving on. But when I use the term —to me an earthbound spirit is someone like Eva and Marie—or how Darlene and Angela were. But Angela and Darlene, like Harvey, are no longer earthbound spirits. They have moved on, to wherever our next leg of the journey is."

"Maybe you should start your own church?" Ian teased.

Danielle flashed Ian an eye roll. "Funny."

"Hey, I heard it's a good way to raise money," Heather said.

"Would that make Dani our high priestess?" Lily asked.

"Oh, shut up," Danielle scoffed.

"ARE YOU FOLLOWING ME?" Chris asked Walt and Danielle a few minutes after their Packard parked behind his car, and they got out of the vehicle. The three had recently left Pearl Cove after lunch and were now standing in front of Chris's house.

"I asked Walt to stop so we could introduce ourselves to Ginny's aunt and uncle. I just figure the little girl spent a lot of time at our house last night, and I think we really should touch base with her aunt and uncle, especially since she plans to come back tonight," Danielle explained.

Chris glanced over to the neighbor's house and then back to Walt and Danielle. "Not sure they're home. I saw them leave this morning. Doesn't look like their car is back."

"I see the Bellemore brothers are doing work for them." Danielle nodded to the truck parked next door.

Chris glanced briefly to the vehicle. "Yeah, I guess so. That was there when the neighbors drove off this morning."

"So they all left?" Walt asked.

"Honestly, I don't know. I just saw their car drive away. I suppose one of them might be home," Chris said.

Danielle looked over at Walt. "Let's walk over and see." She looked back at Chris and asked, "What's their name again?"

"Crawford. I don't remember the first names," Chris told her.

WALT AND DANIELLE walked hand in hand over to the Craw-fords' house. A few minutes later the pair stood on the old front porch, waiting for someone to answer the doorbell. When no one answered, they rang again.

Finally, the front door inched open. Answering it was Chester Bellemore.

"Hello, Mr. Bellemore? We met the other day when you stopped by our house. I'm Danielle Marlow."

The man smiled and opened the door wider. "Yes, what can I do for you?"

"First I would like to introduce my husband, Walt Marlow."

Chester shook Walt's hand, looking him up and down. "Wow, you really do look exactly like your ancestor. I saw the portrait when we visited the museum."

"Actually, he isn't an ancestor, more a distant cousin," Walt explained.

Chester arched his brow. "Really? Wow. The resemblance is unreal."

"We're here to see the Crawfords. Is Mr. or Mrs. Crawford at home?" Danielle asked.

Chester shook his head. "No. I'm sorry, they had to take off to Portland. Some emergency came up. They won't be back until late Sunday. That's why my brother and I are going to be burning the night oil here, trying to get as much of the work done as possible before they come back."

"Oh my, an emergency? I hope everything is okay," Danielle said.

Chester shrugged. "I don't think anyone died or anything. Just something they had to take care of."

When Danielle returned to the Packard a few minutes later, she told Walt, "I think Evan is going to miss having Ginny help him tonight."

"He did say they should be back Sunday. The haunted house is running through Tuesday," Walt reminded her.

"True. And in the meantime, we need to figure out how to prevent another visit from late night pranksters. If we don't, then Pearl Huckabee is going to relish telling us *'I told you so.'*"

FIFTEEN

P arked in the alleyway leading to the garage, the engine running, Walt sat in the driver's side of the Packard and pressed the garage door opener.

Walt watched as the door slowly opened. "That thing is rather convenient."

"Aww, yes, the modern conveniences of my time," Danielle said.

"Technically speaking, the automatic garage door opener is more from my time—my first time around, that is—than yours," Walt said.

"How so?" Danielle asked as Walt drove slowly into the garage.

"When we were having the garage built and you were talking about garage door openers, I googled it."

Danielle grinned. "Googled it? And what did you find."

Walt parked the car and turned off the ignition. "The automatic garage door opener was invented the year after I was killed. 1926. Although they didn't become popular until after World War II."

"Interesting," Danielle murmured. "You are a wealth of information."

Walt pushed the garage remote again, closing the door. "Me and Wikipedia."

Danielle chuckled and opened the car door.

Sunshine was not the only thing to greet Danielle as she stepped outside the garage a few minutes later. Max leapt into her arms while giving a pitiful crying meow.

"Whoa," Danielle said, fumbling with the hefty cat so as not to drop him or her purse. "Good to see you too, Max."

Following Danielle outside and closing the door behind him, Walt furrowed his brow at the cat, who now snuggled in Danielle's arms but peeked over her right shoulder, staring into his blue eyes.

"Danielle, stop," Walt said a moment later.

Danielle stopped walking and turned to face Walt, the cat still in her arms. Walt took Max from her, holding him up so that he could look into the cat's face. He held him there for several minutes, the pair staring at each other, neither one making a sound.

Watching in curiosity, Danielle wondered what the cat was telling Walt—or what Walt was saying to the cat. Normally he repeated whatever he was telling Max out loud so that Danielle could at least hear his side of the conversation. But for whatever reason, Walt remained silent, and she had no idea what the two were discussing.

Finally, Walt set Max on the ground and looked at Danielle. "I think you should go over to Lily's," Walt told her.

Danielle frowned. "Lily's? Why? What is going on? What did Max tell you?"

"It seems we have a visitor," Walt told her.

Danielle glanced quickly to the house and then back to Walt. "Should I call the police?"

"Not that kind of visitor. I doubt they could help."

"I don't understand; who is it?" she demanded.

"According to Max, Harvey is in the house. He wants to talk to you."

"Harvey?" Danielle squeaked. "Presley House Harvey?"

Walt nodded. "Yes."

"I thought he moved on?"

"Apparently not. Unless we've been wrong all along, and Halloween is a time souls from the other side can also visit."

Danielle shook her head. "No. I don't believe that's possible. If it was, then more people would report experiencing Halloween encounters."

"All I know, he is here. So you need to go to Lily's."

Danielle stood in silence for a moment, trying to process what Walt had just told her.

"Danielle, are you listening to what I'm saying? Let's get back in the car, and I'll drive you to Lily's. Or maybe somewhere else. Someplace farther away."

She looked up to Walt. "Not sure why I should go to Lily's. But if I wanted to go over there, I could just walk."

"You don't need to cross the yard and risk running into him. Let me get rid of Harvey. You don't need to deal with him. He caused you enough trouble."

Danielle smiled softly and reached up to Walt, gently stroking his cheek. "I don't think you can just get rid of him. It's not like you can pick him up and show him to the door—even with the gifts you brought over from the spirit world. If Harvey is here, I imagine he'll have to leave when Halloween is over. But until then, I have no intention of staying away from Marlow House. For one thing, we have a fundraiser going on."

"Yes, a haunted house. Lucky us, we picked up another ghost for the event," he said dryly.

"I'm not thrilled about having to see Harvey again, but I don't know how I can avoid it."

"I suppose on the plus side, we now know who was probably here last night breaking things," Walt grumbled.

"You think it was him?"

Walt shrugged. "Max asked him, and he claimed it wasn't him. But I have no reason to believe Harvey. And we know from your last encounter that he is capable of moving objects."

Danielle let out a sigh. "I actually hope it was him. Because if it wasn't, not only is Harvey here, there's also another mischief maker out there who might return to cause more problems."

Walt studied Danielle a moment and then said, "Okay, but I would like to stay with you."

Standing on her tiptoes, Danielle brushed a brief kiss over Walt's lips. Standing back down on the balls of her feet, she smiled up at her husband and said, "I love how you always try to keep me safe. I love how much you care. But I have a feeling that if Harvey is here to talk to me, he will probably want to do it alone. And I'm hoping, the sooner I talk to him, the sooner he will go back—to wherever he has been."

"I don't like this," Walt grumbled.

"I don't either. But we have no other choice. How about when we go inside, I'll go in the parlor, and I'll start reading a book. You can wait in the living room, and if I need you, I'll call for you. Would that work?"

———

WALT ANXIOUSLY PACED the living room floor. The door to the hallway was open, as was the door leading into the parlor. So far he hadn't heard anything out of the ordinary. He began wondering if they were handling this all wrong. Perhaps they should have first gathered together all the mediums, along with Eva and Marie. Eva seemed to know how to handle this sort of thing.

"I know the cat told you I was here. I'm just surprised you're not in there with her. I heard how protective you are of your wife," a strange voice said. Walt whipped around to face the person—or ghost—behind the voice.

"Harvey Crump?" Walt stammered, looking the apparition up and down.

"In the flesh," Harvey said with a grin. He then added, "I suppose that was a poor choice of words. Not the flesh exactly. But you know all about that, don't you?"

Not taking his eyes off Harvey, Walt found himself astonished at what he was seeing. *He is no more than a boy,* Walt told himself. Harvey Crump—the image of a scrawny adolescent, wearing oversized faded jeans, belted at the waist with a worn rope, and a dingy button-down white shirt, its front stained in blood—stood in his bare feet before Walt. His mop of unkempt brown hair looked as if it had never seen a comb.

"You are just a child," Walt stammered.

The smile faded from Harvey's face. "I haven't been a child for decades. That was taken from me—my childhood, any future I might have had."

"I am sincerely sorry about that," Walt said kindly and then asked, "But why are you here?"

"It isn't to talk to you. Although, I have to confess, I was curious. Walt Marlow. I used to hear stories about you when I was alive. How you hanged yourself in your attic. We used to walk by here and look up at the attic window, wondering why you really did it. But you didn't kill yourself, did you?"

"No. I didn't."

"We have a lot in common," Harvey said.

Walt arched a brow. "We do?"

Harvey nodded. "We were both murdered. Our deaths were blamed on the wrong people. We both haunted a house, although I was only allowed to do it one month out of the year. And we both care about Danielle."

"From how you treated her, I have to say you have a peculiar way of treating someone you care about."

Absently holding his hands behind his back, Harvey kicked an imaginary rock with his bare toe. "Yeah, that's why I want to talk to her. I…I need to straighten some things out before I move on."

"Why haven't you already moved on?" Walt asked.

Harvey looked up to Walt and said, "No disrespect intended, but it's really something I should talk to Danielle about." The next moment Harvey vanished.

DANIELLE FELT his presence before hearing his voice.

"Hello, Danielle," Harvey said.

Sitting on the sofa, Danielle closed the book she was pretending to read and set it on her lap. She looked up at Harvey, who sat on a chair facing her.

"Hello, Harvey. I thought you had moved on by now."

"I couldn't. Not without talking to you first," he explained.

She frowned. "I don't understand?"

"I thought I would be able to. After all, the only reason I stuck around, I wanted to right the lie told about my uncle. I wanted the world to know what had really happened to me. But…well, when I went back to the cemetery after the house burned down, I was stuck there."

"This entire time?" she asked.

He nodded. "I was able to leave each October, like before. But returning to a vacant lot, well, there was nothing for me there. And then I realized, I couldn't leave because I had something else I needed to do before I would be free to move on."

"What's that?" she asked.

"I had to make amends to you. If it wasn't for you, the truth would never have come out. But I almost got you and your friend killed. And I never apologized for that. I'm sorry for how I treated you. I'm sorry for scaring you and your friend. Can you ever forgive me?"

Danielle smiled at Harvey. "Yes. In fact, I forgave you a long time ago. But I do have one question for you, and I would like you to answer truthfully."

Harvey nodded. "Go ahead. Ask me."

"Last night someone was here in the house after Walt and I went to bed. They tipped over some chairs and broke a vase. I believe it might have been a spirit. Was it you?"

Harvey studied Danielle for a few moments, saying nothing. Finally he said in a low whisper, "No. It wasn't me. I don't know who it was. But I do know I'm not the only spirit attracted to Marlow House this Halloween season. There are other spirits anxious to move on, and like me, they can't do it until they work things out here."

"What does that have to do with Marlow House?"

"It's not my place to say. But others are coming. I suspect some may already be here—especially considering what happened last night. But for me, I'm free to move on now. Have a good life, Danielle, and thank you for helping me and for forgiving me."

The next moment Harvey vanished.

SIXTEEN

D eath had not diminished Eva Thorndike's flare; it enhanced it. She waited until Marie arrived to make her entrance. All the mediums, except for Evan, sat in the Marlow House living room with Marie, Ian, Lily and baby Connor. Although technically speaking, Connor could be counted among the mediums since he was able to see and hear both Marie and Eva.

She arrived in a whirl of white smoke—befitting a Halloween setting—wearing a long black chiffon gown. Atop her head sat a black pillbox hat, its netting covering the top half of her face. Eva twirled along with the smoke as she made her landing. While Ian and Lily could not see her, they saw the smoke and for a moment seemed a bit panicked that something was on fire. Not exactly the entrance Eva was going for.

Silent screen star during her brief lifetime, many had compared Eva's looks to Charles Dana Gibson's iconic drawing of the fictitious Gibson Girl—which had actually come out before Eva had even been born. While Eva did bear a striking resemblance to the drawing, it was the artist Bonnet who had accentuated that resemblance —playing it up and even enhancing it a bit, making it more than it really was.

Eva didn't attempt to play down the resemblance or dissuade the artist from focusing on the comparison. The Gibson girl had been Eva's inspiration when playing roles on the screen or in the theater. She had mimicked the expressions Gibson had given the drawing, using it as her creative muse.

"I thought something was on fire," Lily said, still clutching Connor as she sat back down after practically jumping from the sofa a moment earlier in an attempt to save her baby from imminent danger.

Eva let out a sigh. "Tell Lily I'm sorry. These things do not always work out as I imagine." A chair appeared to the mediums and Eva immediately sat on it.

"I was just about to tell them about Harvey's visit," Danielle explained. She then went on to tell the group everything that had gone on since they had last seen her.

"Do you think it's dangerous to continue with the haunted house?" Lily asked. "Look how Harvey almost got us killed."

"But he didn't," Eva said.

Danielle looked to Eva. "That was only because Heather got there in time."

Eva shook her head. "From what I understand, if Heather had never showed up, Harvey would have had enough energy to release you from the basement and save you from the fire—which he was willing to do, but he had used all his energy to allow Heather to see him."

"So you're saying it was my fault?" Heather asked.

"Absolutely not," Eva began.

"Her fault for what?" Lily muttered, confused since she couldn't hear Eva's side of the conversation.

"I'm just saying Danielle and Lily were in no real danger—if you showed up or not. Either way they would have gotten out of the house before the fire reached them," Eva said.

"How can you be so sure of that?" Danielle asked.

"Because, as you well know, spirits are generally not allowed to harm the living. The worse that will happen here, your guests might get a good scare, which is why they're coming to a haunted house anyway." Eva smiled. "You can view it as having extra help with the fundraiser."

"We know sometimes spirits can harm people—I'm thinking Darlene," Danielle reminded her.

"Let me rephrase," Eva said. "The universe will not let a spirit harm an innocent."

Seeing Lily's agitation at being left out of the conversation and

Ian's confusion, Danielle quickly summarized what Eva had just told them.

They continued to talk for another thirty minutes, moving on to any proposed changes for tonight's tour. Finally Ian walked Lily and Connor home, planning to return right before the opening to help with the haunted house, while Lily stayed home with the baby.

"Melony should be here in about fifteen minutes," Danielle said after Lily, Ian and Connor went home.

"She's going to do the ticket sales tonight?" Heather asked. Heather, who wore a witch's costume, would be returning to her place in the kitchen, as she had the night before.

"Yeah. She also told me she doesn't think Adam is going to come to the haunted house," Danielle said with a chuckle.

"Why not?" Marie asked.

"I think Marlow House as a haunted house kind of freaks Adam out," Danielle said.

"From what the chief told us, I don't think Brian is coming either," Chris added.

Before they could continue with the line of conversation, a small voice said, "Am I too early?"

They all turned to find Ginny standing at the open doorway to the hallway.

"I hope it's okay. I just walked in. Can I go put my costume on?" Ginny asked.

Danielle stood up. "Certainly. But I thought you'd gone to Portland with your aunt and uncle?"

Ginny smiled up at Danielle. "We got back earlier than we expected. My aunt said I could help again with the haunted house. Do you still want me?"

"Of course. So glad you could make it. I know Evan will be happy to have his haunting partner," Danielle said with a grin. "Go ahead and get in your costume."

By the time the chief arrived with Evan and Eddy, Ginny was already in her ghost costume, and Ian was just walking back from across the street. Not long after the chief dropped his boys off and left, Melony Carmichael showed up to help sell tickets.

The crowds seemed even larger on the second night—and it had been fairly brisk on Friday. Because of the steady flow of traffic, Melony waited for people to leave before letting more in. A line of customers anxiously awaiting entrance to the haunted house stood along the walkway leading from the street to Marlow House's front porch.

JOE MORELLI PARKED his car in the street in front of Marlow House. He looked at the line of people waiting to get into the tour and then glanced at his watch. It was almost 10:30 p.m.

"I wonder if we should have come later—or earlier?" Joe asked Kelly, who sat in the passenger seat, busily sorting through her open purse.

"I texted my brother. He said they have been busy all night."

"So you're talking to him now?" Joe teased.

"Texting is not talking," Kelly grumbled. "And I'm still annoyed at him for not having enough faith in me to watch Conner."

"Don't be so hard on your brother. I remember my sister was pretty paranoid when she was a new mother."

"I'm sure Lily talked him into coming over and checking on me," Kelly said.

"To be honest, I'm just relieved it was Ian who got in the house. The thought of a stranger getting into the baby's room like that freaked me out," Joe said.

Kelly let out a sigh. "I suppose you're right. Freaked me out too. Of course, now I understand why Lily wasn't upset about it. She obviously knew Ian had come over to check on the baby."

Joe unfastened his seatbelt and leaned over, giving Kelly a quick kiss. He then said, "Someday it will be a funny story you can tell your nephew. You know, about how goofy his parents were."

Kelly chuckled. "True."

JOE AND KELLY walked into the Marlow House library. The room was dimly lit save for two spotlights, one shining on the portrait of Walt Marlow, and a second shining on the living Walt Marlow, who sat on a chair adjacent to the portrait. Dressed exactly like the man in the painting, it looked as if Walt had stepped out of the canvas and now sat reading.

Curious, Kelly inched closer. Her eyes widened. Instead of holding the book, Walt's hands rested on the arms of the chair while the book seemingly floated in the air in front of him, a page turning every few minutes. Kelly looked for wires yet didn't see any.

"How does he do that?" Kelly whispered.

Walt flashed her a grin. "Because I'm a ghost, of course."

Joe chuckled and said, "I remember now, you like to dabble with magic. Good trick, by the way."

Walt nodded at Joe. "Thank you."

"That's really cool," Kelly said.

After they left the library, they headed upstairs to see what frights awaited them. When they came back downstairs, they visited the bedroom with the casket, and Kelly let out a scream when Chris popped up in his full mummy garb.

They saved the parlor for last. When they stepped into the room, Kelly glanced around, trying to figure out what spooky thing was supposed to happen. Motion from the coffee table caught her attention. She elbowed Joe and nodded toward the table. Slowly, they both approached it and looked down.

Sitting on the table was a silver tea set. They watched in amazement as the teapot seemingly lifted up off the table of its own accord and then began pouring tea into one of the cups.

"How do they do that?" Kelly stammered.

Joe reached out and moved one hand over the tea set, yet did not detect any wires. Just as he moved his hand back, a sinister laugh broke the silence, and to their surprise a young man materialized, sitting on the sofa, his hand holding the teapot.

He looked up at Joe and Kelly and asked in a low whisper, "Would you like a cup?"

Again he laughed—this time more of a cackle. He became transparent before completely disappearing, the teapot slamming back onto the table, almost tipping over, sending tea splashing.

Kelly had already let out a scream and grabbed for Joe's hand. But they stood there a moment, and finally they both began to laugh.

"A hologram?" Kelly asked.

Joe shook his head. "I don't know. But I have to give it to Danielle, that was one hell of a good trick."

JOE AND KELLY found Danielle on the front porch talking to

Melony. Who they couldn't see was Marie. She stood by Danielle's side, listening to the conversation.

"How did you like it?" Danielle asked cheerfully.

"Impressive," Joe said. "If I didn't know better, I would swear your husband was the ghost of Marlow House."

"How did he do that with the book?" Kelly asked.

Danielle stifled a grin. At the last minute it had been decided Walt and Marie could do a few of their tricks—just to spice things up a bit.

"I really don't know," Danielle lied. "He dabbles in magic, but will never tell me how he does a trick."

"The one that was really impressive was in the parlor," Joe said.

Danielle frowned and cocked her head, trying to remember what they had set up in the parlor.

"I haven't been through the entire house yet," Melony said. "What was it?"

"I don't want to ruin it for you," Kelly said.

"Come on, tell me," Melony begged.

"Yes, please do. I confess, I can't remember what we set up in the parlor," Danielle lied.

"Yeah, right," Joe scoffed, not believing Danielle had forgotten. He looked at Melony and said, "Just be prepared for a ghost to appear before your eyes and offer you a cup of tea."

"And then just disappear and practically dump tea all over. I have to know, how did you get the teapot to do that? It was like an invisible hand was moving it. But we figure the ghost had to be some sort of hologram."

Danielle and Marie exchanged quick glances.

"Oh dear, it looks as if Eva was right. Some spirits showed up to give you a little extra help," Marie said.

SEVENTEEN

"My sister is going to be driving me nuts trying to get me to reveal the parlor trick," Ian said with a groan after Danielle told the small group about the mystery ghost's shenanigans.

"Cute," Danielle said with a chuckle. "Nice play on words."

They sat in the living room, Walt, Danielle, Ian, Chris, Heather, Marie and Eva. The chief had picked up his sons twenty minutes earlier, and Melony had just left. They rehashed the events of the evening, focusing primarily on what Joe and Kelly had witnessed. They compared notes, wondering if there had been any other unusual paranormal activity reported.

"I suppose we should thank whoever it was," Walt said dryly. "Sounds like it was more impressive than my floating book trick."

Danielle thought about the silver tea set and shook her head. "Last time I saw that, it was on the buffet."

"Saw what?" Heather asked.

"The tea set. How did it get into the parlor?" Danielle asked.

"We know how. I'm just surprised one of us didn't see it floating from the buffet into the parlor," Marie said.

"Whoever it was even filled it with tea," Danielle added.

"Helpful in its own way," Eva mused. "It certainly left an impression with your friends."

"I'd like to know who this helpful spirit is," Danielle said. "And is he just here for Halloween mischief or some other purpose? Harvey seemed to think we'd be having some visiting spirits who want something from us."

"You want me to stay?" Chris asked.

"I'd offer, but Lily might kill me." Ian stood up. "Plus, chances are I won't see the ghost, so what help would that be?"

"Sounds like Joe and Kelly saw it," Danielle reminded him.

"True. But I'm out of here before Lily calls a search team," Ian said as he headed to the door.

They all told Ian an additional goodbye, and Danielle conveyed Eva and Marie's words, since he couldn't hear them.

After Ian left, Chris asked again, "Do you want me to stay?"

"I think we're good," Danielle said. "Marie promised she would stick around and keep an eye out for any mischief makers."

"Since Marie has already volunteered to stay," Eva began, "and watch to see who might pop up after you go to bed, I think I would like to take a visit down to the cemetery and ask around. See if anyone knows anything."

"Harvey seemed to," Danielle reminded her.

Walt looked over at Max, who sat on the windowsill looking outside, his tail swishing back and forth.

"Max," Walt called out. The cat turned to look at him.

"I'd like you to sleep on the second-floor landing—watch to see who goes into any of the bedrooms, or if anyone tries to come up the attic stairs," Walt told him.

A guard cat and the ghost of an elderly woman as our protectors, Danielle told herself, trying not to laugh at the absurdity of it all.

"Before everyone leaves, let's give the house, beginning in the basement and moving to the attic, a thorough search," Chris suggested. "If we all go into a different room, it will be more difficult for a spirit to hide. Not impossible, but more difficult."

They searched the basement and then all the rooms on the first floor. Not a ghost or person was to be found. They went through all the rooms—with each of them taking a different one to search. Danielle went through her old bedroom on the second floor. She would have looked into the hidden staircase, but the door to that was locked from the other side. Although their attic bedroom suite had been locked, Walt still looked through it. While there, he checked the hidden staircase but found nothing out of order and the door to Danielle's old bedroom closet still locked.

Satisfied the house had been thoroughly searched, Eva said her goodbyes and disappeared, heading to the Frederickport Cemetery. Eva wondered if the tea-pouring ghost might have returned to the cemetery—assuming that was where he was from.

Not long after Eva vanished, Heather and Chris said their good-byes, with Chris offering to walk Heather home. After the pair left, Walt locked the front door. Walt and Danielle then headed to the attic, Max on their heels. Marie stayed downstairs, patrolling the rooms. After going up to the second floor, Max went to his lookout spot and settled down for the evening, leaving Walt and Danielle to continue on their way up to their attic bedroom suite.

"I HAVE to admit I feel a little better having Marie here," Danielle said as she crawled into bed.

"She does have the advantage of moving through walls," Walt said. "That was one skill I wasn't able to take with me. Also helpful when you're trying to corral a ghost."

Danielle chuckled and snuggled down next to Walt as he pulled the covers over them both and pulled her closer to him.

"Aside from a few party-crashing ghosts, the haunted house seems to be a hit," Danielle said.

Walt kissed her head. "Yes, it does. But I'm glad we're only doing this for five days. It gets a little tedious sitting pretending to read a book while keeping it floating in midair."

"You are a sport," Danielle whispered, giving Walt a little snuggle. Exhausted, both Danielle and Walt fell asleep within minutes.

IF DANIELLE HAD BOTHERED to look at the clock, she would know it was almost three in the morning. She hadn't bothered, because she was asleep. As she rolled over, her body gave her a little nudge, telling her she needed to get up and use the bathroom. Sleepily she opened her eyes, the room dark save for a night-light illuminating the way to the bathroom. Closing her eyes again, she groaned, delaying the trip, reluctant to leave the warmth of her bed.

In the next moment a bright light hit her face and moved to another part of the room. Her eyes flew open and she spied what looked like a flashlight peeking out of the doorway from the hidden staircase. Its beam zigzagged around the room and then went dark. Several moments later she heard what sounded like the door to the hidden staircase closing.

Grabbing Walt's hand, she shook him awake, her heart racing.

"What is it?" Walt grumbled, sitting up in the bed.

She pointed toward the door leading to the hidden staircase. "Someone is in there!"

"A ghost?" Walt asked.

"I don't think so," Danielle whispered. "Ghosts don't normally use flashlights."

Walt jumped out of bed. Danielle wanted to shout at him to come back, but he was moving too quickly, and she was afraid if she shouted, it would just warn whoever was in the house. She reminded herself that Walt had the advantage of his telekinetic gifts.

In the next moment Walt turned on the lights to the staircase and threw open the door. He looked inside, but no one was there.

"They must have gone out the closet in your old room," Walt said.

Now by Walt's side, Danielle looked into the empty stairwell. The overhead light brightly illuminated the narrow space. To their surprise, Marie appeared, coming through the closet from Danielle's old bedroom.

"What are you two doing in here? Ghost hunting?" Marie asked. The illusion of her body floated up the stairwell until she was eye level with Walt and Danielle.

"Marie, someone was just in here. They must have left through the closet. Didn't you see them?" Danielle asked anxiously.

"No, dear. I came in through the closet in your old bedroom. There was no one there. I was out in the hallway chatting with Max —who, by the way, said he hasn't seen anything all evening, when I heard some noise coming from your old bedroom, and when I entered the room, I realized the noise was coming from the closet. There was no one in the closet, so I just popped in here, and I saw you two."

"But someone was just in here," Danielle insisted. "That's the only way they could have gone out, through the closet in my old bedroom!"

"Then I suppose we have some mischievous ghost," Marie suggested.

Danielle shook her head and walked into the stairwell, glancing around. "A ghost with a flashlight? You didn't see a flashlight floating around in my room, did you?"

"I believe I would have mentioned that to you," Marie said patiently.

Walt stepped into the space and looked around. "Maybe you were dreaming," he suggested.

"Dreaming? I wasn't dreaming. I was awake. I was just getting ready to get up to go to the bathroom when light hit me in the eyes!"

"If someone was in here, it had to be a ghost, because whoever it was didn't leave through the bedroom, I promise you that. And the only ones I know who can go through walls are ghosts," Marie said.

"Yes, Marie. But they can't take their flashlights with them," Danielle reminded her.

"Marie," Walt began, "when you heard something in Danielle's old bedroom, was her closet door open or shut?"

"It was shut," Marie told him.

"And when you entered the closet, was the door to the stairwell open or shut?" he asked.

As Walt asked Marie the questions, Danielle made her way down the stairwell to the second floor.

"It was shut," Marie said.

"And still locked," Danielle called out, looking up the stairwell at her husband and Marie.

The one room not included in the haunted house was the master suite in the attic. They had locked their bedroom door prior to opening for the haunted house, to prevent guests from wandering where they were not welcome. With both the attic and the closet entry locked, there was no way for one of their guests to stumble on the hidden staircase.

Walt started walking down the steps toward Danielle. "If this wasn't a dream, then I say it has to be the mischief of a ghost. Perhaps there is some ghostly light trick we aren't aware of."

"You really need to clean the mud off your shoes before you tromp through the house," Marie said.

Walt and Danielle looked to Marie, who had now floated down to where they stood by the door leading to Danielle's old closet.

"What are you talking about?" Danielle asked.

Marie pointed to one of the steps. There were two muddy shoe prints.

"How did those get there?" Danielle asked.

"Obviously Walt stepped in mud," Marie suggested.

With a frown Walt walked over to the muddy footprint and set his bare foot near it. The shoe print was at least one size larger than Walt's shoe size.

After taking a closer look, Danielle could see faint footprints leading from the second floor up the steps to the hidden doorway in their bedroom. It looked as if the mud had gradually worn off the shoes before reaching the attic entrance.

EIGHTEEN

Danielle went to her bedroom and retrieved her cellphone from the nightstand. When she returned to the hidden stairwell, phone in hand, Walt asked, "Are you calling the police?" He now stood on the landing outside their bedroom in the stairwell, while Marie floated by his side.

"Police? No, they're the last people I want to call. Even if it was an intruder and not a spirit, the chief doesn't know about the hidden staircase, and I really don't want him to find out this way—me calling to report another break-in." Danielle looked down at the footprints, gently nudging Walt to one side so she could get a better view.

It appeared to be one set of prints, coming up from the landing on the second floor and ending at the hidden panel leading into the attic bedroom. Yet there were no visible prints going back down—it was as if whoever had come up the stairs had left through the attic bedroom. Danielle knew that was impossible, considering she and Walt had been in the bedroom all the time—and when not in the bedroom attic, they were in the hidden stairwell. That was, of course, assuming whoever had shined a light in her eyes was the one responsible for the shoe prints.

She looked down at the print closest to the attic bedroom entry. Barely visible, it looked as if the shoe responsible for leaving the mark had scuffed off most of the mud before reaching that point.

Leaning down, she aimed the camera of her phone at the print and snapped a picture. She then continued down the stairwell, snapping a picture of each print. They became progressively darker as she made her way down the stairs. When she reached the last one, she leaned down and touched the mud. It felt damp.

"I think this is fresh," Danielle said. "It's damp."

"We are on the Oregon coast, dear," Marie said. "Everything is damp."

"No. Not like that. Someone just made this."

"I'm not sure who. I didn't see anyone," Marie insisted. She had followed Walt down the stairs as he trailed behind Danielle. The three now stood at the bottom of the staircase just outside the closet of Danielle's old bedroom. Walt looked at the hidden panel, and the next moment it unlocked and slid open, revealing the bedroom closet. It was dark inside, and he could see the closet door to the bedroom was still closed. They heard a faint meow. Walt looked at the closet, and the next moment its door opened, and in walked Max, coming from the direction of Danielle's old bedroom.

"Did you see anything?" Walt asked the cat.

Max stared at Walt.

"See, I told you," Marie said.

"Why don't we go downstairs and discuss this," Walt suggested. "I'm hungry."

"Hungry?" Danielle asked. "What time is it?"

"Does it have to be a special time for chocolate cake?" Walt asked.

"No, that's just for alcohol," Marie chirped.

"If I'm not mistaken, there are still a couple of pieces of your double fudge cake left," Walt reminded her. "I think we should eat them before Chris comes back tomorrow."

WHEN THEY WALKED into the kitchen a few minutes later, Walt turned on the overhead light, and Danielle picked up a dishtowel and tossed it over the mock severed head in the jar.

Marie frowned. "Why did you do that?"

"Don't ask," Danielle said, grabbing a carton of milk from the refrigerator.

While Danielle filled two glasses with milk, Walt plated the last

BOBBI HOLMES

two pieces of cake. He carried them to the table while Danielle brought the milk. Marie joined them at the table.

"If it was a living person, wouldn't Marie or Max have seen them?" Walt asked before taking his first bite of cake.

"I would assume so. There is no other way out of that stairwell unless whoever it was went through one of the walls." Danielle speared a bite of cake on the end of her fork.

"If it was someone from my side, then this opens up an entire new range of possibilities," Marie mused. "Ghosts who can leave behind footprints. Ghosts who create beams of light—or possibly find some way to move an object, like a flashlight, through a solid surface."

"The light does not surprise me," Walt said. "Manipulating electricity seems to be one of the first skills a spirit can master. Would it be such a jump to imagine they might be able to harness light, which is a form of energy. And then there is Eva's glitter."

"True!" Marie said brightly. "If Eva is able to toss about glitter, then why couldn't a spirit do the same with bits of dirt to make a shoe print."

"The only problem with that, Eva's glitter disappears before it hits the ground," Danielle reminded them.

"I recall it got in your coffee," Walt said.

"True. But then it vanished," Danielle reminded him.

"Perhaps Eva can shine a light on this?" Marie suggested.

"A ghost with a shining light is what started this," Danielle snarked before stabbing another chunk of cake.

Marie chuckled and then said, "Eva tends to understand these things better than me. She seems privy to more secrets of the universe than other spirits I've met. I know she was going down to the cemetery to see what she could find out. Perhaps I should go down there. See if I can find her. I'll have her come back with me, and perhaps she can help us figure this all out."

Resting one elbow on the kitchen table, Danielle propped her right cheek on a balled fist and yawned. "You might as well see if you can find her and bring her back. Not sure how I'm going to get any sleep with someone roaming around in the staircase, anyway."

DANIELLE GLANCED at the kitchen clock. It was almost 4:30 a.m.

She and Walt sat in the kitchen alone, waiting for Marie to return with Eva—assuming she could find her.

"Maybe we should go back upstairs and see if we can get some sleep. We have a long day tomorrow," Walt reminded her.

"I'm too tired to walk up those stairs. Plus, I won't be able to fall asleep thinking someone might flash light in my face again from the stairwell."

"We could use the bed in the downstairs bedroom," Walt suggested. "It's rather comfortable."

Danielle looked to Walt, her face expressionless. "There is a coffin in there."

"Technically it's a casket not a coffin. And I'm not suggesting we nap in it."

She shook her head. "No. I'm not going to sleep in a room with a casket. As it is, I don't really want that thing staying in the house after Halloween."

"My first body is resting in a coffin, and I don't recall it really being a problem," Walt teased.

"It might have been had you woken up inside it," Danielle snarked.

Walt flashed her a smile and took a sip of milk.

Danielle looked at the clock again. "I wonder if Marie couldn't find her? Where do you think Eva went?"

"I'm here!" Eva said as she appeared in the room, surrounded by a burst of light.

Danielle squinted, the bright lights briefly blinding her eyes.

"That was to prove a point," Eva said as she took a seat at the table with them. The next moment Marie appeared and then sat down on the remaining chair. As she did, she pushed out Eva's chair so that the tabletop was no longer cutting her in half.

"What point exactly? That bright light can be more annoying than glitter?" Danielle grumbled.

Eva arched her brows and glanced briefly to Walt and then back to Danielle. "Oh my, someone really does get grouchy without her sleep, doesn't she?"

"So what was your point, Eva?" Walt asked while giving his wife a gentle pat on the hand.

"The point being: *yes*. A spirit would be capable of shining a bright light on Danielle. Not all spirits, but some could. As for the footprints, I haven't looked at them, so I can't really say one way or the other."

Danielle yawned and then looked at Eva. "Sorry. I'm just overly tired. Did you find out anything tonight? Who is haunting us and why?"

Eva let out a long sigh and then said, "The cemetery was dead tonight."

Danielle's blank stare fixed on Eva. After a moment she asked, "How long have you been waiting to say that?"

"Say what?" Eva frowned at Danielle and then replayed in her mind what she had just said. After a moment she let out a laugh. "No, dear, I mean it was really dead tonight—deader than normal for a cemetery."

"You weren't able to find any spirits?" Walt asked.

Eva flashed Walt a smile and then continued. "Cemeteries are a bit like a train station—always people coming and going. People in a hurry. Some sticking around for a while. Although, that's not exactly like a train station, more like a seaside inn. Eventually, they all move on. But tonight it was dead—not dead like a cemetery filled with dead bodies—dead in that there were hardly any spirits around. Most of the regulars confined to the cemetery are taking advantage of the Halloween season. They have gone on holiday, so to speak."

"And is Marlow House now a B and B for the vacationing ghost?" Danielle asked.

"I do wonder," Eva said. "To be honest, I only found one spirit at the cemetery tonight. He didn't know where they all went, but he did overhear a few discussing coming here—I assume to resolve some conflict so they can ultimately move on."

"Are they just allowed to go anywhere? Is it like a free-for-all haunt once a year?" Danielle asked.

"Oh, no. On Halloween they are allowed to leave, but the understanding is that they need to work on whatever unresolved issue they have that is keeping them here. Although, it's not unusual for a spirit who isn't prepared to move on to use this time for a little harmless mischief. By the way, it sounds like your Harvey has finally moved on."

"Who told you that?" Danielle asked. "I suspected it was the case, but I wasn't sure. After Presley House burned down and the truth about his death came out, I just assumed he had moved on back then, but he hadn't."

"He has this time. Although I can't explain how I know, but I do." She then turned to Walt and said, "And I suspect this recent activity has something to do with unresolved issues left over from your first go-around."

"Me? What does this have to do with me?" he asked.

"I'm not certain. But from what I understand, you hold the key to more than one lost soul, and they're coming here to force you to open the door."

"What does that even mean?" Danielle asked.

"There are some things you just have to work out by yourself, without our intervention. Which means Marie and I can't stay. At least, not for the rest of October."

The next moment both Eva and Marie vanished.

NINETEEN

"I'm not sure how I feel about a Halloween party on Sunday," Chief MacDonald's sister, Sissy, told him as she filled his cup with coffee. They sat together in Sissy's kitchen on Sunday morning while Evan and Eddy sat in the living room watching cartoons.

"Halloween falls on Sunday sometimes. Never recalled a problem taking the boys trick-or-treating then," MacDonald noted before taking his first sip of coffee.

"Maybe once since you started taking the boys out for Halloween." She took a seat at the breakfast bar with her brother.

"Once or ten times, what does it matter? It's just a harmless Halloween party. The boys are looking forward to it."

"You should be taking them to church on Sunday," she admonished. "Not a Halloween party. Bruce's mother feels Halloween is a pagan holiday."

MacDonald chuckled. "I seem to recall you used to enjoy dressing up on Halloween and going trick-or-treating."

"I'm older now. I see things differently," she told him.

"I suppose this means you don't want to go with us this morning?" the chief asked. The reason for stopping by was to ask his sister and her husband if they would like to join them at the children's Halloween party down at the community center. He had left a message about the event on her phone the day before, but she hadn't responded, so he thought he would stop by and see if she was going.

"I asked Bruce," Sissy said. "He really didn't want to go to a kids' Halloween party."

"It's for families. We are family. But if he doesn't want to go, you're still welcome to go with us."

Sissy considered the invitation a moment and then shook her head. "No. But thanks for asking. Although, I really don't know why they didn't have the party yesterday, on a Saturday instead of a Sunday."

MacDonald shrugged. "I don't think they could get the community center yesterday. Someone else booked it. And Halloween falls on a school day, so today was the only time they could have it."

"I understand the haunted house is going through Halloween. Surely the boys aren't going to help on Monday and Tuesday nights; those are school nights," she asked.

"I told them they could. This is an exception. They're having a blast."

"Honestly, Edward, I find Evan's obsession with Marlow House odd. I never understood why he broke in back when you were hijacked."

"I explained all that," the chief said wearily.

Sissy set her cup on the kitchen bar top and turned to her brother, her expression serious. "I've heard around town the haunted house is pretty scary. Are you sure it's wise to let the boys help? I'm sure Danielle Boatman—I guess it's Marlow now—I'm sure she can get people to help her. Heavens, she has enough money she can hire whomever she wants."

"The boys are doing it because they're having fun. Plus, it's for a good cause."

"I've been hearing it's not appropriate for children. Do you know they have a real casket in one of the bedrooms?"

"Yes. Evan climbed in it," Edward said with a grin.

Sissy shook her head in disapproval. "That is not wise. You have no idea what kind of psychological damage that could cause the poor boy! One of my friends went Friday night, and she told me she came home and had nightmares."

Edward considered his sister's words and then said with a smile, "You have to remember, the boys are seeing the haunted house from a different perspective. They can see behind the curtain, where others can't. They know the tricks and what goes on behind the scenes." Although that was not entirely true, Edward told himself. While Evan understood Walt's trick of the floating book, Eddy thought it was very cool yet had no idea how it was done. *It's no different than any other magic trick*, Edward had told his oldest. *It is nothing but a trick, and a magician never tells his secrets.* Of course, that had been a lie. Walt's floating book was about as close to real magic as he would probably ever get.

"I just hope you know what you're doing," Sissy said with a sigh.

MacDonald reached over and patted his sister's hand. "The boys are fine, and if I thought for a moment there was going to be a problem, I wouldn't let them do it."

Once again, MacDonald was not being entirely truthful with his sister. Part of him questioned himself for allowing the boys to participate due to the paranormal activity that had taken place. Spirits like Eva and Marie did not bother the chief, yet the unknown entities troubled him, and he questioned his own judgment. But then he reminded himself he trusted Danielle and the other mediums, and in some ways it was providing Evan with knowledge and skills he would later need to manage his gift.

After they left Sissy and Bruce's house twenty minutes later, they headed for Marlow House. Evan and Eddy planned to wear the costumes from the haunted house to that afternoon's Halloween party, but Evan had left the outer layer of tulle netting in the Marlow House parlor the previous night. He had already called Danielle to let them know they would be stopping by to pick it up. He also wanted an opportunity to talk with her in private, to discover if any unexplained occurrences had happened the previous night after the haunted house had closed down.

"Dad, can we invite Ginny to go with us to the party?" Evan asked after his father pulled their car in front of Marlow House and parked.

"I think Ginny is weird," Eddy said as he climbed out of the car a moment later.

"Dad! Eddy said Ginny is weird," Evan complained.

"Yes, I heard. Why do you think that?" MacDonald asked as he walked with the boys up the sidewalk toward Marlow House's front gate.

"Because she never talks," Eddy told him.

"She talks to me all the time," Evan countered.

"I've never heard her voice. And she never takes the costume off. I wouldn't know what she looks like if I saw her," Eddy said.

"Big deal. It's Halloween," Evan pointed out.

Eddy shrugged. "I still think it's weird she just hides under that thing."

"She isn't hiding," Evan grumbled.

Just as the chief pushed the gate open for his boys, a small female voice said, "Hello."

They turned around and came face-to-face with a young girl with messy blond hair.

"Hi, Ginny!" Evan greeted her.

"I saw your car and thought I would come say hi," she said with a grin.

Evan glanced briefly at his brother and spit out his tongue, and then looked to Ginny and smiled.

"Nice to see you again, Ginny. Without a sheet this time," the chief said.

Ginny responded with a grin.

"I'm taking the boys to a Halloween party at the community center in about an hour. Would you like to join us?" the chief asked. "I would be happy to talk to your aunt and uncle."

Ginny smiled at the chief. "Thank you. But we have to do something this afternoon. And I should probably go now. But I'll see you all tonight!"

After Ginny rushed off and MacDonald and his sons started up the walkway to the front door, Evan looked at Eddy and said, "I told you she could talk."

"I never said she couldn't talk. I said she never talked," Eddy clarified.

"I finally saw Ginny," the chief told Danielle as she led them into the house a few minutes later. "Without her ghost costume, that is."

"There goes all the mystery," Danielle teased.

"Can I get the rest of my costume? Is it still in the parlor?" Evan asked.

"Sure, go on in," Danielle said.

"Eddy, go with your brother. I want to talk to Danielle alone a few minutes," the chief said.

"You boys can turn the TV on in there if you want," Danielle called after them as they dashed to the parlor.

"So what did you want to talk to me about?" Danielle asked, leading the chief to the living room.

The chief studied Danielle's profile as he followed her. "You look pretty tired."

"Is that what you wanted to talk to me about?" she teased, walking into the living room and motioning to the sofa for him to sit down.

"No. Just a side observation," he said.

"Gee. Thanks for noticing," she said dryly.

"You feeling okay?" he asked, taking a seat on the sofa.

"Nothing that a good eight hours' sleep won't fix." She sat on the chair facing him and yawned.

"So does that answer my question?" he asked.

"Which question? That I'm tired. Yes, I am."

"No. One of the reasons I stopped by. I wondered if you had more unexplained activities last night after we all left. But considering you look as if you haven't slept, I have to assume something kept you up."

"No chairs fell over last night. Nothing broke."

"But something happened?"

Danielle considered his question a moment but was hesitant to say what had happened, reluctant to reveal the existence of the hidden staircase. In the beginning she had kept the staircase a secret because she had also been keeping secret her relationship with Walt. Yet now that they were married, and Marlow House was no longer being used as a bed and breakfast, there was no significant reason to keep the hidden staircase a secret. Yet she felt uncomfortable revealing it now, considering she had never mentioned it to the chief before.

"We heard a few things last night. But nothing broken. No chairs tipped over."

"What kind of things did you hear?"

Danielle shrugged. "Footsteps, I guess. Umm...saw some flashes of light."

"Marie saw nothing? I thought she was going to stay and keep an eye on things," the chief asked.

"She didn't see anything. But we talked to Eva later—it was after four a.m. She had gone down to the cemetery to see if she could find out what might be going on." Danielle then recounted her conversation with Eva, leaving out any reference to the secret stairwell.

"And she just left?" he asked.

"Pretty much. Both she and Marie."

"Aren't they coming back?"

"I imagine they will eventually. But I got the impression whoever this is, it's something we need to deal with without their intervention."

"Why?"

"I don't know. Sometimes the universe just likes to screw with me," Danielle grumbled. "But I realize something. You know how they say you shouldn't mess with Ouija boards because it will open a portal to demons or some such thing."

"I have heard that. Is it really true?" he asked.

Danielle shrugged. "How would I know? I've never used one before. I don't need a board to communicate with spirits."

"Then what is it you realize?"

"While Ouija boards might attract demons, if you open a haunted house, instead of demons, you attract mischievous ghosts."

"I thought Eva said something about spirits looking for closure before moving on. That doesn't sound like a mischievous ghost."

"No, it doesn't. Which makes me think, while some spirits may show up looking for answers, I don't believe that's all we're hearing from. Take, for example, the ghost playing peekaboo in the parlor while serving tea. And I'm certain a mischievous ghost made that ghastly head in the jar smile at me."

"It smiled at you?"

Danielle shivered. "It was beyond creepy, but rather funny now that I think about it. Those are the actions of a playful, mischievous ghost—not one coming for serious business. The broken vase and the chairs tipping over, that can go either way. It could have been the result of a ghost learning to harness energy to be heard."

"Does this mean you won't be having a haunted house next Halloween?" he asked.

Danielle shrugged. "I think you should ask me that question on November first. If we survive, of course."

TWENTY

Gray clouds filled the sky and merged with the ocean, making it impossible to see the horizon, where the sky ended and water began. Walking up to Chris's house with Walt, Danielle glanced up to the sky, questioning the wisdom of not bringing an umbrella. But then she remembered a true Oregon girl did not need an umbrella.

According to the weatherman, there would be no rain today; however, the sky told a different story. Thus far the weatherman had not been proven wrong.

"What are we going to tell them?" Walt asked.

Danielle cringed. "I want to tell them everything, but we never told them about the secret staircase, and I feel funny telling them now."

"I suppose we could wait. See what happens," Walt suggested. "And if Eva is right, this has something to do with my first life—which tells me nothing."

A few minutes later Danielle and Walt were being welcomed into Chris's house, greeted by an exuberant pit bull and the smell of bacon frying.

"Smells good," Danielle said when she walked into the kitchen. Heather stood at the stove, turning bacon slices with a pair of tongs.

"He invites me over for brunch and puts me to work," Heather said in greeting.

"Just keep working, minion," Chris said with mock gruffness. He walked to the coffee pot and poured Walt and Danielle each a cup of coffee.

"Yes, master," Heather said in a robotic voice.

"I invited Lily and Ian to join us. But they were already meeting Joe and Kelly for an early lunch," Chris explained, handing them each a cup of coffee.

"Yeah, I spoke to Lily this morning. She told me."

"Does this mean Kelly's no longer annoyed with Ian?" Heather asked.

"Not sure about that," Danielle said with a chuckle.

"Wow, you look terrible," Chris told Danielle after he took a closer look.

"Gee, thanks," Danielle said with a scowl, taking a sip of her coffee.

"And people say Chris is such a charmer," Heather scoffed as she removed the cooked slices from the hot bacon grease and lined them up on the paper-towel-covered plate.

"I'm sorry," Chris said hastily. "But you look so tired. You feeling okay?"

"Our sleep was interrupted again last night," Walt explained.

"Busy spirits or human mischief makers?" Heather asked.

"I'm fairly certain the spirit variety," Danielle said, taking a seat at the breakfast bar, Walt at her side. "At least nothing got broken." She then went on to explain what Eva had told them—leaving out the part about the hidden staircase.

"All very cryptic of Eva. She can be a little dramatic sometimes," Chris observed.

"You think?" Danielle said with a laugh.

"She was always like that. I believe she is truly in her element as a spirit," Walt said.

"I'm just glad she moved on from the glitter," Heather said.

Danielle yawned and then asked, "What do you need me to do?" She glanced around the kitchen.

"We have it under control," Chris said. "Quiche is in the oven. I figure we'll eat in about twenty minutes. I hope that's okay."

"Quiche and bacon?" Danielle asked.

Chris grinned. "Everything goes with bacon."

Danielle stood. "Would you mind if I ran over real quick and introduced myself to Ginny's aunt and uncle?"

"Go ahead," Chris said. "I didn't see their car out there earlier, but it could be in the garage."

"I see the Bellemore brothers are there again," Walt noted.

"They have been putting in some midnight oil," Chris said.

CHESTER STOOD, hands on hips, inspecting the piece of drywall they had hung the day before. "I wish we didn't have to screw with this drywall."

"When they come back, it has to look like we did something when they were gone," Cecil said. "Time is running out, and we're damn lucky they had to go to Portland. Talk about luck. I think old Gramps is watching over us, cheering us on."

"Well, Gramps also said there was a treasure, but we haven't found it yet."

"We will. Everything else was exactly like he said it would be, wasn't it?"

"Unless someone else already found it."

Cecil shook his head. "No way. That treasure is there. We just need to remove more bricks."

The doorbell rang and both brothers looked to the front door.

"Who's that?" Chester asked.

"We won't know until you answer it," Cecil said.

A few minutes later Chester inched the front door open and peeked outside. Standing on the front step was Danielle Marlow.

"Hello," Chester said, opening the door a few inches wider.

"Wow. You guys are really putting in the long hours. And on a Sunday too. I was wondering, are the Crawfords here?"

"I told you, they won't be back until late tonight."

"But they returned yesterday," Danielle said.

"No, they didn't."

Danielle frowned. "Are you saying they haven't come back from Portland yet?"

"It's what I have been saying all along. And my brother talked to Mr. Crawford earlier this morning, and according to him, their plans haven't changed. They won't be back until tonight. So that means we really need to get as much done here before they get back. We were hoping to get finished before they come home. It can be such a mess working with drywall—dusty. I want to get it finished and cleaned, so if you will excuse me."

"Wait, can I ask you one last question," Danielle said right before he shut the door on her.

He eased the door back open and looked outside. "What?"

"Do you have any idea where their niece is staying?" Danielle asked.

"I have no idea." Chester then shut the door. She heard the bolt lock.

Danielle stared at the closed door a moment and then returned to Chris's house.

"I don't understand," Danielle said when she walked into Chris's dining room a few minutes later. Walt and her friends were already seated at the table. "According to Chester Bellemore, they haven't gotten back yet."

"They probably just left again. Ginny did say she couldn't go with Evan to the Halloween party because they were doing something this afternoon," Walt reminded her.

Danielle took a seat at the table and shook her head. "No. According to Chester, they are still in Portland. They haven't come back yet. Claimed they spoke with Mr. Crawford this morning, who was still in Portland at the time."

"Ginny didn't go with them?" Heather asked.

"Apparently not. I asked where she was staying, but he said he didn't know."

"They are obviously having Ginny stay with someone they know in Frederickport, and we just misunderstood about her aunt and uncle coming back," Walt suggested.

"I suppose. That has to be it." Danielle shrugged. "But to be honest, I don't really think I misunderstood her. And it makes me uncomfortable knowing she might be lying to me. I like Ginny. But if she is hiding something…"

"What else did Chester Bellemore say about Ginny?" Heather asked.

"Nothing. I asked about the Crawfords, and just as he was about to close the door, I asked if he knew where their niece was staying, and he said he had no idea and slammed the door on me. Even locked it. What, was he afraid I was going to force my way in the house?"

"Did he even know who Ginny was?" Heather asked.

Confused, Danielle looked at Heather. "Like I said, I asked where their niece was staying, and he said he had no idea."

"Everyone has a niece. Did you ask him if he saw her?" Heather asked.

"Not everyone has a niece. I don't have one. And I don't get your point," Danielle said.

"Welcome to my world," Chris muttered under his breath only to receive a kick to his shin under the table from Heather.

"Ouch!" Chris wailed.

Heather looked at Chris and cringed. "Sorry. I didn't mean to kick you so hard."

"You can be mean," Chris grumbled.

Ignoring Chris, Heather asked, "When you asked him if he knew where the niece was staying, who is to say he knew you were talking about Ginny? Sounds to me like he was just trying to get you out of there so he could go back to work."

"I still don't get your point," Danielle said.

"I think Ginny might be a ghost," Heather said in her most spooky of voices.

All heads at the table turned to Heather.

"Ghost?" Danielle asked.

"Sure. She just shows up out of nowhere," Heather began, her voice low and menacing.

"She didn't just show up out of nowhere," Chris said dryly. "I saw her arrive with her aunt and uncle."

"And who really saw her? You, me, Danielle, Walt, Evan, Eva and Marie. Just the mediums and spirits," Heather went on.

Chris waved his hand dismissively and said, "I quite distinctly recall Eddy talking to her."

"Yes, but did she talk back?" Heather asked. "Me thinks not."

"Me thinks not? Have you gone Shakespeare on us?" Chris asked.

"I don't want to kick you again," Heather warned. She then said, "It would not be unusual for a ghost to move around a sheet, making it look as if someone was under it. And, to clinch it, she refused to wear the white makeup on her face like Evan. It was because..." Heather paused a moment for dramatic effect and then said in a burst, "She has no real face to put it on!"

Danielle studied Heather for a moment and then reached over

and snagged a slice of bacon from the plate sitting in the middle of the table.

"That would be a great theory," Danielle said as she took a bite of bacon, "but there is just one flaw."

"What is that?" Heather asked.

"The chief and Eddy saw Ginny this morning in front of our house. They even talked to her and she talked back. So your little-girl-ghost theory, it doesn't work."

Heather slumped down in the chair. "Drat."

The kitchen timer rang.

"I would prefer she be alive," Walt said.

"Alive is good," Chris agreed as he headed to the kitchen to take the quiche out of the oven.

"I'm still trying to place Ginny. I have seen her before. I know it," Walt said.

"When?" Heather asked.

"If I knew that, I would know where I have seen her before," Walt reminded her.

A few minutes later Chris returned to the table, carrying a crab quiche fresh out of the oven. He set it on the table.

"Ginny is obviously staying with someone else while her aunt and uncle are gone. I can't believe for a minute they would just leave her here alone. Especially considering the Bellemore brothers are working over there at all hours, and for whatever reason she lied to you about them coming back," Chris said as he took a seat at the table.

"Why would she lie about something like that?" Heather said.

Chris considered the question a moment. "Maybe she is embarrassed. Or is staying with someone she doesn't like. But her making up stories is not so surprising to me. While I was fairly young when I got out of foster care, I can still recall some of the elaborate stories a few of the older children would tell. They would make up stories about imaginary families who were going to take them in, or some imaginary aunt or uncle who was about to arrive any day to rescue them from the system. Sometimes all a child has is the imaginary world they create. It's one way to survive."

TWENTY-ONE

G inny stood alone on the beach, looking out to the ocean, her arms crossed over her chest, hugging the oversized sweater to her slim body. She glanced to her right and then left. No one else was on the beach with her, yet considering the weather, it didn't surprise her. Tilting her head back for a moment, she looked up to the sky and studied the dark clouds, wondering when they would release the rain.

She looked forward to seeing Evan again tonight and helping with the haunted house. If it had been possible, she would have accepted their invitation to the Halloween party. With a sigh she turned from the ocean and headed back toward the line of homes. She spied Chris's house and wondered if he was home. When she reached his back patio a few minutes later, she peeked in the window. There, sitting around the dining room table, were Walt, Danielle, Chris and Heather. For a brief moment she had the urge to knock on the window and say hello.

Instead, Ginny smiled sadly. She liked them all, especially Danielle. No one had ever made her anything before—certainly not a Halloween costume. Of course, Halloween was not something she ever celebrated, so there was never a need for a costume. She thought of Evan again, thinking how nice it was to have a friend. In her short life she had never lived in a neighborhood with other children.

Perhaps if her parents had sent her to school, she could have made friends, but her father thought it a waste to educate a girl and felt she would be more useful at home, helping his wife with the chores.

"Everything a girl needs to get by in this world can be learned at her mother's side, cooking and cleaning," he had told her. "School is a waste of time for a girl. And we need you at home."

Taking one final peek into Chris's window, she noticed how they were all smiling, and it looked as if Chris was laughing at something. It seemed as if she had spent her entire existence watching other people's lives—always the outsider. Turning from Chris's window, Ginny made her way home.

She remembered when her aunt and uncle first showed her the house, before they moved in. It didn't feel like home then; it didn't now. Of course, everything was different now. When she got closer, she noticed the construction workers' truck parked out front and assumed the two men were inside. A moment later she peeked in one of the windows and spied the men standing in the master bedroom, obviously in a heated conversation. The taller man used hand gestures to punctuate his comments.

With the two men occupied in the bedroom, Ginny hastily made her way to the side of the house to the kitchen entrance. Once inside, she went to the living room and looked around. She wondered what the men had been doing. They had already removed a section of the living room wall. When she had been there earlier, she had heard them saying something to Mia and Austin about the drywall being moldy. The section they had removed was now piled outside in the back of their pickup truck, but so far they hadn't done anything to complete the repair, aside from nailing up a new piece of drywall.

The boxes she had used as her fort remained piled in one corner. It didn't look like they had been moved, yet there was something sitting on them. Moving closer, she saw the new object was a pair of dirt-covered leather work gloves.

The next moment she heard the men's voices coming in her direction. Ginny ducked behind her makeshift fort. When they entered the living room, she watched as they walked to the brick corner, their backs to her. It was then she realized something was different.

They had removed the brass panel. It now rested on the floor, leaning against the back wall. To her surprise the brick corner was not all brick. With the brass panel now removed, she could see what appeared to be a wooden panel tucked in what looked like a brick frame. She frowned. Ginny had assumed the entire section was made of brick.

Chester glanced at his watch. "If we don't get this done before they return, it's not going to be easy gaining the access we need."

"We will," Cecil said. "Some things are meant to be. I believe that. Everything was exactly like Gramps told us it would be."

"Not everything. We haven't found the treasure yet."

"But it is there," Cecil insisted. "I can feel it."

Treasure? Ginny frowned. *What treasure?*

"We aren't going to find it standing here. I guess it's my turn?" Chester asked.

"Yeah. Let me get the flashlight. I put new batteries in."

Chester glanced around. "Where are the gloves?"

"I set them over there, on the boxes."

While Cecil went to retrieve the flashlight with the new batteries, Chester walked over to the stack of boxes, unaware Ginny remained crouched on the other side.

Reaching for the gloves, he accidentally knocked one of them off the top box. It landed just an inch from where Ginny sat.

Walking around the boxes to retrieve the glove he had dropped, Chester looked down and froze.

"What do we have here?" he asked.

BEFORE ANY OF the haunted house crew arrived Sunday evening, Danielle double-checked the doorway from her old bedroom closet to the hidden staircase, making sure it was locked. She then locked the door into the attic master suite, the one room off-limits for the haunted house.

She was on her way down the attic stairway to the second floor when an apparition appeared before her. It was Marie. The image of an elderly woman dressed in a bright floral sundress and floppy straw hat smiled sheepishly at Danielle.

"You came back?" Danielle said.

"I needed to talk to you. But I'm not staying."

"I thought you were going to help with the haunted house?" Danielle asked as she continued down the staircase.

"I need to apologize. After all, I did tell you I would help, and I believe in honoring one's commitments."

Stepping on the second-floor landing, Danielle glanced over to Marie and arched a brow. "But?"

"Eva and I—well, we have more freedom than others. Something I need to be careful not to take advantage of," Marie explained.

"I don't understand what you're getting at," Danielle said, now heading toward the stairs leading to the first floor.

"Halloween is a time that affords other spirits—those not as privileged as Eva and me—a bit more latitude in dealing with what needs to be done for their eternity. If Eva and I interfere too much, well, it is a bit like playing God, and frankly I don't want to seem as if I've gotten too big for my britches. Because you know what can happen then."

Danielle paused at the top step leading to the first floor and looked at Marie. "What will happen?"

"Not really sure exactly—but what if I get stuck at some dreary place like the cemetery? It would hardly be worth sticking around."

"Is that what Eva told you would happen?" Danielle asked.

"She didn't say exactly, but suggested it might be best if we made ourselves scarce until after Halloween to allow whatever is going on to play out."

"And you can't tell us what is going on?"

"To be honest, I'm not really sure. It's my understanding some spirits might be trying to get Walt's attention. Something to resolve. Beyond that, I don't know."

"Okay." Danielle let out a sigh and started down the staircase. "We'll just have to do the haunted house without your help. I don't suppose we're the first people who had to pull off a Halloween haunted house without real ghosts. Although, from what you're saying, it sounds like there will be some ghosts here—just not to help us."

Marie glanced around quickly as if looking to see if anyone was eavesdropping and then looked back to Danielle. In a whisper she said, "I don't think it will hurt if I tell you one thing—we don't believe those footprints in your secret staircase came from a spirit."

AFTER MARIE DISAPPEARED, Danielle called the chief, asking him if he would mind lending a hand at the haunted house since Marie and Eva would not be helping. She then called the rest of the haunted house crew—just those who were aware of Marie and Eva's existence—informing them of the spirits' pending absence. Chances were, they would not be seeing the two spirits again until November arrived.

WALT, Danielle, Chris, Heather, Ian and the chief huddled in the parlor, discussing what changes needed to be made to compensate for losing two ghostly helpers.

"If we're lucky, maybe our tea-loving spirit will return," Heather said, glancing down at the tea set Danielle had left sitting on the coffee table.

"I'm a little uncomfortable about all this," Danielle said with a sigh. "It's like this really is a haunted house."

"It always has been," Ian reminded her.

"That's not what I mean," Danielle said. "I've never been afraid in Marlow House. A haunted house—like Presley House—it scared me."

"And about killed you," Heather added.

"Yes." Danielle nodded.

"Eva assured us that we have no reason to fear for our safety," Chris reminded them.

"If there is something we need to worry about, I certainly don't feel comfortable having Eddy and Evan here," the chief said.

"I don't doubt what Eva says," Danielle told the chief. "We aren't in any danger. What I meant, it's like we're visitors to the haunted house—not someone just putting it on. Going through a haunted house, you never know what might jump out at you. But if you're the ones responsible for putting it on, like us, we know what to expect around every corner."

"But not now. Now we have a couple of rogue ghosts up to mischief," Chris added.

"I rather like the idea," Heather said. "A nice scary Halloween."

"I don't like being scared," Danielle declared.

"Says the woman who has been seeing ghosts all her life and always seems so blasé about it," the chief snorted.

"I just don't like them jumping at me, yelling boo," Danielle grumbled.

The next moment Evan walked into the parlor, wearing his ghost costume, and said, "Ginny's not here yet."

Danielle glanced at her watch and then looked up at Evan. "We're opening in a few minutes. She's usually here by now. Maybe she can't come."

"She did say they had to do something today," the chief reminded. "Maybe it took longer than she expected, and she can't come now. You'll just have to haunt the upstairs without her."

TWENTY-TWO

Danielle stood in front of Walt, straightening his tie. The two were alone in the library. In five minutes the haunted house would be open for business.

"You look handsome," Danielle whispered, leaning forward to brush a quick kiss over his lips.

"Thank you, love. And while I fully support your desire to raise money for charity, I will confess I'll be grateful when Wednesday gets here."

Dropping her hands from his tie, she looked up into his blue eyes and asked, "You aren't having fun?"

"Sitting for over four hours pretending to read a book while keeping it suspended in air and sending random objects flying about the library can get rather tedious. When I was a spirit, I never suffered from backaches or a sore backside. I could really use an extra cushion to sit on."

Danielle smiled apologetically. "I guess I didn't think this through. We should have gotten more help—but considering the rogue ghosts—as Chris calls them—that might not have been wise. Perhaps a haunted house wasn't such a terrific idea."

"I suppose I should be grateful I'm not Chris. I wouldn't want to be wrapped in that suffocating mummy costume all evening, and that casket!"

"Yeah," Danielle cringed. "He told me it was pretty uncomfortable and that he wished he had gotten one with padding. But that old-fashioned wooden casket was his bright idea."

Walt grinned. "Yes, I believe he's regretting that prop about now."

Danielle gave Walt another quick kiss and said, "It's almost showtime."

SUNDAY EVENING WAS PROVING to have far less foot traffic than the first two nights. Danielle was not surprised considering the next day was either a work or school day for many people.

By the time nine p.m. rolled around, Ginny had still not showed up, and they no longer expected her to come. Evan was disappointed, but he was so busy being the lone ghost on the second floor he didn't have time to miss her.

In the library Walt sat stoically on the chair next to the portrait, an open book floating before him. While he found the chore tedious, there were moments of amusement, which made him rethink his earlier response to Danielle. *Yes, this is sometimes fun*, he thought, entertained by the reactions of the people coming through the library. Minutes earlier a family had come through—a mother, father and two young children. They seemed to be having such a delightful time and were so intrigued by his trick, he began thinking of the family he and Danielle might someday have.

The clock on the wall chimed, telling Walt it was ten p.m., when a group of four teenagers walked into the library—two girls and two boys. Walt assumed the two couples were on a double date. The girls kept staring at him, comparing his likeness to the man in the portrait. But then they jumped when they realized he wasn't holding the book.

"How does he do that, Kurt?" one of the girls whispered to her date.

Kurt looked directly at Walt and asked in a loud clear voice, "How do you get the book to do that?"

Walt smiled at him and then whispered, "Because I'm a ghost." They all laughed.

Kurt reached over to touch the book. Walt shook his head, silently telling him no. He reluctantly took back his hand. A moment later Kurt turned to the other three teenagers to say something, his back to Walt, when motion over their shoulders captured his attention. He froze, his eyes widened. Speechless, he pointed behind his friends.

The three teenagers had been watching Kurt and had failed to notice Walt's startled expression. He had seen the same thing as their friend. There, floating in the air above them, was the transparent image of a young woman.

"Holy crap!" one of them shouted while the two girls let out screams of surprise. They then laughed.

"Oh my gosh, scared me!" one of the girls said. "It must be a hologram."

"That's probably what the book is too. A hologram. That's why he didn't want you to touch it," the other girl said.

They turned to Walt for him to confirm their theories, but Walt said nothing. Instead, he stared intently at the floating image.

"Do you recognize me, Walt Marlow?" the vision asked.

Walt looked from the unexpected apparition to the teenagers, who continued to chatter away as if this was all great fun. It didn't seem as if they had heard the question.

"They can see me," she said. "As can you, Walt Marlow. But they can't hear me. But you can, can't you?"

Walt blinked his eyes, but said nothing. He gave her a slight nod.

"Do you recognize me?" she asked again. "You can answer when they leave the room," the spirit told him.

A few minutes later the teenagers left the library, leaving Walt and the apparition alone.

"You look familiar, but I can't place you," Walt told her.

"I'm Annabelle Fortune. Do you remember now?" She sounded angry.

Recognition dawned. "Yes. Your husband worked for my grandfather. But why are you here?"

"I need to know what happened to my husband," she demanded.

"You don't know?"

"Obviously I don't know, or I wouldn't be here!" she said impatiently.

"I know he left Frederickport after I announced the sale of the company. I remember you came to me looking for him. I told you then I didn't know where he was. I don't know any more now than I did then," Walt explained.

"He would never have left me! I had to go see my aunt in Portland; she was ill. He couldn't go with me. He said he had to stay here and see you. When I came back the next week, he wasn't there. I never saw him again."

Walt looked sympathetically at the apparition.

"Don't look at me like that," she snapped.

"Like what?" he asked.

"Like you feel sorry for me. Like I was a fool and didn't really know my husband. Nothing was missing. He didn't take his clothes, nothing. In fact, the day I left for Portland, I had to come back to the house to get something, and the piano Abe had bought me arrived early. I was so excited, I wanted to stay and play it—I wanted to thank him. But I had to leave and he had already gone to see you. Why would he buy me a piano if he was intending to abandon me?"

Walt shook his head. "I don't know what to say."

"I know you were the last one to see him," she told him.

Frowning in confusion, Walt shook his head. "How can that be? I don't even recall the last time I saw him, but I'm certain it was days before I heard he had left town."

"Then I suppose I'll have to refresh your memory," she said sternly. "After you announced the sale of your grandfather's business, Abe told me he had to speak to you. There was something you needed to know. But your assistant kept telling him you were too busy."

"My assistant?" Walt frowned.

"Yes. I don't know her name. The morning I left, he said he was going to your house instead of the office, and make you see him."

"He never came. And if he did, I never saw him. Did he tell you what he wanted to talk to me about?"

"Of course he didn't. The Marlows and all their secrets. My husband used to say he was the keeper of those secrets. Loyalty to your family and what did it get us? What did you do to Abe!"

"Mrs. Fortune," Walt said in a calm voice, "you are obviously aware of my change of circumstance. I don't believe you imagine I am a ghost."

"No. Of course not. I know all about you."

"Then can you imagine in the grand scheme of things someone responsible for the disappearance of your husband being granted a second chance, as I have?"

"I learned long ago death is no more fair than life," she said stubbornly.

"What motive would I have to lie to you? I sincerely have no idea what happened to your husband," Walt said in earnest.

Annabelle stared down at Walt, doubt seeping in. The image of her body continued to float over the room.

They were interrupted a moment later when Danielle walked into the library carrying a sheet of paper. The moment she spied the floating apparition, she froze and then said dryly, "I thought maybe it was something like this."

Without hesitation Danielle turned from Walt and Annabelle and affixed the paper she had been holding onto the outside of the library door. Neither Annabelle nor Walt could see the 'Closed. Will open in 10 minutes' that had been written on the paper in felt-tip pen, or that it had a bit of adhesive tape affixed to its edges. She shut and locked the door.

Turning to Walt, she asked, "Who is your friend?"

"Danielle, meet Annabelle Fortune. I believe I mentioned her to you. She and her husband used to live in Pete Rogers's house. At least the house that used to be there."

Danielle arched her brow at the spirit and stepped closer, looking up at her. She then turned to Walt and asked, "What does she want?"

"She seems to think I know where her husband went after he left Frederickport."

Danielle looked back up to Annabelle and motioned to the floor. "You think you can come down here?"

Annabelle frowned. "I like it better up here."

"Yeah, well, it's awkward looking up at you floating around like that. If you want us to help you, then come down here so we can talk."

With a frown, Annabelle's spirit floated downwards until her feet touched the floor. "No one is behaving as I imagined they would. Aren't people afraid of ghosts anymore? When I was alive, I would have fainted away had a ghost popped into my house and started floating about. Those young people who were here earlier laughed at me!"

"Sorry about that. But they thought you were a hologram," Danielle explained.

"What's a hologram?" Annabelle asked.

"Think of it as a parlor trick to give the illusion of a ghost. They didn't believe you were real. In fact, that's why I came in here. When they were in the foyer, I heard them talking about the cool hologram of the ghost lady in the library floating about. So I came equipped with a sign to keep people out of the room while I talk to you."

"I just want Mr. Marlow to tell me what happened to my husband."

"I'm sorry, but I don't think he knows. The house you used to live in—well, the lot it was on—it recently sold, and when discussing its previous owners, Walt mentioned you and your husband. He told me your husband left town after he announced he was selling the company. He never said anything about seeing him. Or knowing where he went. I believe him."

"But Abe said he was coming to see your husband," Annabelle whispered. "He said it was important, something Walt Marlow had to be told. And he would never have abandoned me."

"I am sorry, Annabelle," Danielle said gently. "If your husband was on his way to see Walt and never arrived, then something must have happened. Do you have any idea what he wanted to tell him? Perhaps someone stopped him from seeing Walt."

"Are you suggesting someone murdered my husband?"

"Isn't that what you were suggesting I did," Walt asked Annabelle.

Annabelle considered his question a moment and then shook her head. "No. I just…thought maybe you sent him somewhere. Maybe there was an accident. Something you didn't want made public."

"I honestly have no idea where your husband went or what happened to him," Walt said.

Annabelle looked from Danielle to Walt. "Then why am I here?"

"What do you mean?" Danielle asked.

"I feel as if I shouldn't move on. I don't know why, but I know it has something to do with Abe. It's like he's been calling out to me—since before I died."

"Walt told me you died on the beach, from exposure," Danielle said gently.

Annabelle nodded. "I heard him. He called for me. I went looking for him, but then I got so cold…and then…then…I died."

"Have you been at the Frederickport Cemetery all this time?" Danielle asked.

"Yes." Annabelle nodded.

"If Walt can't help you, maybe there's someone else who can. We have to assume whatever happened to your husband, he is obviously dead now. Perhaps you need to talk to Eva Thorndike."

Annabelle shook her head. "No. I won't talk to Eva about this. I don't care for the woman. I'm trapped for eternity at the cemetery, never knowing what happened to my dear Abe, while she has freedom I can only touch once a year. And I know it has something to do with Marlow House."

"I'm curious about something. Why haven't you come before on a previous Halloween?" Danielle asked.

"I...I almost came last year, when I heard Walt was no longer on our side. But something told me this was the year." Annabelle vanished.

TWENTY-THREE

Battery-operated gadgets controlled many of the props on the second floor of the haunted house. Marie's primary job—when she had been there—was to keep an eye on the visitors as they traveled through the dimly lit rooms to make sure none got into mischief, while occasionally moving a random object to spice things up. However, even without Marie's tricks, there was plenty for the visitors to see.

Eva's job had been to direct Evan and Ginny in their ghostly duties. Without Eva to give him direction, Evan tried to recall all that he had been told the first two nights. But he was not alone. His father, dressed as Lurch from *The Addams Family*, wandered the second floor, keeping an eye on things. The Lurch costume had been Eddy's idea. Being asked to help at the last minute, MacDonald had needed a costume in a hurry, one appropriate for a haunted house. *The Addams Family*, being one of Eddy's favorite movies, had inspired the idea, and it was also a costume rather easy to assemble with a black suit and some artfully applied face makeup and hair gel. MacDonald already had the suit, while Heather helped with the makeup and hair.

One of the changes made since learning Marie and Eva would not be helping was to slow down the flow of people going through the open house. It hadn't been a difficult task, since Sunday proved to have less business than the first two nights. The goal had been to let one group of people through the second floor at a time.

The two couples who had been with Walt when Annabelle appeared in the library had just finished going through the second floor when Evan told his father he needed to use the bathroom, which would require his father's help with the costume. They both assumed they would be out of the bathroom before the next round of visitors arrived. What they hadn't expected was a costume malfunction, which kept them in the bathroom longer than they had expected.

While Evan and his father wrestled with the ghost costume, Carla, one of the waitresses from Pier Café, and her date, Kile, made their way to the second floor.

To raise extra money for the fundraiser, Heather had been selling bags of popcorn in the kitchen. She had sold a bag to Carla, who carried it with her up the staircase, eating popcorn as she walked.

"Those illusions have to be some sort of hologram," Kile told Carla as they stepped onto the second-floor landing. "But what was the deal with the guy and the portrait in the library?" Kile, who wasn't from Frederickport, was unaware of local history.

"That's Walt Marlow; his wife owns this house," Carla began. "There was another Walt Marlow, a distant cousin to the man downstairs. He's the one in the portrait."

"Are you saying the guy we saw in the library, that portrait wasn't of him?"

Before shoving more popcorn in her mouth, Carla said, "Nope." She went on to tell him about the history of Marlow House as they went through the rooms on the second floor.

"Come on, I'll show you where the attic is," Carla said when they stepped out of one of the bedrooms. She grabbed Kile's hand, pulling him along with her as she hurried down the hallway leading to the attic staircase. When they reached the foot of the staircase, they found a rope with a sign barricading the attic stairwell.

"Oh drat. I forgot. I guess they converted the attic into their master bedroom suite," Carla said. "I remember now, Adam Nichols mentioned they wouldn't be including the attic in the tour. But that's where they found the body. Hanging from the rafters. For years everyone thought he had committed suicide, but Danielle found some information that pointed to murder."

"Who killed him?" Kile asked.

"I think his wife and brother-in-law."

"For the money?" Kile asked.

"Isn't it always for the money?" Carla snickered.

Kile looked up the dark attic stairwell. "Too bad they didn't include the attic in the tour. Especially since it was really the scene of a murder."

Carla shrugged. "I suppose I understand them not wanting strangers tromping through their bedroom. Plus, from what I understand, the attic was remodeled. So it's not exactly like it was when the murder took place."

"This is a pretty cool house," Kile said, "but I wouldn't want a bunch of strangers coming through it if it were mine."

"I suppose it's different for Danielle. After all, she always ran it as a bed and breakfast, that was at least until her old biddy of a neighbor complained. She's used to strangers coming and going."

"I suppose. Where to now?" Kile asked.

"Let's go in there." Carla pointed to the door leading to Danielle's old bedroom.

Moments after stepping into the room, what appeared to be bats flew overhead. Both Carla and Kile let out a startled scream followed by a laugh. Curious, Kile took a closer look and spied the wires. He suspected whatever had made the bats travel over the wire was triggered by them walking into the room. Or perhaps the plastic bats simply traveled back and forth over the wire every few minutes.

While Kile checked out the mechanism powering the bats, Carla took a close look at the skeleton sitting at the desk, seemingly writing a letter. Dressed in a vintage gown from the late 1800s, the skeleton wore a blond wig and a hat adorned with feathers.

"Lovely. I wonder who she was." Kile snickered after he turned his attention from the wires to the skeleton.

Before Carla could respond, the sound of the closet door opening startled her. She jumped back, bumping against Kile while she studied the closet, wondering what was going to happen next.

Both Carla and Kile stared at the now open closet. It revealed an empty space. There were no clothes hanging on the rod, no boxes or luggage shoved in any corner. However, light seemed to be leaking out from around the seams of the paneling on the back side of the closet.

"What's that?" Kile whispered, leaving Carla's side for a closer inspection.

With a giggle, Carla clutched her bag of popcorn as she trailed close behind Kile, anticipating something jumping out at her.

Standing in the closet, Kile reached for the back wall, but before his fingertips touched it, the paneling slid to one side. The motion caused Carla to gasp, but Kile did not budge. He continued to stare.

"It's a secret passage!" Kile announced when the panel fully opened, revealing a glimpse into the hidden staircase.

"Oh, how cool!" Carla said, getting closer to the opening.

Kile stepped into the passageway first, his attention focused to the right, leading up the dimly lit stairwell.

Carla followed him in, looking in the same direction, when a sound from her left drew her attention. She turned toward the sound, and the unexpected sight made her scream and jerk her hands up, tossing popcorn out of the small paper sack she was holding. There, sitting in the corner, sat what appeared to be a dead man, his eyes staring blankly in her direction.

Carla had never seen the man before, and she had met just about everyone in Frederickport at one time or another. He looked to be in his late twenties, with short black hair, layered in dust. His white dress shirt and black slacks were also covered with dust, as were his scuffed-up black shoes. The way he sat, leaning against the back wall and his legs spread out in front of him, looked like someone who had been walking a long time and had become so exhausted that he had just plopped down to sit a moment.

"Oh my god!" Carla reached for Kile's hand and clutched it firmly. "Is he real?"

Kile could feel his own heart racing. "Umm...no, I'm sure it's fake."

"It doesn't look like a dummy. But he isn't moving. How can he look at me without blinking? Oh my god, is he really dead?"

"Maybe it's wax. I don't think someone could sit like that without moving," Kile suggested.

"Touch him," Carla urged. "Either he has a pulse, is made of wax, or..."

"I'm not touching him. But I'm sure it's all part of the show," Kile said.

"How can you be so sure?" Carla backed out of the passageway.

"For one thing, they had the closet doors rigged so this would open up. At the exact time we were in the bedroom. They obviously wanted us to see it. It's all part of the haunted house. It's certainly not a real dead body."

"Are you sure?" Carla asked nervously as Kile followed her back into the bedroom.

Standing by the foot of the bed, the pair watched as the back panel of the closet closed on its own, followed by the closing of the closet door.

"Yeah, now I'm sure. But let's get out of here. This place is giving me the creeps," Kile said.

A few moments later Carla and Kile hurried down the staircase. When they stepped onto the first floor, Carla spied Danielle walking in their direction. She paused a moment, waiting for Danielle to reach them.

"Hi, Carla," Danielle greeted her a moment later. "I hope you enjoyed the haunted house."

"I did. But it was a little too real for me," Carla told her with a shiver.

"I have to agree," Kile said.

Danielle glanced to the man with Carla. She had never seen him before.

"Oh, Danielle, this is my date, Kile. He lives in Astoria. Kile, this is Danielle Marlow. She owns Marlow House."

"Nice to meet you, Kile," Danielle greeted him. "I'm sorry if the haunted house was too scary."

"It's not that," Carla said. "You did a great job."

"I have to agree. This is probably the best haunted house I've ever been to," Kile said.

"Let's just say our nerves are a little rattled. We both could use a beer," Carla said.

"I was thinking of something stronger," Kile snorted.

"I thought the smiling head in the jar you have in the kitchen was pretty awesome—in a gruesome way. And I'm still trying to figure out the tea set in the parlor—although the ghost who pops in to pour and disappears is not too hard to figure out. After all, I have been to the Haunted House at Disneyland. But that dead body in your hidden staircase—well. It looked too freaking real." Carla shivered.

"Hidden staircase?" Danielle frowned.

"Impressive how you got the closet to open right after we walked into the room. And then the way the back panel of the closet slid open. Timing was perfect," Kile said. "But I agree with Carla, the dead body looked too real. Still creeps me out just to think of it."

"I had never heard you had a secret staircase before. That's pretty cool. Especially for the haunted house. But the dead body! Yikes. Is it made of wax? I can't believe someone could sit that long without blinking his eyes. But he looked so real—like flesh and blood." Carla shivered again.

"So what is he made of?" Kile asked.

"Umm…I'm not sure. But please don't tell anyone," Danielle said. "It…well, we want to keep the element of surprise."

"To be honest, I sort of wish I had known. Might not have been so freaky," Carla said. "But okay. I get it. It would be like telling someone how a book ends before they have a chance to finish it."

Danielle forced a smile and stood numbly, listening to Carla chatter on for a few more minutes before saying goodbye. After the pair exited through the front door, Danielle grabbed the closed sign she had used earlier and dashed to see Walt.

TWENTY-FOUR

"We have a problem," Danielle told Walt. The two stood alone in the library.

"Surely this is just another spirit playing some Halloween prank?" Walt asked after Danielle finished recounting what Carla and Kile had told her minutes earlier.

"I can't imagine it is a real dead body. After all, the chief has been up there all evening. I don't think anyone is going to be murdering people with the police chief down the hallway. I'm just more concerned about the spirit revealing the staircase to more people." Danielle groaned. "And of all people, Carla?"

"We'd better go check it out," Walt told her.

When they stepped out of the library, Ian was waiting for them in the hallway. "Is there a problem?" he asked.

"We need to check out something in the attic," Danielle told him. She looked over at the grandfather clock in the entry hall. It was almost 11 p.m. The flyers had not specified when the haunted house would close down, leaving it open depending on the crowds. "It's getting late. How many more people are waiting in line?"

"No one at the moment. Our last group just left," Ian told her.

"Then can you please tell Melony to put up the closed sign? I think we need to shut down for the night."

"What happened?" Ian asked.

"I'll explain later. But can you tell Mel it's okay if she wants to leave after she closes up. I think it would be for the best."

Ian looked uneasily at Danielle and then to Walt, who stood quietly at his wife's side, one palm placed on her lower back.

"Okay," Ian muttered, leaving to tell Melony they would be closing the doors.

"Are you going to tell the chief what Carla saw?" Walt asked.

"I think we should check it out first and then decide," Danielle whispered.

"You mean in case it's a real dead body?" Walt asked, only half kidding.

Danielle cringed. "Please, that is not even funny."

When they reached the second-floor landing, Danielle forced a smile when greeted by the chief.

"What are you two doing up here?" MacDonald asked.

"We've decided to close for the night," Walt said.

"I was wondering if you might close early. Probably a good thing. I think Evan is ready for bed," MacDonald said. "And it is a school night."

"Umm…where is the little ghost?" Danielle asked, glancing around nervously.

"He just went to the bathroom again, trying to fix his costume. We had a bit of a malfunction tonight, and he keeps trying to fix it," the chief explained.

"Umm…did Carla and her date say anything to you when they were up here tonight?" Danielle asked.

"Carla? She and her date came up here when I was with Evan in the bathroom earlier. I saw them going down the stairs. I didn't talk to them, and I'm afraid they didn't get the full ghost treatment —Evan and I were trying to fix his costume."

"Oh, I think they got their money's worth," Walt muttered under his breath.

As soon as Edward and Evan headed down the staircase, Walt and Danielle hurried to Danielle's old bedroom. The moment Danielle walked into the room, bats flew by on the wire. She flipped on the overhead light, fully illuminating the room and making the wires more visible. They looked to the closet. It was closed. Danielle stood at the foot of the bed and watched as Walt opened the closet door. He then stepped into the small space and tried opening the panel. It would not budge.

"It's locked," Walt told her when he stepped out of the closet.

"I locked it earlier," Danielle told him. "Let's go upstairs."

With a nod, Walt followed her out of the room and down the hallway, to the attic staircase. When they reached the rope barricading access to the stairs, Walt moved it. Instead of letting Danielle go first, as he normally would, Walt sprinted up the steps. Once he reached the attic landing, he realized he did not have the room key, and since he was too anxious to wait for Danielle to give it to him, he used his telekinetic powers to turn the lock mechanism. After he did, he entered first, motioning for Danielle to stay back.

She watched as Walt opened the door to the hidden staircase. She could see it was dark inside. A moment later light flooded the narrow space when Walt turned on the overhead light. Slowly approaching the doorway to the stairwell, she watched as Walt looked down the steps.

"There's no body," Walt called out.

Danielle exhaled, releasing the breath she had been holding. Stepping into the stairwell, she followed Walt down the steps.

"But there is something down here…" Walt muttered as he reached the landing behind Danielle's old bedroom closet. Bending down, he picked something off the floor and looked at it. Standing straight, he turned to Danielle, who stood halfway down the stairwell, watching him.

"What is it?" she asked him.

He held it up for her to see. "Popcorn."

"Carla was eating popcorn. I guess this proves they were actually in here. She obviously spilled some of it," Danielle said.

"What now?" Walt asked.

With a sigh, Danielle made her way down to Walt. When she reached him, she looked around and called out, "Hello? Are you there?"

No answer.

"Please, I want to talk to you!" she called out again.

"Looks like you're being ignored," Walt said.

Frustrated, Danielle stomped her foot and said angrily, "Come on, show yourself. I know you're there!"

Nothing.

"I just wish Marie and Eva hadn't taken off," Danielle grumbled.

AFTER THE HAUNTED house closed on Sunday, Walt and Danielle went with Heather, Chris and Ian across the street to Ian and Lily's house. When they walked in the door, they were greeted by both Sadie and Hunny. Lily had been dog sitting for Chris.

"I didn't expect to see you all tonight," Lily said in surprise, her voice a loud whisper.

"We need to talk," Danielle said, sitting on a chair in the living room.

"Is Connor sleeping?" Heather asked.

"Yeah, he's been down for a couple of hours now. But I expect him up soon for a feeding. What's up, guys?" Lily asked.

"Some things happened tonight that I think you all should know," Danielle began. She waited for them all to take a seat before telling them about the evening's strange haunting—from Annabelle Fortune to the body Carla claimed to see.

"I can't believe you have a hidden staircase," Heather blurted when Danielle finished.

"When did you find it?" Chris asked. "When Bill remodeled the attic?"

"Bill doesn't know about the staircase," Danielle said.

"So you found it before you had the attic remodeled?" Heather asked.

Danielle looked guiltily to Walt, who returned a sheepish smile.

Chris began to laugh.

Heather turned to Chris. "What's so funny?"

"Think about it, Heather—the staircase led from Danielle's room to Walt's. No one would ever know...tsk, tsk, tsk," Chris teased.

"We were married," Walt huffed.

Chris laughed again.

Heather looked to Lily, "Did you know?"

Lily shrugged and flashed Heather a smile.

"What else haven't you told us?" Heather asked.

Danielle then told them about the unexplained beam of light and the footprints on the hidden staircase.

"And you're sure one of you didn't make the footprints?" Chris asked.

Danielle shook her head. "It was larger than Walt's shoe."

144

"Did the dirt disappear, like Eva's glitter?" Heather asked.

"Not until I washed it with a rag. But I took pictures." Danielle pulled up the images on her cellphone and then handed the phone to Heather.

"Do you know if Carla's dead body looks like the tea-pouring ghost in the parlor?" Heather asked, studying the pictures before handing the phone to Chris.

"I didn't ask her to describe what he looked like," Danielle said.

"No, I don't imagine you would," Chris said with a chuckle. "That would be a little awkward. After all, you are supposed to know about all the fake dead bodies lying around your house."

"How many ghosts are crashing the haunted tour?" Heather asked.

"I suspect at least two. We know the name of one—Annabelle Fortune," Danielle said. "But she seems to be there for a more serious reason."

"Like Harvey," Heather said.

Danielle nodded.

"I assume the other spirit is male," Chris said. "The one pouring the tea in the parlor, and possibly responsible for the smiling head in a jar."

"Is he also responsible for the dead body?" Heather asked.

"I don't know. That stunt feels different somehow," Danielle said. "The tea in the parlor—the smiling face—those seem more, well, lighthearted."

Chris laughed, handing Danielle back her phone. "Light-hearted? Says the woman who won't go in there until she covers the jar with a towel."

"I know what Dani means," Lily said. "Those stunts feel more like something you'd see in an Abbott and Costello movie, but the body in the hidden stairwell feels more Stephen King."

"You said you called for the spirit? Asked him to show himself," Heather asked.

"Yes. But to be honest, after I called out, it didn't feel like anyone was there, not like I was being ignored. I felt like whatever spirit had been there was gone. Out of range," Danielle explained.

"Perhaps we should have a séance?" Heather suggested. "Or maybe just try a Ouija board!"

"Ahh, the pathway to the devil, the Ouija board," Chris said in an ominous voice.

"You think that's true?" Heather asked. "Do Ouija boards attract demonic forces?"

Chris shrugged. "I don't know. I've never used a Ouija board."

"Me either," Danielle said.

"Are you saying you have never used a Ouija board?" Walt asked in surprise.

"No, have you?" Danielle asked.

"Certainly. It was actually pretty common back during my first go-around. It was amusing. At the time I never seriously believed a spirit was responsible for making the planchette move. Of course, now I'm wondering if we really contacted spirits back then," Walt said.

"I bought a Ouija board from a yard sale when I was in high school," Heather began. "And when I brought it home, my mother absolutely flipped out. I didn't even get to try it. Mom swore it was a portal into hell."

"Did your mother watch *The Exorcist?*" Ian asked with a chuckle.

"I think so, why?" Heather asked.

"Ouija boards were popular and accepted during the first part of the twentieth century. Like Walt said, they were quite common. I read an interesting article about the history of Ouija boards on the Smithsonian Magazine website. Talked about how it wasn't until *The Exorcist* came out in the early 1970s did the Ouija board assume its demon-attracting reputation. Especially among the Christian churches," Ian explained. He then added, "It was around for about a century before it became a portal to hell."

"Some people think Harry Potter is evil too," Danielle said.

"So what are you going to do?" Lily asked. "I mean about the ghosts crashing the haunted house."

"I suppose all we can do is wait until they tell us what they want—assuming it's something more than Halloween mischief," Danielle said.

"There is always the Ouija board," Heather reminded her.

TWENTY-FIVE

Leaning against one arm of the sofa, her bare feet tucked under her on the cushion, Danielle stared blankly at the space in the library where Annabelle Fortune had been floating the night before. Still wearing her flannel pajama bottoms and an oversized T-shirt, Danielle considered all she must do today before the haunted house reopened. Tomorrow was Halloween, and then the random hauntings should stop.

Walt walked into the room, carrying two cups of coffee. He handed one to Danielle.

"Thank you," she murmured, shifting slightly on the sofa to make room for Walt.

"Any visitors this morning?" he asked as he sat down.

"No." Danielle sipped her coffee and then asked, "And you?"

"No. But I keep thinking about Annabelle."

Danielle turned on the sofa so she could better see Walt. "And?"

"I wonder, did she leave for good last night? I answered her questions, so does that mean she has no reason to come back?"

"Maybe she's still here somewhere," Danielle suggested.

"You think so?"

Danielle took another sip and considered Walt's question a moment and then said, "How peculiar it is she would wait so long to come here to talk to you, especially since she believes the unanswered question is holding her back. But then I remember she is a spirit, and their notion of time is so different from ours." She paused and looked seriously to Walt, studying him a moment before asking, "Do you notice the difference now? From when you were a spirit?"

Cupping the warm mug of coffee between the palms of his hands, Walt leaned back on the sofa, stretching out his long legs. "I noticed a difference after you first moved here."

"Yes, but you were still a spirit. I mean, a difference now that you're alive again."

"I believe spending more time in the living world—even when one is a spirit—tends to give you a more human grasp of situations, as opposed to the perspective of one dwelling primarily in the spirit world. And then, of course, once I did cross back over, there are some elements from my time as a spirit that have slipped from my memory, just out of reach, vaguely there. But I instinctively know, when it is my time again, I'll remember."

"Whatever the reasons for Annabelle coming now and not sooner, I can't believe she's simply going to accept your answer and return to the cemetery and never come back. Just because you didn't have the answer she wanted doesn't mean you can't find it. I'm curious, what did Abe Fortune do for your grandfather?"

"That's the thing, I'm not really sure. My grandfather had always been a robust, healthy man. I imagine he assumed he would be around for many more years. And because of that, there were elements of his business he didn't share with me. Truth was, it didn't particularly bother me. I dreaded the idea of taking over the company. I didn't want it. But neither of us counted on the influenza taking him. It almost took me."

"Did he work in your grandfather's factory?" Danielle asked.

"No. That I'm sure of. I understood him to be something of an errand boy—one my grandfather depended on. But when the company sold, there really wasn't a place for him, so it didn't surprise me he left town. Part of his employment with my grandfather included the house down the street. I would have worked something out with him if he had wanted to stay, but we never had the opportunity to discuss it. He just left."

"And he didn't take his wife with him," Danielle added.

"True. But it was not uncommon for some men when they had a change of fortune to take off and abandon their wives, their families. I felt bad for her, but I didn't really know either one of them."

"I wonder what he wanted to talk to you about?" Danielle murmured.

Walt shook his head. "I have no idea. But he didn't come to the house. Or if he did, I wasn't home."

"Perhaps we should consider that séance," Danielle suggested, only half joking.

"Or pick up a Ouija board? See if we can summon the spirit of Abe Fortune, ask what happened to him," Walt teased.

"This proves one thing," Danielle said.

"What is that?"

"When I was younger, I always imagined a spirit could easily reach out to any other spirit, even someone they hadn't known in life. Heck, even one who had moved on. Like they all had access to this spiritual intercom system. *Hello, ring up Elvis Presley.* Oh, wait, that wouldn't work anyway. I heard he isn't really dead."

Walt smiled at Danielle and quietly sipped his coffee.

"But now I know that's not true. It certainly isn't for Annabelle."

"You are forgetting, it's also possible some spirits may not want to be found by another. No different from when they were alive," Walt reminded her. "Look at Eva, she avoided the local cemetery because Angela was there. And if Abe did run away from his wife, why would he suddenly want to see her again just because they're both dead?"

Danielle let out a sigh and said, "True. If he really did abandon her, there's no reason to believe he'll want to see her now."

Walt nodded. "Exactly."

"If that's true, it's rather sucky of him. Leaving her hanging like that."

"Agreed. So what are you going to do today?" Walt asked.

Danielle glanced at her watch. "Well, I need to get dressed. Have something to eat, and then see if Ginny's aunt and uncle are back."

"You're going to try meeting them?" Walt asked.

"Yes. I'd like to introduce myself. But I don't want Ginny coming over tonight and helping. Not with all that's going on. And then I need to go over and talk to the chief. You want to come with me?"

"I think I should stay here," Walt said. "If Annabelle comes back, I can talk to her. She must know more about her husband's job with my grandfather than she told me. Perhaps if I know more, we can figure out what happened to Abe Fortune."

"You might try some internet sleuthing," Danielle suggested. "It is very possible he will pop up somewhere. Another job in another town. Maybe even another family. At least then she'll know what happened to him," Danielle suggested.

"Good idea."

"And, Walt, if you run into the spirit responsible for the body—find out why. Is it just a Halloween prank? If so, maybe convince him—or her—to stop leading people to our hidden staircase."

THE AIR WAS damp and chilly, and the sky looked more gray than cloudy. Danielle wore blue jeans, an untucked flannel shirt, knee-high boots, a knit cap and a heavy jacket, her hands buried deep in its pockets as she walked up the street. When she reached the Crawfords' house, she noticed their car—she assumed it was their car—in the driveway, and there was no sign of the Bellemores' pickup truck.

Standing on the Crawford front porch a few minutes later, she rang the bell and then quickly tucked her hand back in her coat pocket for warmth. A moment later the door opened, and she found herself facing a man she had never seen before. He briefly looked her up and down before fixing his eyes back on her face.

"Mr. Crawford?" Danielle asked hesitantly.

"Yes. Can I help you?" he asked.

"Hello," Danielle smiled and then offered her right hand. "I'm one of your neighbors, Danielle Marlow."

He took her hand and shook it, a slight frown of confusion on his face. "Which house is yours?"

"I'm Danielle Marlow from Marlow House," she said.

"Who is it?" a woman called from inside the house before appearing by Mr. Crawford's side. She looked Danielle up and down curiously.

"Mia, this is our neighbor Danielle Marlow. She tells me she lives at Marlow House." He turned back to Danielle and asked, "Where exactly is that?"

"Marlow House, you know, where the haunted house is," Danielle explained.

He still looked confused, and then his wife gave him a little nudge and said cheerfully, "I showed you, that big old Victorian on the other side of the street a few doors down." She looked back to Danielle and said, "I normally would love all that spooky Halloween stuff. If we had the time, I'd love to go through your haunted house. But we have been so busy with the move, doncha know."

She glanced at her watch and then looked back to Danielle. "It was nice meeting you. Although I don't believe we were properly introduced. I'm Mia Crawford. You've already met my husband, Austin. But I really must run, I start a new job at the elementary school, and I need to be there in thirty minutes. I'd like to be early on my first day."

"School? Are you a teacher?" Danielle asked. "My friend Lily, also one of our neighbors, was a second-grade teacher there until she took off for maternity leave."

"Teacher? Oh no. Secretarial. I'd much rather be in an office than a classroom." She flashed Danielle a smile and turned, prepared to dash off.

"I was just wondering if I could talk to you a moment about your niece," Danielle said quickly.

Mia turned in her tracks and faced Danielle with a frown.

"Niece?" Austin asked.

"Yes, Ginny. Very sweet girl. We've really enjoyed her," Danielle explained.

"I have absolutely no idea what you are talking about," Austin said.

"We don't have a niece," Mia said. "I have two nephews. Horrid little demons. Not sure a niece would be much better. But, no, we don't have a niece."

"I'm talking about Ginny," Danielle said.

Austin shrugged. "I'm sorry. You must have us confused with another neighbor. I don't know a Ginny." He turned to his wife and asked, "Do you?"

Mia shook her head.

"Cute little blonde girl, around nine or ten years old. Big blue eyes?" Danielle said.

The man shrugged. "Sorry. I have no idea who you're talking about."

"I do hope you find your Ginny," Mia said. She turned and went back into her house and grabbed her purse and car keys. As she rushed out the front door by Danielle a moment later, she said a hasty goodbye before getting in her car and driving off.

Danielle stared dumbly at her neighbor as she drove away.

Austin cleared his throat to get Danielle's attention. She turned back to him.

"Was there anything else?" he asked.

"Umm…no. I guess not," Danielle stammered, reluctantly adding, "Welcome to the neighborhood."

A few minutes later Danielle stood on Chris's front porch, ringing the bell. When he opened the door a minute later, Hunny greeted Danielle with a wiggling backside and sloppy kisses.

"Any more ghost sightings?" Chris asked as he opened the door wider for Danielle to enter.

"Ginny isn't their niece," Danielle blurted.

"What are you talking about?" Chris asked.

Ten minutes later Chris and Danielle sat together at his breakfast bar, drinking coffee and eating cinnamon rolls. Danielle had just told him what the Crawfords had said. Chris sat quietly, digesting the information and tearing off pieces of cinnamon roll before popping them in his mouth.

"But I saw her with them," Chris finally said. "She went in the house with the wife right after they got here."

"I described what she looks like. They acted like they had no idea who I was talking about."

"Maybe she'll show up tonight and you can ask her what's going on," Chris suggested.

"If she shows up. She said she would be there last night. And we know she probably did lie. When I asked her about her aunt and uncle being out of town, she claimed they had come back early, but the Bellemore brothers said they were still out of town."

"But according to the Crawfords, they are not the aunt and uncle," Chris reminded her. "So perhaps she was talking about someone else, and we just assumed it was the neighbors."

"But you just said you saw her with them. And when I described her, they acted like they had no idea who I was talking about."

With a sigh, Chris set his coffee cup on the counter and said, "I think you need to turn this over to the chief. Let him look into it."

TWENTY-SIX

Before leaving for the police station, Danielle called the chief, letting him know she needed to talk to him. It was almost eleven a.m. when she finally arrived.

"What's going on?" the chief asked once Danielle took a chair after closing his office door for privacy.

"I'm not sure where to begin," Danielle said. "So much has happened since last night. But I think for the moment I'm most concerned about Ginny."

"Ginny? What's the problem?"

Danielle went on to tell the chief about her encounter with the Crawfords and what Chris had told her about seeing Ginny with his new neighbors.

When she finished with the telling, MacDonald let out a sigh and leaned back in his chair. "Do you happen to have a picture of her? I know you were taking pictures every night."

"Only with her costume on. I was always so busy when she arrived—before putting on her costume—I never got a chance to get her picture," Danielle told him.

"Evan told me some disturbing things about her," the chief said.

"Disturbing how?" she asked.

"When they had some downtime—waiting for the next round of people coming through the haunted house—they'd talk. She told Evan about how her parents had died. Sounds like her father was fairly abusive, and her mother wasn't much better. There was a fire; she was the only one to get out. According to her, her only family was her uncle and his wife. But he wasn't thrilled to take her in. Ginny told Evan how lucky he was to have a father who loved him. She said she didn't know what that felt like."

"That's horrible," Danielle said.

"But now I'm wondering what is going on. If the Crawfords aren't her aunt and uncle, did she lie about everything? And where is she?" the chief said.

"Maybe the Crawfords lied. I know they lied or conveniently forgot about her being with them when they moved in," Danielle reminded him.

"Which is a chilling thought." He sat up straight and pulled his phone to him.

"What are you going to do?" she asked.

"First, I want to get a picture of Ginny so it'll be a little easier to ask around. Find out who she really is. I noticed the clothes she was wearing the other day looked to be pretty old and didn't fit her properly. Is she homeless?" he suggested.

"If so, and if she was with the Crawfords and they are denying it, then I don't even want to consider what that might mean." Danielle shivered.

Picking up the receiver, he said, "I'm going to call in a favor."

For the next few minutes Danielle sat quietly and listened while the chief made a phone call to Elizabeth Sparks. Sparks, a local artist and art teacher, occasionally worked for the local police department, drawing police sketches. When he got off the phone, he grinned up to Danielle and said, "I hope you can stick around and help Elizabeth with the sketch."

Danielle arched her brow. "I heard you dropping my name a number of times."

"Elizabeth is still grateful to you for your donation to the art department for the fundraiser. When she heard I was working on a case important to you, she seemed quite willing to come right over."

He picked up his phone again and placed an in-office call. When the party answered, he said, "Can you come to my office? I need you to look up something for me."

A few minutes later a knock came at the door. It then opened and in walked Brian Henderson.

"Hi, Danielle," Brian greeted her. "I didn't know you were here."

Danielle gave him a nod. "Hi, Brian."

He looked at the chief and asked, "What do you need?"

"See what you can find out about the Crawfords." He looked at Danielle and asked, "Do you know their first names?"

Danielle told him.

The chief looked back to Brian and said, "They're the ones who bought Pete Rogers's house, next door to Chris. See what you can find out about them. Check to see if either one of them has a niece."

Brian frowned. "What is this about?"

"It's a long story. But I need to go over and talk to the Crawfords this afternoon, and before I do, I would like to learn as much about them as possible. I would do it myself, but I have Elizabeth Sparks coming over in a few minutes, so I'm going to be tied up for a while."

After Brian left the office a few minutes later, Danielle told the chief about Annabelle and then about the hidden staircase, and about the body that had appeared and disappeared.

When she was done, the chief sat back and shook his head in disbelief. "You want to know what I find most surprising—which only illustrates how twisted I've become because of you."

"I've made you twisted?" Danielle sounded insulted.

"A normal person would be shocked to hear a dead body appeared and disappeared in your house. But me, I'm more surprised you have a hidden staircase, and you never told me!"

Danielle shrugged. "I almost told you when Tanya hid that gun in the attic. That's how I really saw her. I was coming up to the attic bedroom by way of the hidden staircase."

He snickered.

"Well, we were married," she reminded him. "We just wanted to keep the staircase a secret. Joanne wouldn't have understood if she saw me going upstairs or Walt going into my room. It just gave us an element of privacy. But...oh, Joanne..." Danielle groaned. "Now that Carla knows, it's going to come out. I need to tell Joanne. But I really don't want her going in there and seeing a dead body, not until we figure this out. Or maybe not until after Halloween, when all the mischievous spirits return to wherever they belong."

BOTH THE CHIEF and Danielle helped Elizabeth Sparks when she came to do the drawing of Ginny. When she finished, they had a remarkable likeness of the little girl. Danielle left for home while the police chief promised to stop by Marlow House and let her know what he had found out from the Crawfords.

Danielle had been gone for about twenty minutes when Brian returned to the office.

"What did you find out?" the chief asked from behind his desk.

Standing in the office, a pad of paper in his hand, Brian looked down at his notes. "The Crawfords have been married five years, no children. He worked for a manufacturing company for almost eight years." Brian then told the chief the name of the company and added, "He quit six months ago, about a year after his mother died. He's an only child. His mother left him a hefty inheritance, which is how he was able to buy that house. His wife works for some temp agency. She has two siblings and two nephews, no nieces. Neither have any priors. Nothing particularly interesting came up on either one of them. But I'm not sure what you were looking for, aside from if they have a niece, which they don't."

MIA CRAWFORD SAT at her desk at the elementary school, sorting mail, when Officer Brian Henderson stepped up to her desk and asked, "Are you Mia Crawford?"

She looked up from her work to the tall officer looming over her. "Yes. How can I help you?"

"I'm Officer Brian Henderson." He showed her his identification and handed her a business card. "We're looking for this little girl, and I wonder if you've seen her." He handed her a copy of the picture Elizabeth Sparks had drawn earlier that day.

Holding the picture in her hand, she stared at it a moment and then shrugged and handed it back. "I work at an elementary school. I see lots of kids. But she doesn't look familiar."

Brian frowned down at her. "Are you certain? Perhaps you might want to look at it again."

With an annoyed sigh, she took back the picture, looked at it briefly, shook her head, and then shoved it back at Brian. "No. Doesn't look familiar."

"That's odd, I have a witness who says he saw that little girl with you on Thursday, at your house."

"Well, he is obviously mistaken. She wasn't with me. I have never seen her before," she insisted.

"I believe her name is Ginny. Does that ring a bell?"

Mia frowned at Brian. "Ginny? About nine or ten? Blond? Blue eyes?"

"So you do know her," Brian said.

Mia shook her head. "No. But one of my neighbors, a Danielle Marlow, she came by my house asking about her this morning. For some reason she thought the girl was my niece. She isn't, of course. I don't have a niece, and I have never seen that girl before. Now, if you don't mind, I really need to get back to work."

AT THE SAME time Brian questioned Mia Crawford, the police chief was making a visit to her husband, Austin Crawford.

Austin stood on his front porch, staring down at the drawing. He looked at it a moment and then shook his head, handing the picture back to the chief.

"Like I told that Danielle Marlow this morning, we don't have a niece. And I have never seen that kid before. Hope you find her."

"We have a witness who claims she was with you on Thursday."

"Thursday?" Austin frowned. "That's the day we moved in. Where does this witness claim he saw us?"

"Here, while you were moving in."

"And the movers were here too?" Austin asked.

"Yes, that's my understanding. They were moving furniture into your house, and she was with you and your wife outside, but then went into the house with your wife."

"Really? Well, I don't know what that witness was smoking, but I'll give you the name of my movers, and they can tell you themselves if there was a kid with us or not." Austin then told the chief the name of the movers, along with the first name of the driver of the truck. "Now, if you don't mind, I have a lot to do." Austin shut the door, leaving the chief alone on the front porch.

MacDonald was just walking back to his police car when the

Bellemores pulled up and parked their truck along the street. He recognized the truck and remembered Danielle and Chris discussing the work the Bellemores were doing at the Crawfords' house. Clutching the picture of Ginny in one hand, he changed directions and walked to the Bellemores' vehicle.

"Excuse me," the chief said when Chester Bellemore climbed out of the driver's side of the truck.

"Is there a problem, officer?" Cecil asked as he got out of the vehicle and walked over to the sidewalk. He pulled a handkerchief out of his shirt pocket and in doing so flipped several business cards from the pocket onto the sidewalk. With a grumble he picked up the cards, stuffing them back into his pocket. While listening to what the police officer had to say, he blew his nose with the handkerchief.

"I'm Police Chief MacDonald, and I'm looking for any information on this little girl." He handed the picture to Chester, who looked at it and then handed it to Cecil.

"Wow, this must be pretty serious if the police chief is out in the field," Cecil said as he stared down at the copy of the drawing in his hand and then shoved his handkerchief into one of the back pockets of his blue jeans.

"Have you seen her?" the chief asked.

The brothers exchanged glances and then looked back to him. They shook their heads no at the same time as Cecil handed back the picture.

"Are you certain?" the chief asked. "She might have been here, at the Crawford house."

Chester looked at his brother and said, "I've never seen any kids at the Crawford house, have you?"

"No. Never," Cecil agreed.

TWENTY-SEVEN

Joanne Johnson, the housekeeper at Marlow House, opened the front door for Police Chief MacDonald on Monday afternoon. She had been holding a dustpan in one hand and a whisk broom in the other, yet moved them both to one hand so that she could open the door.

"Afternoon, Chief. Walt and Danielle are in the library," Joanne greeted him. "Danielle told me she was expecting you. Go right in."

"How have you enjoyed working in a haunted house?" the chief asked her as she closed the front door.

"I haven't been here when it's open. My job is to clean up the next day," she told him. "But I do wish Heather had not suggested selling popcorn. I keep finding it in all sorts of unexpected places. I hear your boys have been a great help and that you pitched in last night."

"Yes, it was fun. So you haven't seen all the ghostly special effects?" MacDonald wondered exactly what the housekeeper had seen.

"No, but I have heard about them—mostly from my friends who ask how they do it. Of course, I have no idea. A magician never tells his secrets. I've always known Walt Marlow likes to dabble in magic. I remember when he was recuperating from the accident. I could swear a box was floating across this entry hall! That man has a gift for magic."

"Yes. Yes, he does."

They exchanged a few more words before Joanne went on to the parlor to tidy up, while the chief headed for the library.

"Hello, Chief, so you have nothing?" Danielle asked. When MacDonald had called earlier, telling Danielle he was going to stop by, he had mentioned he had not found Ginny, but would explain more when he saw her.

"Hello, Chief," Walt greeted him, standing briefly.

MacDonald gave them both a nod and then said, "I haven't found anything, and this is all most peculiar. I'm not sure what to think." He took a seat in one of the chairs facing the sofa where Walt and Danielle sat.

"What did the Crawfords say?" Danielle asked.

"Pretty much what they told you. I also spoke to the men who've been doing work over there, from Bellemore Construction. I showed them the picture, and they claimed they have never seen her. I also called the moving company and talked to one of the men who was there that day. He said he didn't see any children at the house when they moved the furniture in. Just Mr. and Mrs. Crawford. Said if there was a little girl there, they didn't see her."

"But Chris saw her. And the movers were there then," Danielle said.

The chief shrugged. "It's like the child doesn't exist. I had Brian go to the school at the same time I went to talk to Mr. Crawford. I didn't want to give one of them the opportunity to give the other a heads-up about our visit. And after he spoke to Mrs. Crawford, he showed the woman in the admission department the picture of Ginny. She didn't recognize her. Brian returned during lunch hour and had all the teachers look at the picture. Whoever Ginny is, she is not enrolled at the local elementary school."

"Do you have the picture on you?" Walt asked.

"Yes." MacDonald reached into his shirt pocket and pulled out a folded piece of paper.

"Can I see it?" Walt stood up and walked to the chief, who then handed him the paper. Walt unfolded it and returned to the sofa. Sitting back down, the paper in his hand, he looked at the drawing.

"At this point I would suggest Ginny was a spirit—but you and Eddy both saw her, heard her," Danielle said.

"I know where I've seen her before!" Walt blurted. Both the

chief and Danielle looked to Walt, who continue to stare at the picture.

"Where?" Danielle asked.

"It was at the cemetery, during Maisy Faye and Kenneth's funeral. I almost walked into her. She smiled at me and kept walking."

"Who was she with?" the chief asked.

"She was with a group of adults—but I didn't know them. And frankly, I only noticed them in passing. But I also remember thinking, when she smiled at me, that she looked familiar. I thought for a moment I knew her. I almost said hello, but she had already walked by, so I didn't say anything."

Danielle considered his words a moment and then sat back on the sofa. "Ummm…maybe Heather was right."

"Right about what?" MacDonald asked.

"Ginny. Perhaps she is a ghost."

"Like you just said, both Eddy and I saw her. We can't see ghosts."

"No, but I believe we all have some psychic ability. And while you generally can't see ghosts, tomorrow is Halloween," Danielle reminded him. "Remember, Harvey made himself visible to Heather on Halloween."

"But Heather can see spirits," the chief argued.

"True. But back then she couldn't. And don't forget, there are some who normally aren't able to see spirits who saw Darlene, and it wasn't even Halloween. But Halloween does seem to give spirits more ability to make their presence known. I suspect Carla and her date don't normally see spirits, but they saw that body in the staircase, and I don't believe for a moment there is a real dead body playing hide-and-seek in the house."

"There is also that tea-pouring ghost," Walt reminded them. "Many of our visitors report seeing flashes of him."

With a sigh, the chief slumped back in his chair. "This does put an awkward spin on things. I have Brian out helping me track down Ginny, and if she turns out to be a ghost, one from Walt's first life, how exactly do I explain to Brian when I drop the search?"

"Danielle will come up with some cover story for you," Walt suggested with a grin.

"How odd to think learning the child might be dead would actually be a relief," the chief said.

"Yes, life and death do take on a new perspective when we become aware of lingering spirits," Danielle observed.

The three sat in silence for a few minutes, considering what they intended to do. Finally, MacDonald looked at Walt and asked, "Have you found out anything more about your Abe Fortune? Danielle told me you were doing some internet sleuthing."

Walt shook his head. "No. I couldn't find a trace of an Abe Fortune from Frederickport who started a new life somewhere else. It's like he vanished in thin air—like Ginny."

"Sometimes when people want to disappear, they change their names," the chief suggested. "And if he abandoned his wife, maybe he didn't want her to find him."

"Like Pearl Huckabee's grandfather?" Danielle suggested. "He had several different families and was buried under an alias."

"Annabelle Fortune was a beautiful girl," Walt said. "I didn't know them well, but I do remember back then having the impression he was quite besotted with her—and her with him. Of course, Angela was beautiful in appearance, but she also conspired to murder me. So we never really know what goes on between a husband and wife."

"Has Annabelle returned?" the chief asked.

"No," Walt told him.

"While things are a little—unpredictable—perhaps it might be best if Eddy doesn't help tonight. I know he planned to go trick-or-treating with his friends tomorrow anyway. But maybe there's something you can say to him so he doesn't think he needs to keep helping us?" Danielle suggested.

"I was thinking the same thing," the chief said. "To be honest, I don't believe Eddy will be too disappointed if he doesn't help again. This morning he told me he had fun at the haunted house, but now he's mostly looking forward to going trick-or-treating with friends."

"Unlike Evan, if random spirits decide to show up, it might prove too confusing for Eddy, considering they've been making themselves seen to those who I assume are typically non-mediums," Danielle said.

"I'm wondering if I should also be concerned about Evan," the chief mused.

"Under normal circumstances, Eddy is unlikely to experience something like Carla and her friend did last night. But for Evan, it is his normal. It might be best if he's allowed to experience the worst that Halloween has to offer while in the company of supportive mediums he trusts. And then later, when we're not there to help him, he'll be better prepared," Danielle explained.

"When I think about all this—what you just said—I realize how different—how horribly different Evan's life might be if I hadn't met you," the chief told Danielle.

Tilting her head slightly, Danielle studied the chief's earnest expression. "What do you mean?"

"Imagine my little boy claiming to see something as horrific as a dead body, and me by his side seeing nothing," the chief told her.

"And you thinking your precious boy is mentally ill?" Danielle asked in a whisper.

The chief nodded.

———

ABOUT FIFTEEN MINUTES after MacDonald said goodbye and left Marlow House, Walt sat alone in the library. He had just picked up a book to read when the space before him began to sparkle with bright light. For a moment he thought Eva was about to make an appearance. But then Annabelle showed herself. Instead of hovering in the air overhead, she stood before him.

Walt glanced quickly over his shoulder to the open doorway to the entry hall. Knowing Joanne was on the first floor cleaning, and not wanting her to overhear him seemingly talking to himself, he willed the door closed and then locked it.

"I heard you retained some of your gifts when you returned to the other side," Annabelle said.

"Yes. My wife calls it telekinesis." Walt closed the book he was holding and set it on the side table. He looked at Annabelle.

"I've never been able to do that," Annabelle said as she took a seat on the chair facing him.

"Why are you here again?" Walt asked. "I told you I don't know what happened to your husband."

"I have so little time. Tomorrow is Halloween, and after that, I'll have to return to the cemetery."

"Why don't you move on?" Walt asked.

"Because I can't move on without Abe. When we married, we promised we would be together forever."

Walt was tempted to ask, *"And how has that worked out so far?"* But he could remember what it felt like to be a spirit in conflict, and Annabelle looked rather pitiful sitting there as if she were about to cry.

"We've experienced unexpected paranormal activity in the last week," Walt said.

"I imagine you have." A faint smile turned Annabelle's lips.

"We've had someone pouring tea, another playing with one of the props in the kitchen, and someone opening doors and showing our guests what appears to be a dead body, which then vanishes."

"It is Halloween," Annabelle reminded him. "What better time to play tricks? It's all very harmless, but I've no appetite for silly games. I just want to know what happened to Abe."

"But if you move on, certainly you will see your Abe again. Considering how long it's been, he's obviously dead by now. Wouldn't your questions be answered if you simply moved on?"

Annabelle's smile vanished. "He hasn't moved on. I know he hasn't."

"How do you know?" Walt asked.

"I feel it. Abe and I were always so connected. That's why I was so desperate to find him. I knew something was wrong. It's why I can't move on. Not until we are together again."

Walt studied Annabelle a moment, thinking how she didn't consider they might not have been as close as she had imagined. Perhaps he, like Pearl's grandfather, had simply gone away to start a new life. Or another alternative, he had been murdered for some reason, and like Danielle's first husband, Lucas, his confused spirit had been trapped somewhere.

"What do you want from me?" Walt asked.

"I want you to help me find Abe. He's here somewhere; I can feel it. He has always been here."

TWENTY-EIGHT

A dam Nichols sat in a booth at Pier Café, waiting for Melony Carmichael to arrive with Angeline Michaels, Pete Rogers's sister-in-law. He had never met the woman before, but he had heard about her. According to his grandmother, there had been a scandalous legal fight over the estate of Pete's late wife—Charlotte—some thirty years earlier.

Knowing what they all knew now, the wrong person had won back then. The estate should have gone to Angeline, not Pete. But that was all water under the bridge, and Angeline, who had done well managing her portion of her parents' estate, seemed content knowing Pete was now locked up and his estate depleted, with most of the money going to Melony.

Angeline had reached out to Melony after Pete's arrest and had seemed remarkably supportive, especially considering Melony's father had been instrumental in cheating Angeline out of the inheritance.

The reason for meeting today was to discuss Frederickport real estate. Angeline had stayed away from Frederickport since her sister's death, finding it too painful running into her brother-in-law around town. But now that he was locked up and the house he had once lived in sold, she felt it time to come home again.

Adam was just glancing up from his menu when Melony walked

into the diner with an attractive older woman, who he assumed was Angeline Michaels. She went by her maiden name, and according to Mel, she had never been married. She had short dark hair with gray tinges along her temples, and a slim body wearing denim slacks, and a shirt with a black tailored jacket. Her stride when walking toward his booth bespoke confidence and a no-nonsense attitude—or perhaps it was just what Mel had told him about the woman that put those thoughts in his head.

"Hey, Adam," Melony said cheerfully when she reached his booth. She made introductions, Adam stood and shook Angeline's hand, and then the three sat together in the booth.

They were there a short time when Carla showed up at their table, asking if any of them wanted anything to drink while looking at their menus. After they told her what they would like, instead of going for the beverages, Carla asked, "Have any of you been to the Marlow House Haunted House yet?"

"Mel has been helping sell tickets," Adam told her.

Carla flashed Melony a smile and said, "That's right, I saw you there." She looked back at Adam and asked, "Have you gone through it yet?"

"No. I'm going to skip. Haunted houses really aren't my thing," Adam said.

"He's just a chicken," Melony teased.

"In defense of Adam, I'm not fond of haunted houses myself. Some creepy things used to happen in the old house I grew up in. These days I prefer new—more modern houses," Angeline said, flashing a smile to Adam.

"Carla, this is Angeline Michaels. She grew up in Frederickport," Melony introduced her.

"Really?" Carla frowned. "I don't remember seeing you before."

"I haven't been back for years. But I'm hoping, if Adam here can find me the right property, to make Frederickport my home again." Angeline smiled at Carla.

"Welcome back. But you're not going to the haunted house?" Carla asked.

Angeline shook her head. "I don't think so."

"I have to ask, Adam, did you know about the secret staircase?" Carla asked.

"What secret staircase?" Adam frowned.

"At Marlow House, of course. Danielle asked me not to say

anything—she didn't want me to spoil the fun for the others. But if you aren't going to the haunted house anyway, and Melony obviously knows all about it, I don't think Danielle would care. So, did you know?"

"I have absolutely no idea what you're talking about," Adam said.

"Danielle set up this really creepy thing on the second floor. Actually, there were a few of them. I'm pretty impressed. Anyway, this was off one of the bedrooms on the second floor. When we walked into the room, bats flew across the ceiling, and there was this skeleton sitting at the desk. But what really got our attention, the closet door opened—like it opened on its own. If that was not creepy enough, the back wall of the closet slid open, revealing a hidden staircase leading to the attic."

"You're kidding me?" Adam frowned.

Carla flashed a curious look to Melony. "You didn't tell him about it?" She then looked back to Adam and said, "But the really creepy thing, we stepped into the hidden passage, and what do you think we saw?"

"I have no idea," Adam muttered.

"A dead body! Of course it wasn't really a dead body. But it sure looked real."

"Who was playing the dead body?" Adam asked. He glanced briefly to Melony, who only shrugged, as if she had no idea what Carla was talking about.

"I'd never seen him before. But I don't think it was a real person. Some sort of bizarrely realistic dummy—I think it was made of wax. Had to be. Like one of those wax sculptures you see at the wax museum and you think it's going to come to life at any minute. It had to be something like that, because his eyes—really eerie—just stared ahead, never blinking. And he didn't breathe."

"Did you touch it?" Angeline asked. "I would have been compelled to touch it."

"No. It was too creepy." Carla shivered. "But it was one impressive haunted house. Of course, considering Danielle's money, she can afford the best Halloween decorations."

After Carla left the table to retrieve their drinks, Adam looked at Melony and asked, "Why didn't you tell me about a hidden staircase?"

Melony shrugged. "That is the first I've heard of it. But maybe she's confused. The staircase to the attic is tucked in the corner on the second floor; maybe she's talking about that one."

"You haven't seen this so-called wax body?" Angeline asked.

Melony picked up her menu and said, "First I've heard of it."

"I grew up down the street from Marlow House, and I have never been inside. When we were children we'd dare our friends to climb the fence and run up to ring the bell," Angeline told them.

"We used to do the same thing," Adam said with a laugh.

Angeline set her menu on the table and looked from Adam to Melony. "My sister, Charlotte, used to swear she would see someone standing in the attic window. She insisted it was Walt Marlow. The Ghost of Marlow House, that's what she would call him."

"There is a Walt Marlow who lives there now," Melony said. "And he looks eerily like the one who died in that attic."

Angeline nodded. "Yes. I've read all about him. In fact, I'm a fan of his book. He's quite talented. Does he really look that much like the portrait? I've seen pictures, but I know those things can be doctored."

"Yeah, it's more than a likeness. I swear they could be twins. According to Danielle, a few generations back in the Marlow line, a set of identical twins married another set of identical twins. The Marlow who died in the house descends from one of the couples, and the Walt Marlow who lives there now descends from the other. Danielle believes that's a contributing factor to the remarkable likeness," Adam explained.

The next moment Carla brought their drinks and took their order.

After Carla left the table again, Melony looked at Angeline and asked, "Was your sister a great tease, or do you think she believed she saw Walt Marlow's ghost?"

"Charlotte was a dear sweet thing—but jokester, no. She had an overactive imagination—and was also high strung. Not a terrific combination. When we were children, late at night she would insist she heard voices in our room. Actually one voice—a man's voice. He was calling out to Annabelle."

"Annabelle?" Melony frowned.

"My father told her it was mother's wind chimes hanging outside our window. He took them down once, but she kept insisting she could still hear it. Father told her she was imagining things and put the wind chimes back. Of course, this was when she was fairly young, not a teenager. When she was older, she used to laugh about how silly and over imaginative she had been as a small child."

————

CARLA WAS JUST BRINGING Adam's table their food when Joe and Brian walked into Pier Café and took a booth at the far end of the diner. Moments after they arrived, Kelly joined them.

"So what exciting things have you two been up to today?" Kelly asked as she sat down, giving Joe a quick kiss on his cheek and tossing her purse on the bench seat with her.

"I've been catching up on paperwork, and Brian has been looking for a missing kid," Joe said.

Kelly's eyes widened as she looked from Joe and Brian. "Who's missing?"

"Technically speaking, we really don't know if she's missing— and it's unofficial business," Brian explained.

"I don't understand." Kelly frowned.

"Evan met a little girl who supposedly moved to Beach Drive," Brian began. "He asked her to help him be a ghost at the haunted house."

"You don't mean Ginny?" Kelly asked.

"You know her?" Brian asked.

"Evan introduced her to us when we were going through the haunted house," Joe explained. "After they both jumped out and scared us. I thought I mentioned that to you."

"What do you mean she's missing?" Kelly asked.

"It's just that she doesn't live where they thought she lived, and they want to find out where she's from."

"Can't they just ask her? I thought she's been helping at the haunted house?" Kelly asked.

"She didn't show up last night. And when Danielle went to introduce herself to Ginny's aunt and uncle this morning, they claimed they had no idea who Danielle was talking about."

"Oh, how embarrassing." Kelly cringed. "I can see how that can happen. When I was in high school, I got a phone call from someone who said she was Jim's mother. I was dating Jim at the time. But it was actually Tim's mother, one of my close friends. She was asking me for dinner. It wasn't until the very end of the phone conversation that I realized who I was really talking to. I would have absolutely died had I showed up at Jim's house for dinner!"

"Not sure it was a matter of Danielle misunderstanding the girl," Brian said.

"I'm sure she's okay. Kids love to play those kinds of tricks on adults," Joe said.

The next moment Carla showed up to take their drink order. Like she had with Adam's table, one of her first questions was, "Have you been to the haunted house yet?"

"We went Saturday night," Kelly told her. "It was fun. Pretty sophisticated haunted house, if you ask me."

Carla looked at Brian. "How did you like it?"

Brian shook his head. "I'm not going. Haunted houses really are not my thing."

"You and Adam Nichols," Carla said with a laugh.

"What do you mean?" Brian asked.

"He doesn't want to go either. But you really should. Well worth the money. I hope they do it again next year," Carla said.

"It's a good setting for a haunted house," Brian muttered. "It's a natural."

Carla turned to Kelly and said, "What did you think about the dead body in the hidden staircase? Did it freak you out, or did you already know about the staircase? I can't stop thinking about it. I just couldn't believe when the wall in the closet moved!"

"What hidden staircase?" Kelly asked.

"Yeah, I'd like to know that too," Joe said.

"Oh, come on, didn't you see it?" Carla asked. "I thought you went through on Saturday?"

"This is the first I'm hearing of it. Are you saying there's a real hidden staircase at Marlow House? You know there are two staircases. The one coming up from the first floor, and then the one from the second floor to the attic. You don't mean one of those?" Kelly asked.

"No. There are three staircases. There's a hidden passage behind one of the bedroom closets. That staircase leads up to the attic. I'm really surprised you didn't know about it."

"Which bedroom?" Joe asked.

After Carla described the room, Joe said, "Danielle's old bedroom."

Brian chuckled and said, "That must have made it pretty convenient when Walt was living alone in the attic and Danielle's room was on the second floor."

Carla's eyes widened at the thought. "Oh, you're right!" She began to giggle.

TWENTY-NINE

Danielle walked into the library on Monday afternoon and found Walt sitting alone on the sofa, book in hand, staring blankly ahead. He heard her enter the room and looked her way.

"You don't look like you're getting much reading done," she said, now standing by the sofa.

"Annabelle was just here," he told her.

Danielle arched her brows. "And?"

"She wants help finding out what happened to Abe. When I was searching online, I never found anything to indicate he started a new life somewhere else, at least not under his real name. If his spirit was still lingering somewhere near Frederickport, I would expect it to be fairly easy for him to find her. But then I remember what you told me about Lucas, and how his spirit was trapped in a building for a year because he didn't understand he was dead. I was in this house for almost a century not truly comprehending my reality. I just don't know how else I can help her."

"Which would explain why she's normally confined to the cemetery," Danielle suggested.

"How so?"

"Some force is obviously keeping Annabelle here, preventing her from moving on. Maybe she could if she really wanted to, but something is urging her to stay. If she's meant to be reunited with Abe, and he needs to find her, the cemetery is the best place for her. It's where spirits often go before moving on. Remember, the only reason Maisy Faye ever met Angela was because she'd gone to the cemetery during her confused state. And Maisy Faye's body was not even there yet," Danielle reminded him.

"It would be nice if we could discuss this with Eva and Marie, get their perspective," Walt said with a sigh.

"While I understand Eva and Marie aren't supposed to interfere with other spirits on Halloween, I don't believe we aren't supposed to talk to them."

"Eva often takes things to the extreme," Walt noted.

"Why don't we drop in and see Adam? You up for a little car ride?" Danielle asked.

"Adam? What for?" Walt asked.

"If Marie isn't here, there is a good chance she's hanging out with Adam. Let's see if we can find her. We just want to talk to her. It's not like we're asking her to levitate anything."

"I thought the chief was going to drop Evan off after school," he reminded her.

"We should be back before then. But even if we aren't, Joanne will still be here. We can stop at the police station first, so we can let the chief know where we're going."

"You could just call him," Walt suggested.

"I'd rather stop by."

———

"I HAVEN'T FOUND GINNY. But I suppose the good news, I couldn't find any missing person report with her description," the chief told Walt and Danielle after they arrived at his office thirty minutes later.

"On one hand, I keep telling myself it's pretty farfetched to imagine she's a ghost, considering you and Eddy so clearly saw and heard her. After all, the most rational explanation, she's staying with someone else in Frederickport. But then I remember, why did Chris think he saw her with the Crawfords over at their house? Is there something sinister going on? Does Chris need glasses? Or was only Chris capable of seeing her?"

"Hopefully Ginny will show up today and shed light on this mystery." The chief paused a moment and glanced at his watch. "I have to leave in about ten minutes to pick Evan up at school. I was going to drop him off at your house. You want me to bring him by later?"

"That's one reason we stopped by. Walt and I are on our way over to Adam's office. We're hoping to run into Marie and see if she can help us."

"I thought she couldn't?"

"We're thinking maybe she can brainstorm the Annabelle thing —also with Ginny. Maybe Marie has seen her at the cemetery. I know she and Eva aren't supposed to intervene with other spirits on Halloween. But, gee, we don't even know if Ginny is a spirit or not. And with Annabelle, I'm hoping Marie can at least suggest something that might help. But as for Evan, go ahead and drop him by the house. We won't be long, and Joanne is there. I already told Joanne to expect him."

"Before you bring him over, since we may not be there when he arrives, please explain to him what has been going on. And if he sees something frightening, remind him that Eva promised a spirit is not capable of hurting a human—at least not an innocent, which describes Evan," Walt said.

"I will. And I will probably just stay with Evan until you get back," the chief said.

***

WHEN WALT and Danielle walked into Adam's front office that afternoon, they both glanced around, on the lookout for Marie. But the only one sitting in the front office was Adam's assistant, Leslie, who sat at her desk and greeted them when they walked in.

"I was wondering if Adam is here?" Danielle asked Leslie.

"Yes, but he's with a client right now," Leslie told her. "But if it's important, I can tell him you're here."

Danielle flashed Walt a disappointed glance and then looked back to Leslie. "No, that's okay. We just stopped to say hi."

As Walt and Danielle turned from Leslie's desk, a female voice called out, "Walt! Danielle!"

They turned to the voice and found Melony walking toward them from the direction of Adam's office.

"I saw you coming in," Melony said as she walked toward the pair.

"Hi, Melony. We just stopped by to say hi to Adam—and harass him for not coming to the haunted house. But if he's with a client, we'll come by later," Danielle said.

"No, come on in. I have someone I would like you to meet," Melony urged.

A few minutes later Walt and Danielle were being introduced to Angeline Michaels. To Danielle's disappointment, there was no sign of Marie.

"So what is this about a secret staircase?" Adam asked Danielle after introductions and pleasantries were exchanged.

"Who told you?" Danielle asked. She already suspected the answer.

"We went to Pier Café for lunch," Melony answered for Adam. "You know, none of the people leaving the haunted house ever mentioned it to me. What, did you swear them to silence before leaving?"

"Why is it I never knew about a secret staircase before now?" Adam asked.

"It wouldn't be a secret, then, would it?" Danielle said with a smile.

"Not a secret now. Not with Carla knowing," Adam snorted.

"We felt it was for a good cause. What better time to reveal the existence of a secret staircase than a haunted house?" Danielle lied.

"Has the fundraiser been a success?" Adam asked.

"Yes. And while it's been fun, I have to admit I'll be glad when we're done." Danielle looked at Melony and said, "We really appreciate all your help. Especially since it can't be particularly fun for you, sitting outside in the cold."

Melony shrugged. "It hasn't been that bad. I've dressed warm. I've seen people I haven't seen since I moved back. Like old home week."

"And you're moving back to Frederickport?" Walt asked Angeline.

"Yes, I hope so. If Adam here can find me the right property. And I want to say, Mr. Marlow, I truly enjoyed *Moon Runners*."

"Thank you. But please call me Walt."

"And you, please call me Angeline. I hope, Walt, *Moon Runners* won't be your only book."

"Walt's working on his next one." Danielle spoke up. "But I'm afraid the haunted house has put that on hold."

"Have you found any good prospects?" Walt asked.

"A few properties look promising," Angeline said. "I would love to live on Beach Drive again, but unfortunately nothing is currently for sale."

"I imagine your childhood home was sold before you started looking," Danielle said.

"Oh, I would never buy that house," Angeline said with a shake of her head. "The house I grew up in burned down not long after my sister died. Pete had that house built. I could never live in it. Of course, even if it was the original house, I would never live in such an old place." She paused and said, "No offense to you. I know Marlow House is one of the oldest houses in Frederickport—and it is beautiful. At least, from what I see from the outside. But personally, I prefer something a little newer, more modern."

"I learned your family bought that house from Walt Marlow," Danielle said. She glanced at Walt and then back to Angeline and said, "The other Walt Marlow. Was it your grandparents who bought it, or your parents?"

"It was my grandparents. When my parents first married, they rented a little house in town, but then my grandmother passed away and they moved into the house with my grandfather. Not sure if it was to take care of him as much as to keep him company—plus it gave them a place to live rent-free," Angeline explained.

"Walt Marlow grew up with his grandfather too," Danielle noted.

"I loved my grandfather, but he could be such a fussy man!" Angeline chuckled again. "I have never seen a man who could worry like him! But he was also very loving. He spoiled my sister and me shamelessly, but at the same time he fretted whenever we stepped out of the house and insisted on accompanying us everywhere. My mother used to have to step in and ask him to give us a little space. I suppose today one might misinterpret his behavior as something suspect, but it was all very innocent. He was such a kind, loving man. But he worried so much. If he weren't already dead, my sister's death would have killed him. I can't even imagine what he would have done to Rogers!"

"By any chance, do you know anything about the people who lived in that house before your grandparents bought it?" Danielle asked impulsively.

"I heard one of Frederick Marlow's employees lived in the house. That was years before I was born."

THIRTY

"Dad, you don't need to stay. I'm not a baby. Anyway, Joanne is here," Evan told the chief after Joanne let them in the house and then went back upstairs to finish her vacuuming.

The chief glanced toward the stairs, and when he was confident the housekeeper was out of earshot, he led Evan to the parlor and sat down with him.

"As it is, I feel a little uncomfortable letting you even come over here—considering there seems to be several ghosts playing mischief. I told you what happened upstairs."

"I can't believe there's a hidden staircase. How awesome! I hope Walt will show it to me," Evan said excitedly.

"And what if you saw what looked like a dead body?" his father asked. "It would be pretty scary for you. I don't want to leave you alone."

Evan shrugged. "Even if it was real, dead bodies can't hurt you. If I thought it was real, I would look for its ghost. It might need my help to move on. Eva said that's what I'm supposed to do. It's why I have this gift—that's what Eva calls it. I'm supposed to use the gift to help spirits move on. They can get confused after they die, and they don't understand. I have to help them."

"And that doesn't scare you?"

Evan wrinkled his nose. "It used to. But it doesn't anymore. Not now. Now I know that when you become a ghost, you don't really change who you are. In horror movies ghosts are evil and scary. But they would only be that way if they were evil and scary when they were alive. And if I have to run into someone like that, I would rather it be their ghost. Because Eva told me a ghost can't really hurt someone like me, not like a living person could."

The chief looked down at his young son and sighed. "You sure are a brave boy."

Evan grinned up at his father. "I want to be brave like you."

The chief gave Evan a hug and then said, "Okay. I'll go. Walt and Danielle should be back soon. But remember what I told you about Ginny. If she comes, see what you can find out. And one more thing…"

Evan frowned. "What?"

"If Ginny shows up, Danielle told me to tell you, don't come out and ask her if she's a ghost."

"Why not?"

The chief chuckled. "Well, if she isn't a ghost, just imagine how that question would sound to her."

Evan giggled. "Yeah, I didn't think about that. She would think I was a real weirdo."

Ten minutes later Evan stood at the living room window, watching as his father drove away. He was about to turn around when a smiling face looked in at him. It was Ginny. Grinning, Evan pointed toward the front door and then dashed from the room to let her in the house.

"Where have you been?" Evan asked the moment he threw open the front door. "We were worried about you."

"I'm sorry. Something came up yesterday, and I couldn't make it. Is Danielle here?" Ginny peeked into the house.

"No, but they're going to be here soon. I was just getting ready to go in the kitchen. Joanne said I could have some cookies. You want some? I know she wouldn't care."

"Sure. That sounds good." She stepped into the house.

Five minutes later, the two sat alone at the kitchen table. Ginny looked down at the cookie Evan had set on the napkin before her. She reached out and broke off a piece, fiddling with it as she waited for Evan to sit down.

"This morning Danielle went over to meet your aunt and uncle, and they said they didn't know you," Evan told her.

Ginny set her cookie piece on the napkin and looked up to Evan. "Who did she talk to?"

"My dad said their last name was Crawford. Next door to Chris's house."

Ginny smiled. "The Crawfords aren't my aunt and uncle."

"They aren't? So you don't live with your aunt and uncle?" he asked.

"I didn't say that. I just said the Crawfords aren't my aunt and uncle."

"You don't live at the house next door to Chris?" he asked.

With a sigh Ginny slumped back in her chair and said, "It's complicated."

"I know my dad and Danielle want to meet your aunt and uncle."

Ginny looked up to him and frowned. "Why?"

Evan shrugged. "I don't know. My dad always wants to meet my friend's parents. And I think Danielle wanted to meet them because you've been helping here."

"But they aren't my parents." Ginny picked up the piece of cookie she had abandoned a moment earlier, but instead of eating it, she crumbled it.

"They are sorta like your parents now."

Tossing the crumbs on the napkin, she looked up to Evan. "I suppose they are like my parents since they didn't want me any more than my parents did."

Evan wasn't sure what to say. The two sat in silence for a few minutes, Evan eating a cookie and Ginny looking at the cookie crumbs. Finally, Evan asked, "Are they mean to you?"

Ginny looked up. "Who?"

"Your aunt and uncle."

She shrugged. "They don't hit me. But they don't want me. No one ever did."

"Oh, Virginia dear, we love you," the elderly ghost said when she suddenly appeared in the kitchen. Evan's eyes widened, but he didn't scream. The woman looked so familiar all he could do was stare.

"Hello, Evan. Do you recognize me?" she asked, the lines around her friendly eyes crinkling.

A moment later recognition dawned. "Grandma Kat!" Evan blurted.

BABY CONNOR HAD JUST FALLEN asleep. In the next room his father worked on his current article. When Lily walked into her husband's office, he looked up at her and smiled.

"Did he finally fall asleep?" he asked.

"Yes. He has been fed, changed, and he should sleep for at least an hour. I'm going to run across the street and visit with Dani a little. Text me if you need me."

"I'm sure we will be fine," he told her as she leaned down to give him a parting kiss.

JUST AS LILY crossed the street, she heard a woman calling for her. "Mrs. Bartley!"

Looking to her right, she spied Pearl rushing in her direction. She paused a moment on the sidewalk, Sadie by her side on a leash, waiting for Pearl to reach her.

"Yes, Mrs. Huckabee?" Lily asked a moment later.

"Do you know when your friend is going to remove those dreadful headstones from her backyard?"

"I imagine when the haunted house is over."

"And exactly when will that be? You have no idea what a nightmare it is for me to look outside my bedroom and see all those headstones. It's like I'm living in a cemetery!"

Lily resisted the temptation to point out the irony in the crotchety neighbor's statement. Around town people had been referring to Pearl's property as Beach Drive Cemetery because of the dead bodies that had been buried in the backyard for over fifty years. Instead Lily smiled sweetly and said, "Tomorrow is Halloween, and the last night of the haunted house tours. So I imagine Dani and Walt will be putting their yard back to normal. Now, unless there is something else, I really must be going."

Instead of a response or a parting goodbye, Pearl turned abruptly and scurried back to her house. With a shake of her head over Pearl's rudeness, Lily continued up the street. She paused a moment to inspect the padlock on Marlow House's side gate. It was unlocked. With a smile, Lily opened the gate and entered the yard, heading for the kitchen door.

With Joanne's car parked in front of the house, Lily didn't feel as if she was invading Walt and Danielle's privacy by just walking in the kitchen door without knocking. Marlow House would always be her home away from home, and she didn't imagine, with Joanne in the house, Walt and Danielle would be doing anything crazy in the kitchen.

Once in the backyard, Lily spied Max sitting in a nearby tree, looking down at them. Lily gave Sadie a pat. "You stay out here with Max. I suspect Joanne is cleaning the house and won't want you getting underfoot."

As soon as Lily walked in the kitchen, she latched the pet door to keep Max and Sadie outside. But then she stopped abruptly when realizing it wasn't Danielle or Walt at the table, nor Joanne, but Evan MacDonald with an elderly woman and a little girl. The three turned to look at her.

"Hi, Lily," Evan cheerfully greeted her. "Did you bring Sadie?"

Shutting the door behind her, Lily smiled at Evan and then glanced briefly at the two strangers. "Hi, Evan. Yes, but she needs to stay outside. Is Dani here?"

"She's supposed to be here pretty soon. Come meet my grandma. You already know Ginny."

Lily walked up to the table and looked from Ginny to the older woman. "Nice to meet you, Evan's grandma." She looked to Ginny and said, "I didn't recognize you without your sheet on."

"Hi, Lily." Ginny grinned.

"You know, Dani has been looking for you," Lily said.

"I told her," Evan said.

Lily looked to the elderly woman and smiled. "I didn't know Evan's grandmother was in town. I'm Lily Bartley. I live across the street."

"Nice to meet you, dear. My name is Katherine, but you can call me Kat."

"I assume you're the chief's mother-in-law?" Lily asked, recalling all the times the boys had spent time with their mother's parents.

"Oh, no, dear, I am Edward's grandmother," the woman told her.

"Really? So you're actually Evan's great-grandma," Lily asked.

"I haven't seen her since I was really little," Evan told her.

"If you don't mind, dear," Kat said, standing up. "Evan and

Ginny were going to give me a little tour of the house. I've always wanted to see it."

"You aren't going to stick around for the haunted house?" Lily asked.

"No. I spend enough time with ghosts."

Lily wasn't sure how to respond to the comment, so she said nothing and just smiled as the three left the kitchen. Glancing around the room, Lily spied two napkins sitting on the table. Cookie crumbs littered one napkin while a smashed cookie covered the other. Deciding to make herself useful while she waited for Danielle's return, Lily removed the napkins with the crumbs, tossed them in the trash, and wiped down the table.

Helping herself to some of Danielle's cookies from under the covered cake plate, she took them with a fresh napkin and sat down at the table. Just as she took the first bite, Danielle and Walt walked in the back door.

"Drat, you caught me pilfering your cookie jar," Lily said as she took a second bite.

Danielle laughed and tossed her purse on the kitchen counter. "I don't even have a cookie jar."

"Cookie plate?" Lily suggested, taking another bite.

"Afternoon, Lily. You know you're always welcome, as long as you leave me some," Walt said as he snatched a cookie for himself and joined Lily at the table.

"Oh, by the way, Ginny is back, so I guess you can find out where she really lives," Lily told her.

Danielle had just removed a glass from the overhead counter. She paused and faced Lily. "Ginny is here? Where is she?"

"She and Evan are giving Evan's grandmother a tour of the house."

Danielle set the empty glass on the counter and turned to Lily. "Evan's grandmother is here?"

"I guess it is really Evan's great grandmother. She introduced herself as Katherine, but told me I could call her Kat." Lily popped the last bite of her cookie into her mouth.

"Very interesting," Danielle stammered, abandoning the glass she was about to fill with water. She took a seat at the table with Walt and Lily.

Walt looked quizzically at his wife. "What is it?"

Danielle turned to Lily and stared at her a moment. In response, Lily frowned. "What is it, Dani?"

"Don't you remember? The chief's grandma Kat passed away about three years ago."

THIRTY-ONE

"Are you saying I was just talking to a ghost?" Lily asked.

"If it's Evan's great-grandma Kat." Danielle glanced to the doorway leading to the hallway and then back to Lily and Walt. "Why don't you two stay here and let me see what I can find out."

"I can come with you," Walt suggested.

Danielle shook her head. "No. I'd rather Kat stick around. Maybe she'll tell me what's going on. She might spook if we both approach her."

"Spook the spook? Really, Dani?" Lily giggled.

Ignoring Lily's quip, Danielle left the kitchen and went in search of the visiting ghost. Or was it ghosts? The jury was out on Ginny. She found them in the library, looking at Angela Marlow's portrait. They didn't hear Danielle enter the room.

"She might have been a pretty thing, but rather a self-centered young woman," Kat was telling Evan and Ginny.

"I never liked her," Ginny said. "She was always telling me to stay out of her part of the cemetery."

Danielle had her answer. Little Ginny, like Kat, was a ghost. But why was she here?

"Hello," Danielle greeted them. The three who had been studying the portrait turned to her. "I'm glad you came back, Ginny. Nice to see you again, Kat."

"This is my grandma Kat!" Evan told Danielle.

184

"Yes, Evan. I've met her before. I was hoping Kat and I might have a private chat."

"Can Ginny and I go in the backyard and play with Sadie?" Evan asked.

Danielle nodded. "But please stay in the side yard."

Ginny and Evan raced from the room. Kat watched them leave, a soft smile on her face. When alone with Danielle, Kat turned to her and said, "He's one of the reasons I haven't moved on."

"Evan?"

Kat nodded. She walked to a chair and sat down and then pointed to the sofa. "Why don't you sit down, dear. I imagine there are things you would like to ask me."

Danielle took a seat on the sofa and then said, "I thought you stuck around to make sure your grandson remarried?"

Kat laughed. "Really, dear? Confined to the cemetery? Do you imagine I was waiting for some lovely grieving widow to stop by, and then I would try sending her Edward's way?"

"You did send me his way," Danielle reminded her.

"Yes, I did, didn't I? But not for the reason it seemed at the time. I was something like you when I was alive. Oh, not as sensitive, but I would occasionally glimpse a spirit crossing over, or one lingering. But it didn't take long to figure out some things were best not shared with others. If you know what I mean," Kat said.

Danielle nodded. "Yes, I do."

"I could see my husband after he passed—his spirit hadn't moved on. The dear man wanted to wait for me. And I was happy for him to stay. After all, I knew my time here was limited. It wasn't like I had many years left to start a new life without him. So I would visit the cemetery every day, often using the excuse they didn't tend the grounds properly. When I died, I fully expected to move on with my husband, but then something unexpected happened at my funeral."

"Evan could see you?" Danielle said.

"Exactly. It was quite startling to me because I realized his gift was much stronger than mine had been. He even managed to see several other spirits at the funeral. Of course, he didn't realize they were spirits, and seeing me just confused him." Kat sighed.

"How did you think sticking around—especially if you were confined to the cemetery—would help Evan?"

"What I wanted was for you to go to Edward, tell him what I had said, and then he would know. He would know the truth."

"The truth?" Danielle frowned.

"Yes, of course. That people like you—like Evan—exist."

"I'm not sure I understand. How did you even know about me?"

"Perhaps it is best I start at the beginning. It is always best to start at the beginning, isn't it, dear?"

"Umm…yes. I suppose it is." Danielle studied Kat.

"I hadn't figured it all out at first. I just knew I couldn't go. But then I met your great-aunt's mother," Kat explained.

"Katherine O'Malley?" Danielle asked.

"Yes. You know, I was never called Kat when I was alive. Only by dear Edward, and then his boys, who knew me as Grandma Kat. Once I took residence at the cemetery, I decided it best to use the nickname, to make it less confusing with the other spirits still lingering."

"So she was known as Katherine and you Kat?" Danielle asked.

"Yes. She wasn't here long after I arrived, but we became very good friends in that short time. I rather miss her. It will be nice to see her again when we move on."

"We?" Danielle asked.

"My dear husband is still here. You haven't met him. He is rather shy and prefers not to converse with mediums. Anyway… Katherine told me about you. She had been visiting her daughter in her dreams and had learned about her son-in-law's great-niece who had the gift. Katherine managed to convince Brianna to leave you Marlow House, believing when you came, you could help Walt Marlow. And I thought if you could help Walt Marlow, perhaps you could help Evan."

"Help him how?" Danielle asked.

"Help him to understand his gift. To help his father understand so he wouldn't think there was something off about the dear boy. And my plan worked, didn't it?"

"I suppose it did." Danielle smiled. "But you're still here."

"I did rather expect you to bring Evan to the cemetery to see me and his grandfather so we could say goodbye one last time. But you are a medium, not a mind reader. And I suppose Edward would not be comfortable with you whisking his young son off to a cemetery where he might encounter any type of spirit. Of course, he is allowing him to help here on Halloween, and Marlow House does seem to be attracting its share of spirits this year."

"Ginny is a spirit too, isn't she?"

Kat smiled gently and glanced to the window leading to the side yard. She could see the two children running by, chasing Sadie.

"Her real name is Virginia. I suspect she wanted to reinvent herself for Halloween, while passing herself off as a living child. To be honest, Virginia is another reason I am reluctant to move on," Kat said with a sigh. "She needs me."

"Why hasn't she moved on? What's her story?"

"The girl came from the most unfortunate circumstances. Not loved, as are Eddy and Evan. Children should be loved, don't you think?" Kat asked.

"Most certainly."

"Her mother was weak, addicted to opioids. Her father drank and took the adage 'spare the rod, spoil the child' to extremes. During a drunken rage, he caused a fire that burned down his house. Virginia was the only one to escape. She went to live with her aunt and uncle, who, according to Virginia, wanted her no more than her parents had."

"The Michaelses? She was the niece of the Michaelses who used to own Pete Rogers's house?" Danielle asked.

Kat nodded. "Yes."

"According to Walt, when he returned from Europe, she was no longer living with them. He never knew what had happened to her," Danielle told Kat.

"She never felt welcome, but one must remember she was also a troubled girl, and it is not easy for anyone to take in someone else's child. Her aunt and uncle were very young, newlyweds, and had been renting a room when Virginia came into their care. According to Virginia, her father had taken out a life insurance policy on her mother. She found that out while overhearing a conversation after her parents' death. I believe the man intended to kill his wife and collect on the policy, but he ended up killing himself too. The money went to purchase the house they all moved into. But Virginia hated her bedroom and insisted there were strange sounds late at night. One evening she snuck out of the house with her blanket and pillow and climbed into the back of her uncle's car to sleep. She didn't want to sleep in the house, something scared her, and her aunt and uncle didn't take her fears seriously. She didn't wake up the next morning. She was dead."

"Do you know why she died?" Danielle asked.

"No. I don't."

"Maybe she froze to death during the night?" Danielle suggested.

"I doubt it. It was during the summer, and according to Virginia, she rolled up the car windows and was very warm inside the vehicle," Kat explained.

"Is that why she can't move on? She needs to know why she died?" Danielle asked.

"I don't think so. Since spending time at a cemetery, I've learned most children who have a loving parent or grandparent on the other side, waiting, are anxious to move on."

"But Ginny has no one," Danielle said.

"Exactly. She has no desire to see her parents again. And she was never close to her aunt and uncle. I've asked her to move on with us when we go, but she seems determined to stay. I was actually surprised she decided to venture out this Halloween. From what I understand, it's the first time she ever has. She, of course, has been at the cemetery much longer than I have."

"If she came here, maybe she's seeking answers," Danielle suggested.

"I suppose that's possible. But answers to what questions?"

"Who are you talking to?" Joanne asked Danielle when she walked into the library a moment later. By the way she looked around the room, it was obvious Joanne could not see Kat, as Lily had.

"Oh my, I suppose I used up my energy making myself seen to your friend Lily," Kat murmured. "I confess I am rather a novice at all this. Like Virginia, this is my first Halloween away from the cemetery."

"I was talking on the phone," Danielle lied.

Joanne frowned, obviously wondering how that could be possible since Danielle wasn't holding a phone to her ear.

Danielle pulled her cellphone from her pocket and held it up. "Speakerphone." Because of where Joanne stood, she couldn't tell if Danielle had picked the phone off her lap or pulled it from a pocket.

Joanne laughed. "I was wondering."

Danielle smiled and set her phone down. "I was just saying goodbye."

If Joanne questioned Danielle's explanation, considering it didn't sound as if she was ending a phone call, she said nothing. Instead, Joanne walked to the window and looked outside. Placing her hands on her hips, her back to Danielle and Kat, she shook her head. "I was watching Evan and Sadie from upstairs. That boy certainly has energy!"

"Yes, he does," Danielle said, flashing Kat a smile.

"The way he and Sadie are running around those headstones, I think he's pretending to play with someone." Joanne laughed. "Maybe a ghost."

"A ghost?" Danielle asked.

Joanne turned to Danielle. "Yes. It looks as if he's talking to an imaginary friend, the way he keeps pointing and chattering on."

"He's probably talking to Sadie," Danielle suggested.

Joanne shook her head. "No. Sadie ran off to the other end of the yard to catch a ball Evan had thrown, when the boy started up a conversation with his imaginary friend. Since it looks like a cemetery out there and he has been playing ghost here the last few days, I wouldn't be surprised if that's what he's doing. The child has such an active imagination. Perhaps he'll be a writer someday like Walt."

Danielle and Kat exchanged glances. "Perhaps he will," Danielle murmured.

THIRTY-TWO

K at vanished before Joanne left the library, not giving Danielle a chance to say goodbye—or ask additional questions. She wasn't sure if the chief's grandmother had returned to the cemetery or was still lingering somewhere in Marlow House. It sounded as if Kat and her husband were prepared to finally move on, yet Ginny was making Kat reluctant to go—death had not dampened her maternal instincts.

Danielle went first to the kitchen to update Walt and Lily on what she had learned, and then she called the chief to let him know he could stop looking for Ginny. He wouldn't find her. She was outside in her backyard, still playing with Evan and Sadie, and considering Joanne had not seen her, and Lily could no longer see her, she doubted Ginny had enough energy left to lift a sheet. Although it was entirely possible she would have enough come Halloween night if she didn't spend it all making herself visible.

Had the chief not been so busy, she would have asked him if there was anything in his old files about the death of Michaels' niece. She tried doing a brief search online, but found nothing. Knowing she would be able to find Ginny at the cemetery after Halloween, she focused her energy on the haunted house, since there were only two nights left.

Ginny stayed to visit with Evan during the Monday haunt, yet since no one could see her but the mediums, no one mentioned her presence to people like Melony. Kat didn't show herself again on Monday, and by evening's end, Danielle was fairly confident Kat had returned to the cemetery. Annabelle showed herself again to Walt, but to no one else.

To the disappointment of that evening's guests, there was no dead body on the second floor—and no glimpse of a hidden staircase. A number of guests, who had heard of the secret staircase, attempted to find it, but with the panel door locked, it looked like nothing but a solid wall.

"I knew Carla was making it up," one of the disappointed guests said after he stepped out of the closet. "There's no secret passage."

Fortunately for the guests, the tea-serving ghost remained in the parlor, as did the flirtatious head in the jar, which didn't just smile at those passing by, but had begun giving winks to the pretty girls.

HEATHER HAD JUST FINISHED her morning run. Wearing a black jogging suit, with orange ribbons securing her two long ebony braids, she sat alone in a booth at Pier Café, her feet up on the bench seat as she leaned back against one padded side of the booth, menu in hand. It had been a fun week helping at the haunted house, but she was ready for November to arrive, yet dreaded playing catch-up at the office. Since the haunted house had opened, both she and Chris had been putting in just a few hours each day at work. But Halloween had finally arrived, and tonight would be the last viewing of Marlow House.

"Excuse me, but aren't you the one I've seen over at our neighbor's house?" a woman in the next booth asked Heather.

Heather, who hadn't realized someone had just sat down in the next booth over, removed her feet from the seat, set them on the floor, and sat up straighter so she could better see the woman now peering over the booth at her.

"I suppose that would depend on who your neighbor is," Heather said, still holding her menu open.

The woman turned in Heather's direction, sitting on her knees so she could get a better view, giggled and said, "I suppose you're right. It's that gorgeous guy with the most amazing blue eyes and abs you just want to touch, if you know what I mean." The woman practically drooled.

Heather groaned and closed her menu. "I suppose you're talking about Chris Johnson?"

"Yes, yes! That's his name! Such a common name for such an uncommon specimen. Is he your boyfriend? If so, you are one lucky girl. I am absolutely green."

"No." Heather set the menu on the table. "Chris is just a friend. He's also my boss."

The woman arched her brows. "Really? Wow, with a boss who looks like that, workplace sexual harassment sounds rather appealing."

Heather frowned. "Not sure about that. You said you live next door to Chris?"

"Oh, sorry." The woman giggled and then extended a hand in greeting. "I'm Mia Crawford. My husband and I just moved into the house next door to your boss."

Husband, Heather thought. *Wonder if your husband knows how you're talking about your new neighbor.* Reluctantly, Heather shook the woman's hand.

"Is Chris meeting you for breakfast?" Mia asked, looking around anxiously as she took back her hand.

"No. I also live on Beach Drive. Just stopping to have breakfast after my morning jog."

"Oh, you are an ambitious thing," Mia said. "Where do you live exactly?"

"Do you know where Marlow House is?" Heather asked.

"Don't tell me you live there?"

"No," Heather said, "I live two doors down from Marlow House."

"My husband and I met the owner of Marlow House. She was looking for some missing girl. In fact, the police questioned me at work. Do you know anything about it? I wondered if they found the child."

"They did. She's fine. There was just some sort of misunderstanding."

"Glad to hear that."

"Are you going to be visiting the haunted house?" Heather asked. "Tonight is the last night. It's for a good cause."

"Normally, I would love to. But we have been so busy, moving and all. And then we had to go to Portland unexpectedly. My mother-in-law died last year, and it seems there is always something new coming up with her estate. Believe me when I say put your estate in a trust. If my mother-in-law would have just listened to her son, everything would have gone so much smoother! I really expected to be all settled in our new house by now, but it has been one thing after another."

Before Heather had a chance to comment, a man showed up at Mia's booth.

"I would have been here sooner, but I was talking to Chester and Cecil," the man told Mia as he took a seat in her booth.

"Austin," Mia said as she turned around to face her husband, no longer sitting up on her knees, "this is one of our neighbors." She looked back to Heather and said, "I just realized I didn't get your name."

"I'm Heather. Heather Donovan."

"It's been so nice meeting you, Heather. This is my husband, Austin."

Heather and Austin exchanged nods and brief smiles before they each picked up a menu and turned their attentions back to their own booths.

"They say we need to get a room somewhere while they deal with the mold. Say it's worse than they initially thought," Austin grumbled, his voice drifting over to Heather, who was trying to read her menu but was unable to ignore her neighbors' conversation.

"Move? I have to work today, when am I going to have the time to move again?" Mia asked. "I've never heard of such a thing."

Unable to resist, Heather set her menu down and looked over at her neighbors' booth. "Excuse me, I didn't mean to eavesdrop, but I couldn't help but hear, you have mold?"

"Yes. I suppose that's what we get for buying the property as is. It was a great price, but now I know why," he grumbled.

"You aren't alone. My house had some serious mold a couple of years ago," Heather told them.

"Did you have to move out of your house when they were dealing with the mold?" Mia asked.

"I did. I stayed at Marlow House. Back then, Marlow House was a bed and breakfast."

"It isn't anymore?" Mia asked.

Heather shook her head. "No. It closed down the first of the year."

"Now they just run a haunted house out of there?" Austin asked.

Heather smiled. "It's for a good cause. Walt and Danielle Marlow—that's who own Marlow House—are active philanthropists. Occasionally they use Marlow House to help raise money for a charity."

The next moment Carla arrived to take Heather's order, ending the conversation between the two booths. About that time Brian Henderson walked in, taking a seat at the counter. A few minutes later he was joined by Joe Morelli.

"I understand your missing girl has been found," Joe said when he took a seat next to Brian.

Brian nodded and then asked, "How did you hear?"

"Kelly talked to Lily last night. Said something about there being a misunderstanding about where she was staying. I guess she was just visiting family in Frederickport, and Danielle misunderstood."

"I thought Chris saw her with the Crawfords?" Brian asked. While he had heard the girl had been found, that question had not been answered.

"Lily told Kelly the girl—I guess her name is Ginny—was watching the movers unload furniture, and Chris assumed she was with the new neighbors. I guess the Crawfords and movers were so busy they didn't notice her."

"But I thought Chris saw her go inside the house with Mrs. Crawford?" Brian asked.

Joe shrugged. "Chris was mistaken."

Brian turned his attention back to the menu. "I guess one mystery has been solved."

CHESTER BELLEMORE STOOD in the Crawford living room, watching his brother add a few extra screws to the copper paneling they had reaffixed to the brick wall before the Crawfords had returned from Portland the night before.

Stepping back from the wall, Cecil inspected his work for a moment before saying, "This should keep them out of there in case they decide to poke around before we're done. No way are they going to get that off without the right tool. And I don't think Crawford even owns a screwdriver."

"Now what?" Chester asked.

"How long did they say they'd be gone?"

"He told me they were going into town after they have breakfast," Chester said.

"The last thing we need is for them to return while we're in the middle of adding mold to the inside of their bedroom walls. But we're going to have to do that if we want to convince them they have to move out for a few days. Did you bring the bottle of dye?"

"Yeah. But do you really think it's going to convince him?"

"It has so far, hasn't it?" Cecil asked.

"But what if he decides to ask someone for a second opinion?"

"I can't think about that now," Cecil said impatiently. "We need to find the treasure. I know it's there. Everything else we were told has panned out."

"Unless someone else has gotten to it first," Chester grumbled.

THIRTY-THREE

Fitting the fleece cap on Connor's bald head, Lily gently wiggled it in place, carefully adjusting the bear ears attached to the headgear. Made from the same brown and gold fleece fabric as the pajamas, it helped transform her son into a cuddly teddy bear for Halloween. Satisfied with his outfit, Lily stepped back from the crib and picked up her cellphone and then used it to snap picture after picture of the baby bear.

"Are you sure you don't want to come over to Marlow House with me and bring Connor?" Ian asked when he walked into the nursery a moment later. "You could hang out in the library with Walt."

Lowering her phone, she glanced over her shoulder at Ian.

"I hate you spending Halloween alone," he added.

"I won't be alone. I'll have Connor, Sadie and Hunny. Anyway, I really don't want Connor exposed to all those people coming through the haunted house. Too many germs."

Now standing over the crib, Ian looked down at his son. Connor's face broke into a wide smile the moment he noticed his father. Exuberantly he wiggled his feet and waved his tiny hands.

Glancing from his son to Lily, Ian said, "You're probably right. No reason to expose him to all that. Not worth the risk."

"Anyway, I have to hand out candy," Lily reminded him.

"Let's go eat dinner," Ian said. "I have everything on the table, and I moved the baby swing. It doesn't look like he's ready to go to sleep, and if we want to enjoy dinner, I think the swing by the table might be a good idea."

Leaning over the crib, Lily picked up her son and said, "You're a good husband." She then pulled the cap off Connor's head and tossed it on the dresser before following Ian out of the nursery to the dining room.

CARLA REFILLED Joe's and Brian's coffee cups. The two officers sat at the lunch counter at Pier Café.

"You ready for all the ghosts and goblins?" Carla asked.

"Halloween doesn't seem to be the headache it used to be," Brian said. "Ever since Presley House burned down."

"I think Marlow House's haunted house has been good for Frederickport," Carla said as she set the coffee pot on the counter. "It gives the teenagers something to do without burning anything down."

Joe glanced at his watch and then looked at Carla. "Are our burgers about up? We need to get back to work."

"Just a few minutes." Standing on the other side of the counter, she propped her elbows on the countertop and looked down at the two officers. "I heard they didn't have the hidden staircase open last night. Why do you think that was? They must have spent a fortune on that wax dummy. I mean seriously, if I didn't know it wasn't real, I would have thought the guy was really dead. You'd think they'd want that open every night."

"Why are you so sure it was a dummy?" Brian teased.

"If it wasn't a wax dummy, it was a real dead body. The eyes, they just stared. Didn't blink. And no one can sit like that without moving. I know he wasn't breathing. No, either a wax body or a real dead body."

"Knowing Marlow House, I wouldn't be surprised to find it was a real dead body," Brian said with a snort.

HALLOWEEN CANDY HALF-FILLED the black plastic witch's cauldron. Mia had set it on the entry table next to the front door before grabbing a handful of the candy and going to the living room. There she found Austin sitting on the sofa, his stockinged feet propped up on the coffee table while he watched television, a can of beer in hand.

"I wonder if we'll have a lot of trick-or-treaters?" Mia asked as she sat on the sofa next to Austin and handed him several pieces of the candy.

He accepted the offering without looking away from the television. "I have a feeling we might get swamped with that haunted house going on."

"What if we run out of candy?" she asked.

"Then we turn off the lights and don't answer the door," he told her.

With a sigh, she picked up the wineglass she had left on the coffee table earlier. Leaning back on the sofa, she took a sip and then said, "So what are we going to do? Are we going to find someplace to stay while they get rid of the mold?"

"I really should have paid for a more thorough inspection before we bought this house," Austin grumbled.

"It's too late to worry about that now. We have to figure out what to do. As it is, I'm not thrilled about sleeping in our bedroom tonight, not since they removed that piece of drywall and exposed all that mold. It's not healthy."

"We can sleep in this room tonight," Austin suggested. "On the sofa bed. At least there's no mold in here anymore, and they've nailed up new drywall. Tomorrow I'll give one of the rental offices a call and see what we can find."

Mia glanced briefly at her watch. "That scary movie is going to start in about five minutes."

"I thought you didn't want to watch it?" he asked with a chuckle. "You said those things give you nightmares."

She scooted closer to him. "Oh, it's Halloween. Let's watch it."

"ARE you sure you don't want to go trick-or-treating with your brother? Danielle said it was okay if you came later to the haunted house," Chief MacDonald asked Evan as he helped him into his ghost costume. The two were in the downstairs bathroom at Sissy and Bruce's house, where they had just had dinner. In the living room Eddy played video games with his uncle Bruce while Sissy cleaned the kitchen after dinner.

"No. I told Ginny I was going to be there. I have to be there."

"I suppose hanging out with a real ghost on Halloween is cooler than hanging out with your brother," the chief said dryly.

"She has to go back to the cemetery when Halloween is over," Evan explained. "That's how it works."

"Why doesn't she move on? Did she tell you?" the chief asked.

"There's no one she wants to see. I feel sorry for her. She never had a dad like you. He used to hit her real bad."

With a sigh, MacDonald nodded. "Yes, you told me."

"And her mom just let him. Ginny told me I was lucky. And you know what?" Evan asked.

"What?" MacDonald asked as he crouched before Evan, adjusting the ghost costume.

"I never thought I was lucky before, because Mom had to die, and all my friends have moms. But Ginny told me I was real lucky to have a mom who loved me and took care of me, even if it was only for a short time. And I still have you. Ginny never had anyone. She's right, Dad." Evan threw his arms around his father, giving him a tight hug. "I love you."

"I love you too," MacDonald whispered, unshed tears dampening his eyes.

BEYOND THE HOUSE blocking Pearl's ocean view, the sun had begun dissolving into the sea. Soon costumed trick-or-treaters would be descending like locusts. Pearl suspected the haunted house would attract more than Beach Drive's fair share of the little beggars. Before they started to arrive, she slipped a padlock on her front gate. The locked gate would prevent the children and teenagers from even stepping on her property, much less reaching her front door.

She scurried up her walkway and then into her house, locking the door behind her. Once inside, she went from room to room on the first floor, closing the blinds and turning off the lights. Before going upstairs, she put a bowl of chili in the microwave oven. A few minutes later she set the now boiling hot chili on a serving tray with crackers, a glass of milk, a napkin, and a soup spoon. She spent the next few minutes slowly making her way up the stairs carrying the tray, careful not to fall or spill anything.

Once in her bedroom she set the tray on her bed and then spent the next few minutes visiting all the rooms on the second floor, closing blinds and turning off lights. After she returned to her bedroom, she turned off that light. Someone driving by her house would assume no one was home.

Instead of closing her front bedroom blind, she left it wide open. Pulling a chair to the window, she positioned it so that she would be able to look outside, down on the street and the evening's activity. She then moved a small table next to the chair.

Confident her chili was now cool enough to eat, Pearl picked up the tray off the bed and set it on the table she had just moved. She then sat down on the chair in the darkened room, picked up her bowl of chili and the spoon, and began to eat while looking out at the night.

ADAM HAD AGREED to help at the haunted house on Halloween night, handing out candy. He would share the table with Melony on the front porch. Several hours before sunset Chris had added a rope barrier he had borrowed from the museum. It divided the walkway, sending haunted house visitors to the right of the rope, while trick-or-treaters would be directed to the left for their candy. Those leaving the haunted house would walk behind the table and past Adam, giving them an opportunity to help themselves to some Halloween candy.

Believing they would have increased foot traffic on the final night of the haunted house, Danielle had asked Joanne if she would help monitor those going through the first floor and basement, while she kept an eye on the second floor.

Chris ordered pizza for the haunted house volunteers who hadn't had a chance to have dinner. Since Ian had already eaten, he covered for Adam, handing out candy before the haunted house opened, while Adam joined the other volunteers in the dining room to eat pizza.

While Evan had eaten dinner at his aunt's house, he didn't turn down a slice of pizza. He ate quietly while the adults talked. He glanced around, disappointed Ginny hadn't yet showed up. But he said nothing, considering Adam, Melony and Joanne were sitting at the table.

Danielle glanced at her watch. "Twenty minutes until showtime."

"It's been fun," Heather said, "but I confess, I'm kinda glad it's the last night."

"You think you'll do it again next year?" Adam asked, helping himself to another slice of pizza.

"Not sure yet," Danielle said.

"If you do, please don't sell popcorn again," Joanne said.

"Why not?" Heather asked. "Everyone loves popcorn."

"Not everyone likes cleaning it up off the floor," Joanne grumbled.

"You haven't been through the haunted house yet," Chris told Adam. "I bet Melony can handle the table for a few minutes alone while you do."

"Maybe later, right before it closes," Adam said. "Unless you close up after my bedtime. I need to get up bright and early tomorrow morning for my eleven o'clock meeting with Angeline Michaels."

"Eleven o'clock? I think you could stay up until after midnight and still get up bright and early for an eleven o'clock meeting. You're just afraid to go through," Melony teased.

Adam shrugged. "Why would I be afraid? I've been in Marlow House lots of times."

"But not on Halloween when the spirits are restless," Melony said in a low and menacing voice.

Adam rolled his eyes at her comment while Danielle chuckled and stood up, picking up her now empty paper plate and napkin as she did.

"I'm going to run up to our room and change," Danielle announced.

"I have to go up too," Walt said, standing up.

"I'll take that for you," Joanne told Danielle, nodding to the trash in her hand. "Just leave it."

"Thanks, Joanne." Danielle set her trash back on the table. "See you guys in a little bit."

Together Walt and Danielle left the room. Yet they wouldn't be back when it was time for the haunted house to open. In fact, they wouldn't be back for the rest of the evening.

Walt and Danielle Marlow vanished on Halloween night, and none of their friends knew what had happened to them. Ian and then Adam and Melony had been by the front door and never saw them leave. Joanne and then Heather had been in the kitchen, and they hadn't seen the couple leave through the back door.

On Halloween night, the last time any of the friends saw Walt and Danielle was when they finished their pizza and went upstairs.

THIRTY-FOUR

Walt was already dressed in his vintage suit matching the portrait when they went upstairs to their bedroom. While he didn't need to change his clothes, he wanted to brush his teeth, use the bathroom, and wash up before taking his place in the library. Walt headed to their bathroom, and Danielle went to double-check the doorway leading from the secret staircase to her old bedroom closet.

"Unfortunately, a locked door is not going to keep a mischievous ghost out," Walt reminded her after she told him where she was going.

"I know. But still. I'd feel better double-checking."

Walt walked into the bathroom while Danielle stepped into the hidden staircase and turned on the overhead light. She glanced up at the fixture. One of the bulbs had gone out. Not long after discovering the staircase, Ian had helped Walt install the modern light fixture. Using candles and the old sconces as Frederick Marlow had done hadn't seemed safe. While reaching the fixtures to change light bulbs was difficult for her, Walt's gift made the task relatively easy.

"I need to remind Walt to change that bulb," she muttered to herself before heading down the staircase.

When she reached the landing by the back of the closet on the second floor, she inspected the lock. Like the overhead light fixture, it was something they had added after discovering the staircase. It had actually been added right before their honeymoon. At the time they thought they would be returning to run Marlow House as a bed and breakfast. Since they were officially married, there was no reason to continue with the charade, letting people believe she used the second-floor master suite while Walt used the attic. She thought her old bedroom would be a valuable addition to the bed and breakfast as another guest room, but she didn't want a guest using that room to stumble on the hidden staircase and end up in their bedroom.

Satisfied the panel was locked, Danielle was about to return upstairs when she noticed there seemed to be something different about the panel along the wall adjacent to the doorway into the closet. Turning to that section, she ran her hand along the panel, pressing it firmly. To her surprise it began to move. Startled, Danielle snatched her hands from the wall and jumped back, staring at the piece of paneling. Her eyes widened when she noticed it was ajar a good three inches. There appeared to be a space behind the wall.

Curious, Danielle placed her palms back on the panel and pressed. The next moment it flew open, revealing a hidden passageway.

"Walt!" Danielle called out, jumping back from the wall.

A moment later Walt came to the open doorway from their bedroom and looked down the stairs at Danielle.

"What is it?" he called out.

"Please get a flashlight and come down here!" she called back. "And hurry!"

Minutes later Walt rushed down the staircase, flashlight in hand. "What's wrong?"

Glancing briefly over her shoulder at him as he hurried down the stairs, she said, "It's another passageway."

When Walt reached Danielle, he aimed the beam from the flashlight into the opening and they both peered inside. It looked like an elevator chute, but instead of an elevator, an iron ladder affixed to the back wall ran down the chute.

Leaning farther into the opening, Danielle reached out and touched one of the mud-covered ladder rungs. It was damp. Rubbing her fingers together, she looked at Walt, her eyes wide in concern. "It's like the mud we found on the stairs. Did someone come up here? Was someone in our house? Where does this even lead?"

Walt gently pushed Danielle back from the opening and began climbing inside.

"Where are you going?" Danielle asked, her voice suddenly high pitched.

"I'm going to see where this thing goes."

"You might fall," she said.

"It looks pretty sturdy," Walt said, climbing all the way into the opening. To free his hand, Walt willed the flashlight to hover over him, lighting his way. Danielle watched as Walt slowly descended the ladder. When he reached what she assumed to be the first floor, he stepped onto a small landing. A moment later he looked up at Danielle, the flashlight still hovering over his head, and gave her a little wave. "You might want to come see this."

"Are there spiders?" she asked.

He grinned up to her. "I haven't seen any webs so far."

"Let me get my own flashlight. I'll be right back." The next moment Danielle ran up the stairs, back into their room, and snatched the flashlight from her nightstand. As she ran back into the staircase, she shut the door behind her without thought, and hurried down the stairs. She was more than halfway down the steps when the remaining lightbulb overhead flickered and went out, sending the stairwell into darkness.

"Drat," she cursed, turning on her flashlight. Instead of dealing with the light fixture, she continued on her way to Walt.

After shoving the handle of her flashlight into the back pocket of her jeans, she entered the opening as Walt had done, and slowly made her way down the ladder. When she reached Walt, she was fairly certain they were somewhere on the first floor of Marlow House. She could either continue down the ladder or step off on the small shelf where Walt now stood. She joined Walt.

He pointed to a tiny hole in the wall to her right. She looked through it and could see clearly into the living room of Marlow House.

"That is just creepy," she whispered.

He then pointed to the wall behind her, where there was another peephole. She looked through that and could see into the downstairs bedroom.

Taking hold of his own flashlight, Walt pointed it downward and said, "This must go to the basement."

Stepping off the shelf and back onto the ladder, Walt continued downward, Danielle following him. When they finally reached the bottom of the chute, they discovered a door.

"Does that go into the basement?" Danielle asked, looking from the rustic door to Walt.

"We won't know until we look," he said.

Just as Walt reached for the glass doorknob, they heard a loud slamming sound. It echoed through the chute. Danielle glanced upwards.

"What was that?" she asked.

"Sounded like someone slamming a door," he said.

Turning his attention back to the mystery door, Walt reached for its glass doorknob and turned it, pushing the door open. Instead of leading to the basement, it led to a second passage with two doors, one to the left and one directly in front of them.

Instead of swinging open as the doorway they had just gone through did, the door directly in front of them appeared to move from side to side, similar to the panel door leading into the hidden staircase.

Walt pressed against the door, sending it sliding to the right. To their surprise, they looked into the golden eyes of Max. The cat sat staring at them, his black tail twitching back and forth.

"Max!" Danielle yelped, then gave a little laugh. The cat jumped into her arms while Walt peered into the opening.

"We were right. It's the basement," Walt said.

Danielle set Max down. He began weaving in and out between her ankles.

Reaching down to pet Max, Danielle looked at Walt and said, "If this leads into the basement, where does that go?" Danielle pointed to the second door.

To their surprise, the door to the basement slammed shut. A crashing sound echoed through the passageway.

"I think I know what the other sound was we heard a minute ago," Walt said.

"What?" Danielle asked.

"I'm fairly certain that first doorway we went through slammed close—like this one just did. Sounded the same, and it's the same type of door."

"I'm not overly concerned," Danielle told him. "Considering your telekinetic powers, I doubt you'll have a problem getting it open again. After all, you did pick up a tree."

"It wasn't a tree exactly," Walt reminded her, "just a very large branch."

Danielle turned her attention to the second door. "Where do you think that goes?"

"Let's see," Walt said, opening the second door, its weight noticeable as if made of heavy iron instead of wood. Using the beam from his flashlight to light the way, he walked through the now open doorway, Danielle following close behind him. They found themselves in a dark hallway with a dirt floor, its walls made of brick, and beams overhead supported the passage.

"Where does it go?" Danielle asked as she moved the beam from her flashlight along the walls, inspecting the area.

"I have absolutely no idea. I've heard of tunnels in Portland, but I've never heard of tunnels in Frederickport," Walt said. He glanced down at the cat and said, "Stay with us, Max."

Clutching his flashlight in one hand, Walt slowly made his way down the dark hall, Danielle right behind him, her flashlight zigzagging along the outer walls, looking for—she wasn't sure what she was looking for. They went about ten feet when they reached another flight of stairs. It took them one floor below the basement to a long dark winding tunnel. Where it led, they had no idea.

———

THE LONG-SLEEVED BLACK crepe dress hugged Heather's narrow waist while its full skirt, several layers of shredded fabric, flowed dramatically around her black boots with each step she took. She wore her long dark hair down and straight, a witch's hat covering the crown of her head.

"Where's Walt and Danielle?" Heather asked Chris. "We're opening in a couple of minutes, and Walt isn't in the library, and I haven't seen Danielle." The two stood in the downstairs bedroom by the open casket.

"I haven't seen them," Chris said, already dressed in his mummy costume.

"Has anyone seen Walt and Danielle?" Ian asked from the open doorway.

Heather turned to Ian and said, "I was just asking Chris the same question. I don't think they've come back downstairs."

"You two go ahead and take your posts. I'll go upstairs and see what's taking them so long," Ian said.

Ian sprinted to the staircase and up the steps to the second floor.

"Ginny's still not here," Evan said with disappointment when he spied Ian.

"Sorry, bud. I'm sure she'll show up. Have you seen Danielle and Walt?"

Evan shook his head. "No. Not since they went upstairs after we ate."

"And you haven't seen them come downstairs?" Ian asked.

Again Evan shook his head. "No."

"I wonder if one of them got sick or something," Ian muttered. Instead of continuing to the attic bedroom, he pulled his phone out of his back pocket. First he called Danielle and then Walt. Neither one answered the phone.

With a sigh, Ian headed for the attic staircase. Once on the landing, he knocked on the door leading into the attic bedroom suite. There was no answer. He knocked again, this time louder. Still no answer. Gingerly he tried the door. It was unlocked. He opened it and peeked inside.

"Walt? Danielle?"

No reply.

Stepping into the room, he glanced around. Sitting on the dresser was Danielle's cellphone. He spied Walt's on the bed. Also on the bed was the costume he knew Danielle intended to wear this evening.

"Walt? Danielle?" he shouted.

Walking farther into the room, he noticed the door to the bathroom was open. He looked inside. No one was there. He peeked in the walk-in closet and then opened the door to the hidden staircase. Reaching his hand inside, he tried turning on the light. He soon discovered the light bulbs had gone out.

Pulling his iPhone from his pocket, he turned on the flashlight app and used it to illuminate the hidden staircase. Stepping inside, he yelled, "Walt, Danielle, you down here?"

No answer.

Using his phone to light the way, he made his way down the

stairwell. There was no sign of Walt and Danielle. When he got to the landing behind the closet, he tested the door. It was locked.

"They obviously didn't go in here," Ian muttered.

He then sprinted up the stairs, back into the attic suite. After he left Walt and Danielle's bedroom, he went back down the attic stairs, put the rope up—its sign still attached—barring entrance to the attic, and walked through all the rooms on the second floor. Still no sign of Walt and Danielle. When Ian reached the first-floor landing, Joanne greeted him.

"Where are Walt and Danielle? Melony just let the first group through, and Walt's not in the library. Where are they?" Joanne asked.

THIRTY-FIVE

"I think we should go back," Danielle told Walt. She glanced at her watch. "We have to open up for the haunted house, and everyone is going to wonder where we are. This will obviously be here tomorrow, and I would rather check it out when someone knows where we are."

"I was about to suggest the same thing," Walt said.

They turned around and headed back up the stairs to the last doorway they had gone through. When they reached it, they found it closed. To their surprise, there was no doorknob on their side. Neither had noticed the lack of doorknob when going through the doorway minutes earlier, too curious about the dark hallway.

Danielle pushed on the door. It did not budge. She stepped back from it and looked at Walt. "I guess you're going to have to open it."

Walt stared at the metal door. Nothing happened.

"Are you going to open it?" Danielle asked.

"It won't move. It's locked."

"Then I guess unlock it?" Danielle suggested.

"That only works when I'm familiar with the lock mechanism. I don't know where it is or what to move. I tried focusing my energy along the entire length of the left side of the door—nothing."

"At least we left breadcrumbs. Someone is certain to come," Danielle said.

"Breadcrumbs? Where?" Walt asked.

"When they look for us, I'm sure Ian will check the hidden staircase; after all, it's off our room. And then he'll see the opening."

"Did you forget that slamming sound we heard? Like I said earlier, that was probably the door closing. If it closed all the way, no one will know we're down here," Walt said grimly.

Danielle groaned.

Turning back down the dark tunnel, Walt aimed his flashlight beam into the darkness. "This must lead somewhere."

Together, Walt and Danielle, with Max close at their heels, made their way down the stairs again to the tunnel-like hallway, looking for another way out. They had gone about twelve feet when Danielle spied what looked like a piece of paper along one wall. She walked to it, bent down, and picked it up. After looking at it, she handed it to Walt and said, "It's a Bellemore Construction business card. It's just like the one they gave me the other day."

He glanced at it briefly and then handed it back to Danielle. "This must mean they've been down here."

Danielle smiled. "And it means there is another way out."

Walt aimed the flashlight into the darkness. "Then let's find it."

They continued down the dark corridor, the walls on either side made of brick. A few minutes later they both came to an abrupt stop when the beam from Danielle's flashlight landed on another foreign object. This time it was not a piece of paper. It appeared to be a skeleton. Hesitantly they both approached the gruesome sight. It sat leaning against the wall, its legs outstretched as if he had just sat down to rest. They both assumed it had once been a he, considering the tattered clothes falling off the bones.

"Who was he?" Danielle murmured.

The next moment her question was answered when what appeared to be a man suddenly materialized before them. He wore the same clothes—yet not as tattered—as the poor skeleton sitting on the floor.

"Walt Marlow!" the man shouted exuberantly. "You came!" The ghost sounded giddy.

"Abe Fortune?" Walt stammered, looking the apparition up and down.

"I thought I was going to die in here!" Abe said. "But you found me! Thank god you found me! I've lost all track of time. I don't even know how long I've been down here. Annabelle must be worried sick!"

"Oh my," Danielle muttered, glancing from Abe to Walt.

Abe turned to Danielle and frowned. "Who are you?"

"I'm Danielle Marlow, Walt's wife."

Abe grinned and looked at Walt. "You eloped?"

"Actually, we did," Walt said under his breath, glancing back to Danielle.

"Did you see some other men down here?" Danielle asked, thinking of the business card she had found.

"Oh yes, them," Abe said angrily. "I'm not sure who they are, but they refused to talk to me. I'd been trying to find my way into Marlow House." Abe turned to Walt and added, "So I could talk to you about the tunnel—the secret passageway. But I see you already knew about it."

"What happened?" Walt asked.

"I couldn't get the door to work, but they got it open, and I followed them. I didn't see you, so I came back later. But two people were there. I knew I had to go back through the tunnel. Something is going on and you could be in danger."

"One of the people you found in the hidden staircase, was it a woman with purple and green hair?" Danielle asked.

"Why yes. She was with a man," Abe said.

Danielle turned to Walt and said, "Carla and her friend."

"Can we get out of here now?" Abe asked. "I really need to go find Annabelle."

"Why did you need to talk to me in the first place?" Walt asked.

"To explain about the secret passageway, of course. But since you're here, obviously you know."

"You got trapped down here, didn't you?" Danielle asked.

"Yes. And I thought I was going to die," Abe said.

"Are you thirsty?" Danielle asked.

Abe frowned. "No. I remember being very thirsty. But that passed, and I can't remember the last time I thought about water. Why?"

"Are you hungry?" Danielle asked.

"I was. I think I was." Abe frowned.

"But you aren't now?" Danielle asked.

"No." Abe shook his head.

"Haven't you seen that?" Danielle asked, pointing to the skeleton a few feet away.

Abe glanced briefly at his former self and then shook his head in denial. "I don't want to look at that."

"Why?" Danielle asked softly.

"Because someone obviously got stuck in here and died. I don't want to die like he did. I don't want to look at it."

"I think you tried to help him," Danielle said gently. "You tried moving him into the hidden staircase so someone would find him and you would be rescued. Didn't you? But I think he didn't quite look like that. I don't think he looked like a skeleton when he was in the staircase, and that woman with the purple and green hair and her friend saw him."

Shaking his head again in denial, he turned his back to Danielle. He then heard a meow and looked down. Until that moment he hadn't noticed the cat. Abe stared into Max's golden eyes.

"Dead? You say I'm dead?" Abe shouted.

Walt glared at the cat. "Did you have to be so blunt, Max? Danielle was trying, in her own way, to break it to him gently."

"I HAVEN'T SEEN HER. What do you mean she and Walt are missing?" Lily asked Ian. She sat alone in her living room, with Connor sleeping in the nearby nursery, Sadie curled up under the crib, and Hunny napping by her feet. She held the cellphone to her ear. Ian had just called her moments earlier. She listened as he explained Walt and Danielle's mysterious disappearance.

"Then you have to do something. Call someone," Lily insisted. "I don't know, the police?" When she got off the phone a few minutes later, she stood up and began pacing.

Across the street at Marlow House, the haunted house had been open for an hour—and still no sign of Walt and Danielle. With their friends becoming increasingly uneasy, Ian called Chief MacDonald, who came right over. After interviewing each of the volunteers, it was learned someone else was missing—Max.

THEY SAT SIDE BY SIDE, each leaning back against the brick wall, with Abe sitting next to his skeleton, Walt on the other side of him, and then Danielle, who held Max on her lap. Abe had not

213

taken as long as Cheryl had to come to terms with his new reality—yet not as quickly as Walt had. After about ten minutes of ranting, followed by wailing and then lamenting, Abe settled down as if suddenly exhausted and began recounting the events of his final days.

"The last doorway you came through is designed to lock when closed, so it can only open from the Marlow House side without the key. The key to open that door is hidden nearby."

"I didn't even see where you could fit a key in that door," Walt said.

"It's a little tricky to find, but once you know where it is, it's not too hard. Once unlocked, the door can be pushed inward. But the key wasn't there. Thomas must have taken it with him for some reason."

"Thomas?" Walt asked. "What did Thomas have to do with the tunnel?"

Abe looked to Walt. "His father was the one who designed and built it for your grandfather."

"What did he use it for?" Danielle asked.

Abe only stared at Danielle, yet did not answer.

"Smuggling?" Walt asked.

Abe looked to Walt. "Your grandfather was involved in a variety of projects, some of which occasionally required a hasty departure—or removal of evidence."

"Who knew about the tunnel?" Walt asked.

"Your grandfather, me, Thomas," Abe said.

"What about the construction workers who actually dug the tunnel?" Danielle asked.

"That was years ago, before my time. It's my understanding the workers weren't from this area. And none of them worked on the entire project."

"How did you get trapped down here?" Walt asked.

"When I realized the key was gone, I returned to the other entrance. But it wouldn't open. I don't know why. It wouldn't budge. I called for help, but I knew there was no one to hear me. Annabelle had already left and wouldn't be back for a week. I just kept praying, calling for help, hoping someone would hear me."

"You said you needed to talk to Walt. Why did you use the tunnel instead of just knocking on his front door?" Danielle asked.

"I'm wondering that too," Walt said.

Abe turned to Walt. "I didn't think you would listen to me. I had to show you. Each time I tried to make an appointment with you, that annoying Beatrice Hollingsworth kept telling me you were too busy to see me. I couldn't tell her why I wanted to talk to you. She didn't know about the passageway."

"Who was Beatrice Hollingsworth?" Danielle asked.

"She worked for my grandfather. After he died, Beatrice became a little heavy handed. I think it was her way of trying to make herself indispensable," Walt explained.

"We had promised Frederick Marlow that when he died, we would tell his grandson about the tunnel, and then let him do with it what he wanted," Abe told them.

"Sounds like grandfather," Walt grumbled. "He didn't want to tell me about it himself because he didn't want me to start asking him questions about why it was here in the first place. I think he started to tell me about it, and then for whatever reason, changed his mind and his story about a supposed hidden staircase."

"I don't know why your grandfather didn't just tell you, but he didn't want you living at Marlow House without knowing of the passageway. Anyone who found it could gain access to your house—if they had the key."

Abe closed his eyes and said, "Oh, my poor Annabelle, I wonder where she is now."

"Annabelle died not long after you went missing," Walt told him. "She had gone looking for you and died of exposure. Her spirit has been lingering at the Frederickport Cemetery, waiting for you."

Abe perked up. "She's been waiting?"

"Yes, but…" Danielle began.

"Thank you!" Abe interrupted Danielle's sentence and vanished.

"Nooooo!" Danielle groaned. Pushing Max off her lap, she stood up and shouted, "Abe! Come back!"

"He's obviously gone to find Annabelle," Walt said. "It's rather romantic."

"Yeah, right, and he is also a ghost—and now realizes he is a ghost. Which means he could have gone through the walls and reached out to Chris or Heather and told them where we are!"

Walt cringed. "Perhaps he will come back?"

"I'm not counting on it," Danielle grumbled.

Walt stood up and dusted off his slacks. "We need to find that other entrance. The Bellemores obviously went through it, considering that business card you found."

They began walking down the passageway, flashlights in hand, Max trailing behind them.

"Looks like the Bellemore brothers are in some way related to Thomas," Danielle told Walt as she walked by his side.

"Yes, I think you're right. I suspect they're grandsons, considering their age. And one does share his great-grandfather's name," Walt said.

"And I bet that's who we heard walking around in the hidden stairwell, leaving mud all over the place. I bet their grandfather left them that key and told them about the tunnel."

"Why did they come? To rob us?" Walt asked.

THIRTY-SIX

Danielle slowed down and pointed her flashlight on one wall. She then moved it to the opposite wall.

"I don't think you're going to find a doorway there. I imagine we'll find it at the end of this tunnel," Walt told her.

Danielle stopped walking, focusing her attention to the wall on her right. She moved the flashlight to illuminate one brick. Unlike the other nearby bricks, its side was not smooth but stamped with a word.

"I was just looking…" Danielle muttered, walking closer to the wall. She reached out and ran her hand over the word. It felt like cold sandpaper.

"What's so interesting?" Walt asked.

"These brick walls. Every once in a while there's a brick like this, with a word stamped on it."

"Probably the name of the brick manufacturer. They used to stamp their name on one side. When we were at the home improvement store a while back, I noticed none of the bricks were stamped. I suspect they don't do that anymore."

"Do you think these other bricks are stamped," Danielle asked as she ran a hand over a smooth brick, "but were laid so we can't see it?"

"That would be my assumption."

Pointing her flashlight along the wall they had just walked by, she moved the light up and down. "Oh, look. I didn't notice before. It's a pattern. I guess the bricklayer was trying to get fancy. Looks like they intentionally set those bricks differently, with the stamped ones making a pattern."

Danielle turned away from the wall and started back down the corridor with Walt. A moment later she stumbled. Walt quickly reached out to stop her from falling. She grabbed her injured toe and looked down to see what she had tripped over. It was a brick.

"Dang, no wonder my toe hurts so bad. That thing is hard," Danielle grumbled, lifting her injured foot while she hopped around on the other one, attempting to massage her wounded toe through her sneakers.

"Are you okay?" Walt asked.

Once again standing on both feet, she glanced over at the wall. "Yeah, I think so. Look." She pointed to the wall. One of the bricks was missing. "It looks like someone pried that out of the wall."

Walt started down the dark hallway again and then stopped. He moved the light over one wall and then the next. Random bricks had been removed from the wall, abandoned on the ground.

"Why would someone take those out?" Danielle asked. "Or should I say who? You think Abe did that, looking for the key?"

"If you notice, along that section with the missing bricks," Walt began, shining his light on the area. "Not a single brick with the word showing."

"He didn't say anything about ripping out the bricks. I didn't see any tools with his skeleton. I wonder what he used," Danielle asked.

Walt shook his head. "I don't know. But I think we should hurry up. I'm not sure how new these flashlight batteries are."

"Don't even suggest that!" Danielle groaned. She picked up her step, careful not to trip over any of the abandoned bricks littering the way. It didn't take them long to reach the end of the tunnel.

"I guess this is it," Walt said as he ran his flashlight beam over the back wall. A metal ladder ran up the wall and into what looked like a brick chimney, narrower than the chute they had climbed down from the hidden stairwell.

Danielle looked up into the square hole overhead. The ladder seemed to disappear. "Wow, looks like a long way up there."

"Remember, we went to basement level at Marlow House, which is underground. And then we went down another set of stairs."

"So we are, like, two floors underground?" Danielle asked.

"That would be my guess."

Danielle frowned up at the peculiar exit. "So where does that thing lead? Where are we?"

"I don't think we're a quarter of a mile from Marlow House. So I suspect somewhere on Beach Drive," Walt guessed.

"I wish we could just go back the way we came," Danielle grumbled.

"If Abe couldn't get that door open, I doubt we will be able to. But I can try. We'll have to find the keyhole. At least we know there is one now. But first, let me see if we can get out this way."

"Okay," Danielle said with a sigh. She watched as Walt made his way up the ladder. Once he reached the top, he tried moving the section not made of brick. When it did not move, he began pounding.

NEARBY, the flames from the portable electric fireplace flickered, providing the only light in the Crawford living room aside from what was coming from the horror movie playing on the television set. Mia had moved the cauldron of candy outside, affixing a note with a strip of shipping tape, telling trick-or-treaters to help themselves, but when the cauldron was empty, there was no more candy.

They had pulled out the sofa bed, brought out their blankets and pillows, and made a large bowl of popcorn. Snuggled together under the blankets, Mia wearing a long nightgown and Austin wearing nothing but boxers, they watched the gruesomely frightful movie. Mesmerized by the horror show, Mia stayed close to her husband as she nibbled on popcorn. When the movie became too tense, she closed her eyes.

Austin normally did not have a problem watching scary movies. It was only a movie, he told himself. But this one was sure to give him nightmares. Mia opened her eyes and peeked at the television while Austin held his breath. On the screen the hapless woman was unaware she was about to get her throat slashed by the man whose face looked as if it had been half eaten off by rats, when a loud pounding sound exploded in the far corner, directly behind the television set.

Mia jumped out of bed, pitching the bowl of popcorn she had been holding over her head, sending the fluffy kernels raining over the room. Austin had also jumped out of the bed and was just turning on the lights when Mia said, "What in the world was that?"

"Sounds like someone pounded on the back of the house," Austin said angrily. He turned the television off and looked outside into the dark night but saw nothing. "Damn kids. I think whoever it is ran off."

"I want to clobber whoever did that," Mia grumbled as she began picking up popcorn from the floor.

"That's why I don't like kids," Austin said as he began helping her pick up the popcorn.

Mia paused a moment and listened. "I hear something."

"Where's the flashlight?" he asked.

"In the kitchen, in the drawer next to the refrigerator. Why?" She frowned.

"I'm going to see who's out there messing around."

Absently chewing her lower lip, she glanced over to the corner where the sound seemed to be coming from. "Is it safe?"

"I'm sure it's just a couple of Halloween troublemakers." Austin stomped off to the kitchen and then returned with the flashlight.

"I still hear something. Like squeaking. Maybe we should call the police?" she asked in a whisper.

"We don't need to call the police," he said as he stormed out the door, flashlight in hand.

When he returned a few minutes later, he found Mia standing by the sofa bed, waiting anxiously. "And?" she asked.

"They were gone," he said.

"But I still hear that squeaking sound."

"That has to be the wind," he told her, tossing the flashlight on a chair.

She glanced at the bowl of popcorn. "Do you want me to make more? I have to throw this out."

Before he could answer, pounding came again from the corner of the living room.

DANIELLE WATCHED as Walt made his way down the ladder.

"Well?" she asked.

"If it is a doorway, it seems to be boarded over," Walt said.

"Can you get it unboarded?" she asked.

"I'm not saying it's impossible, but it will take time. For me to get something like a screw to twist around and remove itself from a hole, I need to know where it's located, and there seems to be a number of them. Plus it's very dark in there and not much space. I tried keeping the flashlight overhead so I could see what I was doing, but I found it almost impossible to keep it afloat while trying to figure out how to remove those boards."

"I could hold the flashlight for you," Danielle suggested.

"Let's go back to the other door first. If we can find that keyhole Abe told us about, perhaps I can trigger the lock."

THIRTY-SEVEN

R eluctantly, Chris made the decision to close the haunted house early. He didn't see any other way. It had been open for over two hours, and there was still no sign of Walt and Danielle. He had even made an appeal to the mystery ghost serving tea in the parlor. Either the ghost was not interested in helping, or he had no idea where Walt and Danielle might be.

Ginny had eventually showed up, but since she hadn't been around when they went missing, Chris was not surprised to discover she was as clueless as the rest of them. Adam suggested it might all be some prank—something to add mystery to the haunted house, but after they remained missing for over an hour, he abandoned that idea.

Most of the haunted house volunteers gathered in the Marlow House living room. Before assembling in the room, Heather, Chris and Ian had gone through the house, turning on all the lights, transforming the once darkened haunted house into a brightly lit space. Lily had come over to join them, while Connor slept in her arms.

Chief MacDonald sat with them in the living room while Joe and Brian searched the house again, beginning at the attic and moving toward the basement. Ian accompanied them, to show them the location of the hidden staircase. Joanne went to the kitchen to make sandwiches and lemonade. Earlier they had checked and rechecked the grounds and the garage.

"Max is definitely missing too," Heather told the chief.

"I keep thinking about that secret staircase," Melony said.

"I still haven't seen it," Adam muttered, glancing up to the ceiling.

"Maybe there's another secret passage in the house. Something Walt and Danielle didn't tell anyone about," Melony continued.

"She didn't tell most of us about the staircase," Adam said.

"Exactly. And maybe there's another hidden space. These old houses often have hidden passages. Maybe they got locked inside."

"There is only one problem with that," Chris said.

"What?" Melony asked.

"I'm sure if they got stuck in some secret passage, they would start pounding on the wall. We've had people going through this house for two hours, and no one mentioned any knocking. Ian and I have been checking and rechecking the rooms all evening. Nothing," Chris explained.

Melony let out a sigh. "True."

A moment later Joanne walked into the library, carrying a tray with sandwiches. She set it on the table and then returned a few minutes later with a tray of beverages and cookies. "Help yourselves," she said.

"And the Packard is still here?" Lily asked. She had asked the question earlier.

"Yes. It doesn't look like it has been moved," the chief said. "And both of their phones are still in their bedroom."

"You don't think they have been kidnapped, do you?" Heather gasped.

"How would kidnappers get them out of the house?" Chris asked.

"They are obviously not in the house, so someone, somehow got them out of here!" Heather snapped.

When Brian and Joe walked into the living room with Ian a few minutes later, Joe said, "We couldn't find anything. No sign of them."

"Chief, we just got a call about a disturbance down at the Crawfords' house," Brian added.

"Next door to my place?" Chris asked.

"Yes," Brian said. "He claims someone keeps pounding on his back wall in their living room, and then they run off before he can get out there. He's pretty upset."

"Do you want us to go check on the Crawfords or stay here?" Joe asked.

Ginny jumped up and looked at Evan. "I think I know where Walt and Danielle might be. Tell your dad to have them go to the Crawfords'." She then vanished.

Heather and Chris exchanged quick glances.

"Dad, have them go to the Crawfords'," Evan said anxiously.

MacDonald frowned at Evan, momentarily confused by his unsolicited suggestion.

"Listen to him, Chief," Chris said quietly.

"WHAT WAS THAT ABOUT?" Joe asked as he and Brian drove down to the Crawfords'.

"I have no idea. But these days, nothing that happens at Marlow House surprises me. Even an eight-year-old kid telling the police chief what to do."

"Where do you think Walt and Danielle are?" Joe asked as he parked along the curb in front of the Crawfords' house.

"Your guess is as good as mine."

DANIELLE SAT on the hard ground by the opening at the end of the tunnel, Max by her side, waiting for Walt. She had refused to cry thus far, but she wasn't certain she could hold out much longer.

"I don't think we're going to die down here," Danielle said hopefully when Walt climbed back down off the ladder and sat next to her.

"That's good to know." Walt wrapped an arm around her and pulled her closer, kissing the top of her head. "I'll figure it out."

"I mean, well, if the Bellemore brothers were down here, they will probably come again, won't they? And when they do, we can make them let us out, can't we?"

"Even if they don't come back—"

"Don't say that!" she interrupted.

"I was just going to say, even if they don't come back, I will figure out some way to open one of those doors. At least we found the keyhole on the other one."

"Yeah, but you couldn't trip the lock." She glanced up at the opening overhead. "And I'm not sure you'll be able to open that one."

Walt didn't need to reassure Danielle again, because in the next moment Ginny appeared before them.

"Ginny!" Danielle squealed. "You found us!"

Ginny grinned at Danielle. "Everyone is looking for you."

"I imagine they are. How did you find us?" Walt asked.

"I was hanging out at the Crawfords' house. I used to live there, you know. Not in the house that's there now, but the house that used to be there. Those two men came. The ones who've been ripping off pieces of the Crawfords' walls."

"You mean the Bellemore brothers?" Danielle asked.

Ginny nodded. "The reason I didn't show up the other night, I followed them down here."

"Did you know about the tunnel?" Danielle asked.

"Not until I followed them. Funny thing. For a moment I thought one of them could see me. I was hiding behind a stack of boxes, watching them, and one looked straight at me. I was sure he could see me. But he couldn't. He was looking at some sort of card that had dropped out of his pocket."

"What do the Crawfords have to do with the tunnel?" Walt asked.

Ginny pointed up the narrow chute. "That comes up in their living room. When the Crawfords were in Portland, those men removed the metal panel and went inside. That's when I followed them in. The passageway goes through that brick corner in the house. It was in the other house too. But I didn't know it had a secret door. But maybe that explains the strange sounds I'd sometimes hear."

"So how do we get out? Have Ginny go tell Chris and Heather where we are?" Danielle asked.

"Two policemen are on their way over to the Crawfords'. Did you pound on that wooden door?" Ginny again pointed up the chute to indicate what panel she meant.

"Yes, why?" Walt asked.

"Because the Crawfords heard you and called the police. Maybe if you pound some more, they'll let you out," Ginny suggested.

JOE AND BRIAN stood in the open front doorway of the Crawfords' house, while Mia and Austin stood in the entry hall talking to them.

"We just walked the entire perimeter of your property, and whoever it was, they aren't there now," Joe told them just as the pounding started again.

"There it is!" Mia squealed.

Both Joe and Brian dashed from the front porch, Joe running to the right while Brian ran to the left. But when they got to the back of the house, no one was there. They could, however, hear the pounding from outside.

"Did you hear that?" Joe asked, glancing from the brick corner to Brian.

"It's coming from the house."

Just as Brian and Joe returned to the front porch of the Crawford house, Police Chief MacDonald walked up with Heather, Chris and Ian. Ginny appeared by their side a moment later, her presence only known to the mediums.

"With Walt and Danielle missing, we thought we'd check the neighborhood again," MacDonald said. "And we wanted to see what you found."

"Did you get him?" Mia asked as she rushed to the open doorway. She stopped suddenly, stunned to see the new arrivals.

"Are they the ones who were knocking?" Austin asked, stepping outside and looking accusingly at Chris, Heather and Ian.

"No," Brian said with a sigh. "But I have to ask, did you or your wife just knock on your wall?"

"Of course not!" Austin snapped.

Mia gasped and swung around, her back to the police. She stared into her house. "There it is again!"

A few moments later they all huddled in front of the brick corner. If Austin and Mia wondered why their neighbors had joined the police, they said nothing, both too preoccupied with the noise coming from the brick corner to wonder. No longer was it random tapping. Now it sounded like a musical tune.

"Someone is trapped in there," Heather blurted.

"What do you mean, trapped in there?" Mia frowned at Heather.

"You can hear it, can't you?" Heather asked.

They then heard a faint voice call out, "Help! We're trapped."

"Damn, someone really is in there!" Austin said.

IAN WAS the only one who had the necessary tools nearby to remove the copper paneling. They all sat quietly and watched as he removed each screw.

"I don't see how anyone could be in there," Mia muttered. "It's too small."

"And how would they even get in there?" Austin asked.

In spite of their disbelief at the possibility of anyone squeezing into their brick corner, neither of the Crawfords objected to Ian's intervention, and they stood by quietly with the others and watched. To all their surprise, when Ian removed the copper panel, they didn't find a hole—nor more brick. Instead, it appeared to be a wooden door.

Mia gasped at the sight. "Where does it go? How can it go anywhere?"

In the next moment the wooden door swung open, and they found themselves looking into the smiling face of Walt Marlow.

DANIELLE SAT IN THE CRAWFORDS' living room, drinking a glass of brandy Mia had given her. She had brought Max out of the tunnel but immediately released him outside, and Walt told him to go home.

Several people from the coroner's office had arrived fifteen minutes earlier, and they were in the tunnel, discussing the best way to remove the remains. Walt suggested going through the Marlow House basement since that would not require climbing ladders.

Mia was the only one not to take a tour of the tunnel below her home. "I have claustrophobia," she had told them.

Danielle and Walt had already filled them in on how they had found the tunnel and managed to get trapped.

"Any idea who the skeleton was?" Ian asked.

Walt pulled some papers from his pocket and handed them to the chief. "I found this identification on the body. Well, what is left of it. I believe his name was Abe Fortune."

"He worked for Frederick Marlow," Danielle interjected. When

227

Joe and Brian looked at her, she quickly added, "I remember reading that name when I was researching Marlow House."

"This is just too creepy!" Mia shuddered. "First the mold and then this."

"I think you might want to get another opinion on that mold," Danielle said, pulling the Bellemore business card from her back pocket. She showed it to Mia before handing it to the chief.

"I don't understand." Mia frowned.

"Someone entered Marlow House from that tunnel the other night. We found this card in there when we were trapped. I'm certain that someone was one of the Bellemore brothers, if not both of them. I suspect they are in some way related to Chester Bellemore, who built Marlow House and who undoubtedly knew about the tunnel."

"Chester Bellemore?" Austin asked. "One of them is named Chester."

"Perhaps a grandson named after his grandfather?" Danielle suggested.

"But what does that have to do with our mold?" Mia asked.

Danielle couldn't tell them Ginny had witnessed the Bellemore brothers removing sections of the wallboard and spraying a black liquid along the exposed beams. Instead she said, "They obviously got into the tunnel. I think they were looking for something, and they needed you to leave so they could keep looking."

"They did want you to move out of the house so they could work here," Heather reminded them. "Maybe they were faking the mold to get you out of here. I agree with Danielle. You need a second opinion."

THIRTY-EIGHT

"I don't understand why you asked us to come in," Chester Bellemore said, glancing nervously around the interrogation room.

"Why do we have to talk to you in here? Can't we just go to your office?" Cecil asked the chief. The brothers sat on one side of the table while the chief sat on the other.

"Normally we would question you separately," the chief began.

"Do you think we are guilty of something?" Chester asked. "Is this about that missing little girl? Because I swear we didn't see her."

"No. It's not about her," the chief said calmly, pulling a small plastic bag from the file before him. It contained a business card. He slid it across the table. "This was found in a tunnel under Beach Drive. I believe it's one of yours."

Chester picked up the plastic bag and briefly looked at it before tossing it back on the table. "We've been handing these out all over town."

"Are you saying you haven't been in the tunnel?" the chief asked.

The brothers exchanged glances, and then Cecil said, "We don't know what you're talking about."

"Are you sure? You're saying you don't know anything about a tunnel that runs under Beach Drive?"

Chester shrugged. "We just moved here."

"I looked into your background. It seems your grandfather was Chester Bellemore, who built Marlow House." The chief then turned to Chester and added, "You're named after him, aren't you?"

"So? What does that have to do with anything?" Chester asked.

"You have been working at the Crawfords'?" the chief said.

"Yeah. Can you please tell me why you brought us in here?" Cecil said. "Are we under arrest for something?"

"Not yet. But there is a good chance you could be losing your contractor's license and facing a civil suit. The Crawfords are debating bringing charges against you for faking their mold."

"I don't know what you're talking about," Chester stammered.

"It is interesting how the sections you told the Crawfords were mold turned out to be ink," the chief said.

"I didn't know the police department handles complaints against contractors," Chester said.

"You also left some tools in the Crawfords' garage. We had them checked, and the residue on the tools match the bricks in the tunnel you know nothing about. You know, the bricks you pried out of the wall. Do you want to tell me what you two are up to now, or should I just bring charges against you for the murder of that body we found in the tunnel next to your business card?"

"Body? It was a skeleton! It's obviously been down there for decades!" Chester blurted.

MacDonald arched a brow at Chester and smiled.

DEFEATED, Chester slumped down in the chair. "Our father passed away a couple of months ago. About six months before he died, we had to put him in a nursing home. When we were going through his things, we came across a small engraved box. Inside was a key and a note. The note said 'key to fortune.' Curious, we took it to our father and asked him about it."

"Key to fortune?" The chief frowned.

Chester nodded. "That's when my father told us about the tunnel his grandfather had built. Dad had never been to Oregon—in fact, he didn't even know about the tunnel until his own father told him about it on his deathbed. Grandfather insisted there was a fortune hidden in the tunnel and he wanted our father to get it. He begged him to get it."

"But your father never came to Oregon?" the chief asked.

"Dad didn't take his father seriously," Cecil told the chief. "He knew my grandfather had worked in Oregon when he was a young man, but Dad thought the talk of a tunnel and a hidden treasure was nothing but his medication talking. He was on some pretty heavy meds back then and would ramble."

"But you believed him?" the chief asked. "You came here."

"We were kids when our grandfather died," Chester said. "But when we were little, before he got sick, he told us about the tunnel. Described the brick entrance, the copper panel, and how they would hide things behind the stamped bricks."

"But he never told our father about the tunnel, not until his death," Cecil added.

"Why was that?" the chief asked.

"Grandpa used to say he was sharing his secrets with us—so they wouldn't die with him," Chester said.

"But he never mentioned the treasure to you?"

Both Bellemore brothers shook their heads and muttered, "No."

"We never heard about the key—or the hidden treasure—until we found that box and showed it to our dad," Cecil added.

"After Dad died, we decided to come see for ourselves if what Grandfather said about the treasure was true," Chester explained.

"Grandpa had told us about the tunnel that ran from Marlow House to another house across the street. He said he was the only man alive who knew of its existence—until he told us. Of course, we were just boys then," Cecil said.

"We weren't really sure which house it was. In fact, we were surprised it was the Crawford house. It was too new. But then we saw the brick corner and the brass panel covering the hidden door, with our great-grandfather's name engraved on it. Just like Grandpa told us it would be," Chester continued.

"Did you get into the secret staircase at Marlow House?" the chief asked.

"We were exploring the tunnel. It was just that one night, and we left as soon as we realized where we were," Chester insisted. "We weren't going to take anything from the Marlows. We were just treasure hunting. It's not like anyone would miss it. No one even knew the tunnel was there."

DANIELLE STOOD SILENTLY with Walt and Brian in the office next to the interrogation room, watching the Bellemores through the two-way mirror. It was November first. Officially the Halloween season was over.

"What are you going to do about the tunnel?" Brian asked.

"First, we're going to have an engineer look at it, to see how safe it is before anyone else goes in it," Walt said. "My first impulse is to figure out some way to fill it in, but most of it isn't on Marlow property."

"And I suspect when the historical society gets wind of it, they're going to want to preserve it. I have no idea what the Crawfords want to do about it now. The Bellemore brothers made a mess of their house," Danielle said.

Brian began to chuckle.

Walt and Danielle turned to him. "What?" Danielle asked.

"Last night when we were leaving your house after we got back from the Crawfords', Pearl Huckabee flagged me down. I guess she had spent most of Halloween night looking out her window at Beach Drive. She wanted to know what had happened—rather convinced you two had caused more trouble."

"*More* trouble?" Danielle scowled.

Brian shrugged. "You know what I mean. Anyway, I was just wondering how she would feel if she thought you and the Crawfords might successfully pitch to the city an idea to turn your house and theirs into some tourist attraction—you know, haunted tunnel tours. They have them in Portland. Might be a great draw for local tourism."

"I imagine she would be as thrilled as Pete Rogers was when the historical society wanted the *Eva Aphrodite* to stay," Danielle scoffed.

"True. But I don't think that tunnel is going to disappear as easily as that old yacht did," Brian added.

WHEN WALT and Danielle left the police station, they headed to the cemetery. There were several spirits they wanted to see.

"You think they'll still be here?" Danielle asked as Walt parked the car five minutes later.

"I have a gut feeling they haven't moved on yet," Walt said. He turned off the ignition.

"I'm also wondering when Marie and Eva will show their faces. Those two have been scarce the last few days," Danielle grumbled.

They didn't know the location of Annabelle's headstone, and they hadn't encountered any spirits to ask directions. Yet they headed to the older section of the cemetery, and as it turned out, it didn't take them long to find Annabelle and Abe. The reunited pair sat side by side on a headstone.

"We were hoping you would stop by before we left," Annabelle said brightly when they approached.

"I see you found her," Walt told Abe.

"I had to stick around to see you one more time," Abe told Walt. "I must say, I was more than confused when I came aboveground and saw the changes. After all, we had just talked in the tunnel, and, well, I assumed I hadn't been dead that long. But by the time I found Annabelle, I had decided you must have been a ghost. After all, you looked the same—even dressed the same." He paused a moment and looked Walt up and down. "Although, your clothes look much different today."

"Did Annabelle tell you about Walt?" Danielle asked.

"She did. It was hard to believe. But I imagine Annabelle and I will see more spectacular things when we continue with our journey." He grinned at Walt and Danielle.

"Can I ask you a question before you go?" Danielle asked.

"Sure. What?"

"That missing key, where was it normally kept?" Danielle asked.

"Behind one of the bricks in the wall—one of the stamped ones. The one closest to that door," Abe explained.

"We know what happened to that key," Walt told him. "Thomas Bellemore took it, and his grandsons eventually found it."

"Did he know? Did he know what happened to me?" Abe asked.

"I suppose you can ask him yourself when you move on," Walt told him. "But I suspect he knew. By the time he realized you might be trapped in the tunnel, he had to have known you couldn't have survived all that time. I caught him breaking into the house right before the new owners moved in. I don't know if he had time to go into the tunnel and look for your body or not. Perhaps that's one reason he left town so quickly. The guilt—the fear of someone finding you."

"I don't blame him," Abe said. "I blame no one." He looked to Annabelle and asked, "Are you ready to go?"

"First I need to tell them about Virginia," Annabelle told him.

Danielle looked quizzically to Annabelle. "Ginny?"

Annabelle smiled sadly. "We tried to talk her into going with us. She's been here so long. But she still doesn't want to go."

"Where is she?" Danielle asked.

Annabelle pointed down the path and told them where they would most likely find her.

"Thank you," Abe told them right before he and Annabelle vanished.

Danielle and Walt stood a moment, staring at the headstone where the two spirits had been sitting just moments earlier.

"I still don't understand one thing," Danielle said.

"What's that?" Walt asked.

"Why couldn't Abe open the hidden doorway into his house? The only reason you couldn't push that door open was because the Bellemore brothers had added screws from the other side into the copper panel. I would have to assume, for Abe to open the wooden door in the first place, he needed to remove the copper panel. And then when Annabelle was looking for him, she would see the copper panel was removed and see the wooden door. And someone obviously replaced that copper panel after Abe was trapped."

Walt looked to Danielle and smiled sadly. "I suspect because he never completely removed the copper panel to open the door."

"I don't understand." Danielle frowned.

"After Ian let us out of the tunnel, I took a closer look at the copper panel and the wooden door it concealed. That copper panel had been nailed to the wooden door from the outside. If anyone had been paying attention, they might have suspected there wasn't brick behind the panel, because it's not easy to nail into brick. But you can into wood."

"So all someone needed to do to open the door from inside the house was pull on the corners of the copper panel and the door would open?" Danielle asked.

"Exactly. And from inside of the tunnel, all you needed to do was give it a good shove. But then the Bellemore brothers added those screws into the brick along the edge, making it impossible for me to push the door open."

"But why couldn't Abe push it open?" Danielle asked.

"It was the piano," Walt explained.

"Piano?" Danielle frowned.

"Annabelle mentioned there was a piano delivered the day she left to go to Portland. Abe wasn't there; it had come early. I suspect she had the movers put it in the house."

"So?" Danielle frowned.

"I remembered the piano when Ian let us out of the tunnel. The piano Annabelle's spirit mentioned. In the first house, the one the Fortunes lived in, there had been a piano sitting along the back of the room, butted up against the brick wall."

"Are you suggesting the piano blocked the door?" Danielle asked.

"The first time I saw the piano was after Annabelle died and we had to clean out the house for sale. Their family didn't want any of the furniture. I recall feeling sorry for them, so I gave the attorney for their estate some money to buy it all. I just left everything with the house when it sold—including the piano."

"You're suggesting when the movers arrived early to deliver the piano, Abe was already in the tunnel, and Annabelle had them put the piano in the corner, not realizing she was blocking the door her husband needed to use," Danielle said.

"She was gone for a week, so if he pounded on the door like we did, there was no one to hear. And I read once a person can only survive for about three or four days without water."

"What do you think is going to happen when Abe and Annabelle realize why he was trapped?" Danielle asked.

Walt smiled at Danielle and took her hand. "I honestly don't think any of that matters to them anymore. They are together, starting a new adventure."

THIRTY-NINE

They found Ginny sitting by her headstone, watching the clouds move overhead. She didn't notice Walt and Danielle's approach until Danielle said hello.

Ginny sat up abruptly. "You're here."

"We had to come say thank you. You saved our lives," Danielle told her as she sat on a nearby bench.

"You think I did?" Ginny asked brightly.

"I'm pretty sure you did. We just said goodbye to Annabelle and Abe. She told us she wanted you to go with her, but that you didn't want to move on," Walt said.

"Everyone else has someone waiting for them. I have no one," Ginny said.

"But you know Annabelle," Danielle reminded her. "And Kat mentioned she and her husband are ready to move on, and they would like you to go with them. See, a lot of people want you."

Ginny shook her head. "It just isn't the same. You don't understand." Ginny looked down and began fiddling with her hands.

"You and Annabelle lived in the same house," Danielle said after a few moments of silence.

Ginny nodded. "We didn't know each other then. But we died within the same year." She looked at Danielle and said, "I think maybe when I was alive, I might have been a little like Evan, a little like you."

"Why do you say that?" Danielle asked.

"Because those voices that used to scare me in my room late at night, I think it was Abe's spirit calling out for help. He didn't know he was dead. And when he called out, I could hear him. I wish I had known sooner, I could have told Annabelle."

"It all worked out," Walt told her.

"You think Evan would ever visit me here?" Ginny asked. "I like Evan. I never get to visit with other children. When any come through here, they're always in a hurry to move on. There's always some grandparent, aunt, uncle or some relative on the other side they're eager to see or meet."

"Did you see your aunt and uncle after they died?" Danielle asked.

Ginny shook her head. "I don't think their spirits stopped here. Annabelle said many don't. After I died, I was so confused, I don't even remember my funeral—if there was one. By the time I understood what Annabelle was trying to say, my body was already buried. No one ever visited my grave. Some would stop and visit the graves next to me, maybe read my headstone, say something about how sad I died so young. But they weren't really there to see me."

Walt studied Ginny a moment. Finally he said, "If I can convince Evan's father to let me bring him, would you like to see Evan later today? After he comes home from school?"

Ginny perked up. "Really? You would do that?"

"You did save our lives," Walt reminded her.

"WHAT ARE YOU UP TO?" Danielle asked as they walked back to their car.

"Why do you think I'm up to anything?" Walt asked with a smile.

"I can tell."

"Ginny did save our lives, and I think deep down she wants to move on. I have an idea. Didn't Adam say Angeline Michaels was coming to his office at eleven today?"

"Yeah, so?"

Walt glanced at his watch. "Then we need to hurry. It's about a quarter to eleven now, and I would like to be at Adam's office before Angeline gets there."

"What are you up to?" Danielle asked. They had just reached their car, and Walt was unlocking the passenger door for her.

"I'll explain on the way over to Adam's," Walt said as he opened the car door for Danielle.

WHEN THEY WALKED into Frederickport Vacation Properties ten minutes later, they found Adam sitting alone in the front office, waiting for his client.

"How are you two doing after your adventure last night?" Adam greeted them.

"It was harrowing," Danielle said, taking a seat on one of the chairs. "We just wanted to stop by and thank you for helping last night."

"No problem. By the way, I ran into Brian Henderson at Lucy's a little while ago. I guess he'd just left you at the police station after interviewing the Bellemores. I don't think any of our local contractors have to worry about them stealing business. I doubt they'll be in town long."

"You're probably right."

Adam then began to laugh. "And it is typical Danielle Boatman." He paused a moment and looked at Walt. "Sorry, Danielle Marlow." He laughed again.

"What is so funny?" Danielle frowned.

"Brian told me why those two were down there. Looking for a treasure. They didn't find it, but I have no doubt you will. You always seem to end up with the buried treasures around here." He laughed again and shook his head.

"She already found it," Walt told Adam. "Actually, we both found it."

"Damn!" Adam slammed his fist on the desk. "I knew it! So what was it? More gold coins? Some expensive jewels? What?"

Danielle flashed a smile at Walt, but said nothing. She waited for him to finish.

"The Bellemore brothers were looking for a treasure. But I'm fairly certain their grandfather never told them there was a treasure hidden in the tunnel. He said there was a Fortune in the tunnel."

Adam shrugged. "So? Are you saying it was money? A fortune would mean a lot of money."

"It can also be a name," Danielle said. "Their grandfather, in his delirious state at the end of his illness, was telling his son about Abe Fortune—who was trapped in the tunnel. That's whose remains we found. He was never talking about a treasure. He was talking about a person."

WHEN ANGELINE WALKED into the real estate office a few minutes later, she seemed pleased to find Walt and Danielle there and wasted no time in telling them she had already talked to Melony that morning about what had happened the previous night.

"I can't believe I grew up in that house and had no idea there was a hidden passageway in that corner!" Angeline told them. "Of course, that's always where my parents kept the piano."

"You had a piano?" Danielle asked, exchanging a quick glance with Walt.

"Yes. It was an upright. Not that any of us played, although both my sister and I took lessons briefly when we were children. Mother wanted to get rid of it; it was impossible to clean behind. But it had belonged to my grandparents, and my father was sentimental about it. It stayed with the house when my sister got the property. In fact, after the fire, I heard the piano only suffered smoke damage. It was the bedrooms and kitchen areas that suffered the brunt of the fire," Angeline explained. "I heard Pete got rid of the piano."

A few minutes later, after exchanging more words, Walt stood. "We should get going. I know you two have business to discuss. But I will have to say all of this has really given me an idea for another book."

"Really? Oh, I just loved your first book," Angeline said.

Walt turned to Angeline and added, "In fact, if you have any free time, I would love to talk to you more about that house—your parents. Your grandparents. If you don't mind."

"I'd love to. But I'm leaving in a few days."

"Any chance you have some free time this afternoon?" Walt asked.

"Why yes. I should be finished with Adam in a couple of hours. Would you like me to stop by Marlow House?" Angeline asked.

Walt paused a moment as if thinking her question over and then said, "I know this may sound peculiar, but would you mind meeting me at the cemetery?"

"The cemetery?" Adam blurted.

"It's a writer's thing," Walt said quickly. "It may sound odd, but I find cemeteries can provide inspiration. The headstones alone are story fodder."

Angeline smiled. "Yes, that would be fine. Actually, I need to put some flowers on my sister's grave. It has been so long."

"I HOPE you know what you're doing. This could backfire," Danielle told Walt as he drove them toward the cemetery late Wednesday afternoon. Evan MacDonald sat in the back seat listening.

"It's just something Angeline said the first time we met. If it doesn't work, what is the worst that can happen?" Walt asked.

"I hate those *what is the worst that can happen* questions. Never works out well," Danielle muttered.

With a chuckle Walt reached over and patted Danielle's knee. "Have faith, love."

They arrived at the cemetery parking lot just minutes after Angeline. Walt pulled up next to her car and parked just as she was getting out of her vehicle.

"I still can't get over that car," Angeline said, admiring the Packard.

"It belonged to my distant cousin, the other Walt Marlow," Walt explained.

"I'd heard that," Angeline said with a nod. She then looked at Danielle and smiled. When she spied Evan coming out of the Packard, she frowned, somewhat surprised to find a child with them.

"Hello, Angeline," Danielle said cheerfully, taking Evan's hand. "This is Evan MacDonald, the police chief's son. He just got off school and the chief needed me to watch him. I'm going to take him over to visit his mother's and grandparents' graves while you and Walt visit."

Angeline smiled down at Evan. "Hello. Nice to meet you, Evan."

"Evan, this is Ms. Michaels," Danielle introduced them.

Evan smiled. "Hello."

"Well, I'll leave you two to chat," Danielle said before leaving with Evan.

———

DANIELLE AND EVAN walked quickly toward Ginny's gravesite before Walt could arrive with Angeline.

"Remember what you need to tell her?" Danielle told Evan.

"Maybe you should do it?" Evan suggested.

"No, Evan. I think Walt is right. Ginny likes you. She considers you her friend. She trusts you."

———

WHEN WALT and Angeline arrived at her family's gravesites, Danielle and Evan were nowhere in sight. But Ginny was there, sitting patiently on the bench, waiting. Only Walt could see her. He flashed her a smile.

"Evan said I needed to listen in to your conversation. He said it might help me," Ginny told Walt. His only response was a quick smile.

Carrying a bouquet of flowers to her sister's gravesite, Angeline set it by the headstone. "I suppose I should have brought flowers for the others. If I end up moving back to Frederickport, I really should do that more often."

Standing next to Angeline, Walt glanced over the headstones. "By the names and dates, I gather those two are your grandparents, and those are your parents."

Angeline nodded.

Walt then pointed to another headstone. "What about that one? Virginia—she has a different last name. By the dates I see she died rather young. Do you know who she was?"

"Ahh, sweet Virginia." Angelina bent down to her sister's grave and removed half of the flowers. She then placed them on Ginny's grave.

"I don't know her," Ginny said. "Why did she call me sweet Virginia?"

"Who was she?" Walt asked.

"The little girl who broke my grandfather's heart," Angeline said with a sigh.

"What is she talking about?" Ginny frowned.

"Tell me about her," Walt urged.

"She was my father's first cousin. Of course, he never met her. As you can see by the dates, she died before Dad was born. He used to say she was the sister he never met—but would meet someday. I guess he did, didn't he?" Angeline smiled softly.

"Why was she the sister he never met?" Walt asked.

"My grandfather had one sister. He loved her, but she became addicted to drugs. Strange, drug addiction is really not a new thing, is it? I suppose just the type of drug changes each generation. Anyway, she married an abusive man. They had a little girl— Virginia—whom the parents neglected horribly. My grandparents tried to get custody of her, but at the time they had very little money and were only living in a room at a boardinghouse. His brother-in-law may have been a bum, but they owned a house. Maybe a shack, but it was still a house."

"I don't understand," Ginny said, walking closer. "They wanted me?"

"But then there was a fire and both her parents were killed. There was an insurance policy that went to Ginny. The lawyer for the estate convinced my grandfather to buy a house with it. It's the same property Pete just sold. My grandparents didn't feel right about it. They felt the money was Virginia's. But the lawyer convinced them it was really in her best interest, so she could have a house to live in. They eventually agreed."

"What happened to her?" Walt asked.

"My grandparents were so young at the time. They hadn't been married long. They were kids themselves. She was such a confused little girl. I suppose these days they would have counseling for the family. Virginia hated the house. My grandfather feared she also hated him, and he so wanted to save her, like he hadn't saved his sister."

"I didn't hate him," Ginny murmured.

"One night she left her bedroom and went to sleep in my grandfather's car. There were some chemicals on the floor in the back seat, and they spilled—probably when she climbed into the car. Toxic combination. Killed the poor child as she slept. My grandparents were utterly heartbroken. I think that's why my grandfather was so protective of us. He didn't want to lose another child. As for the house, the death was ruled a horrible accident. Since my grandfather was Virginia's only family, the house—which my grandparents had initially insisted be put in her name—went to him and his wife."

"So that's what happened to me," Virginia murmured.

"Your grandparents loved her?" Walt asked.

"Oh yes. My grandfather used to tell me about Virginia. She never cared for dolls, but loved to fish and climb trees. Spunky, that's what he called her."

"Why didn't he ever visit my grave if he loved me?" Ginny blurted. But only Walt could hear.

"I imagine he used to visit her grave often?" Walt suggested.

Angeline shook her head emphatically. "No. After her funeral, he refused to go to the cemetery ever again. My grandmother said it was because he blamed himself for her death. He couldn't bear looking at her headstone. And when my grandmother passed away, he never went to her gravesite after the funeral."

ANGELINE AND WALT talked for about forty-five minutes. Finally she said her goodbyes, and he watched her leave while Ginny stood quietly by his side.

"They loved me," Virginia said.

"It sure sounds that way. Let's go find Evan and Danielle," Walt suggested.

"I have a brother. Well, maybe not a brother, but a cousin who thinks of me as his sister. I would have been his big sister if I had lived."

Walt smiled down at Virginia. "Yes, you would."

"I remember when my uncle would take me fishing. I had fun. I forgot how much fun I had. He never got mad at me when I asked him to bait my hook," Ginny recalled.

"Sometimes we are so overwhelmed by the bad things that happen to us, we lose sight of the good moments. We need to hold on to those good moments and let the bad ones go," Walt told her.

THEY REACHED DANIELLE FIRST. She sat alone on a bench, watching Evan, who stood about twenty feet away at the gravesite of his great-grandparents. Walt took a seat by Danielle while Ginny remained standing. He spied an elderly man and woman with Evan.

"I take it that's Grandma Kat and her husband?" Walt asked, nodding toward Evan and the elderly couple.

"Kat's husband is shy of mediums. But he is making an exception for Evan," Danielle explained. "I believe he is rather excited to see him. They have been chatting nonstop."

"I'm going to go talk to Evan now," Ginny interrupted.

Danielle smiled at Ginny. "Thank you again for saving our lives."

"Thank you—for everything," Ginny told them before turning and walking toward Evan and his great-grandparents.

"How did it go?" Danielle asked when Ginny was out of earshot.

"Better than I expected."

Danielle studied Walt. "You look pleased with yourself."

"If it all works out. Let's see."

With a sigh, Danielle leaned back on the park bench. Walt took her hand and they sat silently, watching as Evan talked to Ginny. After a moment, Ginny walked to Kat and took her hand. The three spirits turned to Walt and Danielle. Kat and Ginny waved briefly, and then the three vanished.

Evan stood alone for a moment, looking at the place where the spirits had been moments earlier. He then turned abruptly and ran to Walt and Danielle.

"They moved on," Evan said with a wide smile. "They said it was time."

"I'm very proud at how brave you are being," Danielle said as she stood up. "I know how much you're going to miss them."

Evan took Danielle's hand. "Aw, there are always dream hops, Danielle. Huh, Walt?"

Walt smiled down at Evan and took his free hand. "Yes, there are. Who wants ice cream?"

FORTY

There was no reason to ask Ian to come over and help move the casket into the truck Chris had borrowed on Thursday. Chris and Walt were able to easily carry it from the downstairs bedroom to the truck parked outside in front of the house. Of course, Walt did most of the work; Chris just needed to create the appearance of carrying his half so some passerby didn't witness a floating casket.

Unfortunately, the best-laid plans can go awry when someone is distracted by a cellphone. Danielle held the front gate open for them as they stepped onto the sidewalk. It was at that very moment Pearl Huckabee happened to drive by. Pearl rarely drove north on Beach Drive. After all, downtown was south from her house, and she normally had no reason to drive by Marlow House aside from checking on her nemesis. But today she had a particular reason for driving by. She wanted to make sure they had finally removed the haunted house sign from their front gate.

The timing was perfect. Seeing them carrying a wooden casket from the house was shocking enough, but as Pearl slowed down to pass by Marlow House, she looked their way just as Chris let go of the back half of the casket to answer his phone. From her vantage point, it looked as if Walt carried the cumbersome wooden casket at the front end, while the rest of it simply floated along—following him.

So startled by the sight she swerved and barely missed taking out one of her neighbors' mailboxes. Fortunately for Pearl—and the neighbor's mailbox—she quickly corrected her error and then sped off, disappearing up the street.

"She does come by at the most inopportune times," Danielle noted as she watched Walt and Chris load the casket into the truck bed.

"You sure you don't want to just keep the casket for next year, in case you decide to do the haunted house again?" Chris asked.

"I'm sure," Danielle said.

"I APPRECIATE you taking the casket back," Chris told Norman Bateman. He stood with Walt and Danielle in the front lobby of the mortuary, talking to the funeral director. They had already unloaded the casket from the truck and placed it in the storage room.

"I had a feeling you would want to bring it back," Norman said with a chuckle. "It always seems that after Halloween most people don't really want a casket sitting around the house."

Danielle was tempted to ask him how his mother was doing, but since he didn't bring the subject up, she thought it best to skip over it. He actually looked rather cheerful, especially considering his elderly mother, whom by all appearances he had been close to, was now facing the possibility of life in prison for murder.

Instead of asking Norman about his mother, she excused herself to visit the restroom, leaving the three men alone to chat. The moment the bathroom door closed behind her, a swirl of light took up the space between her and the bathroom sink. Before her eyes it transformed into a male figure. It was the same ghost she had seen at the funeral home before—when Norman's mother had plotted to kill her. According to Eva, he had died years earlier after falling off the pier in a drunken stupor.

"Someone really needs to explain to you how inappropriate it is to follow a woman in the bathroom!" Danielle scolded.

Instead of showing remorse, he twirled his right hand in a flourish and said, "Tea, anyone?"

Danielle's eyes widened. "Were you the one? Were you the one in the parlor during our haunted house?"

He grinned mischievously. "I must say, I had the most delightful fun! I do hope you do it again next year. And did you like how I made that mask grin and wink?"

Danielle arched a brow. "That was you too?"

He nodded. "I am sorry for breaking your vase. I hope you will forgive me. But here, well, the best I seem to be able to do is occasionally slam a door. I was practicing when I accidentally tipped over those chairs and broke the vase. Please forgive me. But I did have such a jolly time!"

Danielle smiled. "Yes, I forgive you. And thank you for telling me. You know, I had a few visitors from the cemetery—and afterwards they decided it was time to move on. What about you?"

He frowned. "Me, move on? Oh pshaw. You silly thing!" He then grinned. "But I will let you have your privacy now. Ta-ta!"

THURSDAY NIGHT the mediums and a few friends gathered at Marlow House for dinner. Adam and Melony had been invited, but Angeline wanted to take the couple out to dinner at Pearl Cove to thank them for helping her search for real estate before she left town, so they declined the invitation.

Danielle curled up with Walt on the living room sofa, sipping a glass of wine before dinner. Lily rocked Connor nearby as he slept on her lap. The chief sat on one of the chairs facing the sofa. His two sons rolled a ball in the spacious entry hall for Sadie and Hunny; nearby, Max perched on the chair, watching the canine duo. The chief enjoyed a beer while Heather, who sat next to him in the other chair, enjoyed a glass of wine. Chris sat with Ian on the fireplace hearth, and they, like the chief, each drank a can of beer.

"I noticed all the Christmas decorations up at the hardware store today," Heather noted.

"Before we turn around, it will be here," Danielle said before sipping her wine.

"What is everyone doing for Christmas?" Heather asked. "Do you know yet?"

"Staying home," they all replied at once, and then laughed, realizing they had all said the same thing.

"I want to be in our own house for Connor's first Christmas," Lily said, dropping a kiss on the baby's head. "But we promised my folks we would join them in Tahoe for Thanksgiving. They have a timeshare there. Ian's parents are coming too."

"I heard Joe and Kelly might go," the chief said.

"I think that's still up in the air," Lily said.

"My brother is coming to spend Christmas with me," Chris added.

"You haven't seen him for a long time, have you?" Ian asked.

"No. But we talk just about every day," Chris said.

"I would love to host Christmas dinner, if anyone is interested. You are all invited," Danielle said.

"I don't have to cook?" Heather perked up. "I'll be there!"

A few minutes later, after the direction of the conversation turned to the events of Halloween week, MacDonald told Walt and Danielle, "You two were right about the Bellemores' grandfather saying fortune instead of treasure."

"They told you that?" Danielle asked.

"Yes. As far as they know, their grandfather never told their father there was a treasure hidden in the tunnel, just a fortune. They assumed he was talking about a hidden treasure," the chief explained. "They had no idea he was really talking about a man."

"What's happening to them now?" Ian asked.

"They've agreed to pay for all of the Crawfords' repairs before leaving town," MacDonald told them. "If they do everything they promise to do, we aren't pressing any charges."

"So they're leaving Frederickport?" Chris asked.

The chief nodded. "Yes."

"Have any of you seen Marie and Eva?" Ian asked.

"Yes," Walt told him. "They both *popped in*—actually that is a rather literal description—" He chuckled and then added, "—not long after we returned from the funeral home. They left again to go to the local theater to watch a Humphrey Bogart marathon."

"I still don't know why they had to bail on the haunted house," Heather grumbled.

"To make it up to us, before taking off to the theater, they both went through all the walls in Marlow House," Danielle told her.

"And the floors," Walt added.

"And Marie and Eva assured us there are no more hidden passageways—no more secret staircases," Danielle said.

"If Marie needed money, she has several career options—now that she's a ghost," Ian said before taking a swig of beer.

"How so?" Heather asked.

"She did a great job painting Connor's room. And now she's performing home inspections," Ian said with a chuckle.

"I suppose it is handy when you can walk through walls," Heather said.

"Now that we are confident Marlow House has no more surprises, let's all enjoy a calm and peaceful holiday season," Danielle said as she raised her wineglass in mock salute.

"Yeah, right," Lily scoffed under her breath. "What else could go wrong?"

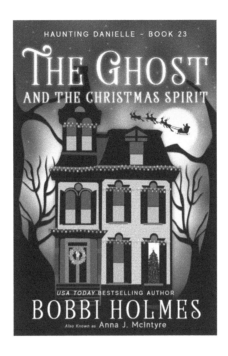

RETURN TO MARLOW HOUSE IN

THE GHOST AND THE CHRISTMAS SPIRIT

HAUNTING DANIELLE, BOOK 23

It's once again Christmastime at Marlow House and the mediums of Beach Drive have all decided to stay in Frederickport for the holiday. Surprises await for them when the true Spirit of Christmas comes for a visit.

Do you believe in Santa Claus?

NON-FICTION BY

BOBBI ANN JOHNSON HOLMES

Havasu Palms, A Hostile Takeover

Where the Road Ends, Recipes & Remembrances

Motherhood, a book of poetry

The Story of the Christmas Village

BOOKS BY ANNA J. MCINTYRE

COULSON FAMILY SAGA

Coulson's Wife

Coulson's Crucible

Coulson's Lessons

Coulson's Secret

Coulson's Reckoning

UNLOCKED 🔓 HEARTS

Sundered Hearts

After Sundown

While Snowbound

Sugar Rush

CPSIA information can be obtained
at www.ICGtesting.com
Printed in the USA
LVHW090142270222
712100LV00003B/577